SHIP OF DREAMS

KELSEY PAINTER

To my sister, Haley.

Thanks for watching *Titanic* with me like, a hundred times while I wrote this book. You and your amazing children are the first people I would get to a lifeboat.

AUTHOR'S NOTE

While this is a work of fiction, and my main characters are all from my imagination, there are many historical figures taking part in this story. I have done my best to portray them accurately and respectfully, especially those who did not survive the sinking of the Titanic. I in no way intend to dishonor their memories in my depictions. All characterizations are based on research and testimonies from survivors. I have taken artistic liberty in some events.

Content warnings: This book contains discussions of pregnancy termination/miscarriage, on page depictions of domestic abuse (not between the two main characters), mild physical violence between characters, strong language, and disaster related violence. It is not intended for readers under the age of 18, as it also contains on page, explicit sex scenes. Please read only if you are comfortable.

CHAPTER ONE

March, 1912

There was blood on the sheets.

Thank God, Sybil thought to herself. She faced Iris, who was already shedding a soiled chemise, but Sybil beat her to the wardrobe for a fresh one.

"Allow me, m'lady," she said. "It must have been a rough night for you."

"Physically, I suppose," Iris replied, kicking the bloodied garment away with her bare foot. Her deep blue eyes remained fixed on the stained sheets, her mouth turned down as she heaved a sigh. "Though I'm relieved. The pharmacist's new medicine works."

"Thank heaven for that." Sybil slid the clean chemise over Iris's pale shoulders before wrapping her in a dressing down. "Would you care for a bath, m'lady?"

"Yes, have one drawn for me while I have my breakfast."

"Of course. And I'll have the maids come up to change the bedding before they start on anything else."

"Thank you, Sybil."

Sybil nodded and picked up the other dirty clothes to bundle them in her arms. She hurried to the door, getting one hand on the knob before Iris spoke again.

"Sybil."

Sybil turned, catching her lady's eye in the mirror. That blue, frosty gaze that had earned Iris the nickname 'Ice Princess' from the household staff. It didn't intimidate Sybil the way it once did. Not after everything they had been through.

"Don't forget to have some breakfast of your own. I'm sorry I had to call you up this early."

"Yes, m'lady."

She swept out of the room and down the stairs, past Nellie, the scullery maid, who was beginning to stoke the fire in the front hall. Sybil told her to pause on that and get a bath drawn for Lady Iris. Nellie nodded, and Sybil continued on. She dodged an eager footman on her way down to the servant's stairs, which led to the house's main kitchen. Two maids, Bridget and Flora, yawned as they made their way into the laundry room. Everyone was still just waking up.

"These need washing," Sybil said, adding Iris's things to the pile. "And Lady Iris needs fresh sheets. She's having a bath this morning, so you'll have plenty of time to turn the bed."

"All right," Bridget said through another yawn.

Flora's gaze landed on the crimson stained chemise. "Another one?"

"I'm afraid so," Sybil said with a grim nod.

"Mr. Mooring won't be happy," Flora replied. "Remember Christmas?"

"How could any of us forget?" Bridget said with a shudder. "I don't think I've ever seen a grown man behave that way."

"What way? Like a toddler?"

"Well, *I* wasn't going to say it."

They giggled together before remembering Sybil standing there.

Flora cleared her throat. "And. . . how is Lady Iris?"

"She's fine," Sybil said stiffly. "Maybe this will be the one that convinces Mr. Mooring to take the doctor's advice and leave his wife alone for a while before trying again."

"Good luck convincing a man to stay out of his wife's bed," Bridget said.

"His wife's, his mistress's, a maid's," Flora joked.

"With all that company, you'd think it'd be easier to leave his wife out of it," Sybil said, without humor.

Bridget and Flora shifted their weight to their heels and glanced at the floor.

"Sorry, Sybil," Bridget said. "We know it must be taking a toll on Lady Iris. We'd never dream of poking fun at her."

"Not to worry." Sybil offered a half-smile, only somewhat appeased. "I know it isn't at her expense. But do get to work, we haven't got all day."

They nodded and gathered the washing. Sybil slipped out and went straight for the kitchen. Many of the other servants were still eating, and a place was set beside Mr. Oliver, the gray-haired, stern-faced butler of Buckland Hall. He met Sybil's eye and beckoned her over to sit. Her stomach gave a rumble as she did.

"Good morning, Chambers," he said, ever the man for formality despite knowing her since she was a child. Her parents had worked under him, after all.

"Good morning, Mr. Oliver," she replied, scooting up the bench to reach for her tea. Remarkably, it was still warm.

"Mrs. Pratt said you were up early this morning with Lady Iris," Mr. Oliver continued. "Is everything all right?"

"She's fine, Mr. Oliver. Nothing to concern yourself with."

"Is there anything I should prepare Mr. Mooring for while he has his breakfast?"

"Nothing Lady Iris can't tell him herself if she so chooses."

She sipped her tea, and he sipped his as an understanding look passed between them.

Sybil scarfed down her eggs and toast and only took a few more sips of tea before getting up and heading back upstairs. Her foot was already on the first step when the bell for Lady Iris's room rang.

Iris was back at her vanity, putting on her wedding band, when Sybil walked in. She was still in the dressing gown, but her skin had a warm pink tint to it beneath the silk. Sybil frowned when she spotted the stained sheets had still not been removed. Iris glanced up when Sybil came through the door.

"Did you eat?" she asked.

"Yes, m'lady."

"Good."

Sybil offered a smile and approached the vanity, reaching for Iris's blonde hair. It was in stark contrast to Sybil's dark brown and still in the braids her lady slept in, wrapped up and pinned to her head. Sybil gently removed the pins and let the hair fall in front of her before untying the ribbons and working the braids apart with practiced fingers.

Lady Iris let her eyes fall closed at Sybil's touch, and her shoulders dipped slightly. It was the only time Sybil ever saw her drop her posture. She ran her fingers along Iris's scalp, giving it a light scratch to relieve any tension, before fluffing out her curls. Then she reached for the hair brush and began to tug the bristles through the hair, starting from the bottom and working her way back to the scalp.

"How would you like it styled today, m'lady?" Sybil asked.

"Something simple, please," Iris answered. "I don't have any plans today, though I may go for a light walk around the grounds later if it doesn't rain."

"I'll have your boots ready just in case."

"Thank you."

She got to work on rolling Iris's hair into a loose bun at the nape of her neck, not unlike the one Sybil wore herself. When Iris's hair was secured and she was happy with it, Sybil helped her into a pair of drawers and fastened the button in the back. For the corset, Sybil picked out the one Iris had owned the longest, as that would be the most comfortable for all day wear. She was still lacing Iris in when there was a knock on the door.

"Who is it?" Iris called.

"Only your husband," said the voice on the other side with a smooth, New York accent.

Iris rolled her eyes, but reached for Sybil's hand. Sybil gave it an encouraging squeeze.

"Very well, come in," Iris said with a sigh.

He opened the door with a swift click of the knob and walked in, closing it shut behind him. Sybil didn't bother to look up. She was all too familiar with the slick black hair, slender frame, and wickedly dark eyes of Lewis Mooring. Her eyes slid over to the stain on the bed. Maybe if she was quick and careful, she could move the duvet over it before he saw it. But she couldn't stop lacing the corset now.

"Tighter, Sybil," Lewis said. "She's put on an unattractive amount of weight in the last few weeks."

"Yes, sir," Sybil said quietly, and made a show of dragging the laces through her fingers, but without actually tugging them. She knew exactly how Iris wore it, and she was not a fan of tight lacing.

"Is there something you want, Lewis?" Iris demanded.

It used to shock Sybil the way those two greeted each other. No pleasantries or affection, they got straight to business. But after all these years, she'd grown used to it.

"Another letter from one of your brother's tenants," Lewis said, holding up an envelope from what must have been the morning's mail delivery. "Apparently, one of them has died, and the sons are asking for an extension to pay their rent so they can bury him."

Iris let Sybil finish tying her corset before marching over to her husband and snatching the letter out of his hand. "I told you not to read my letters."

"They aren't *your* letters, they're for your brother. He is the earl, after all."

"Believe me, I'm aware. But seeing as he is on his honeymoon, I'm the one responsible for his correspondence."

"Foolish. What sort of man leaves his sister in charge when he has a perfectly capable brother-in-law? With a mind for business, at that."

"The kind of man who understands who will prioritize his wishes."

Sybil took the argument as her chance to cover the sheets. She stole a glance at Lewis to ensure he was still focused on Iris reading the letter while she flipped the duvet over.

"You can't honestly be considering granting the extension," Lewis scoffed.

"Of course I am," Iris said. "They've lost their father."

Sybil went to the wardrobe and pulled out a walking skirt and blouse for Iris. She retrieved a coat, scarf, and gloves as well, since there was still a spring chill in the air. Iris hadn't confirmed she would be going out for a walk, but Sybil needed something to do other than watch this disagreement unfold.

"Oh, no, that's the Percy farm," Iris said.

Sybil's heart skipped a beat, and she dropped the hat box in her hand. Both pairs of eyes turned on her as she scrambled to pick it back up. Her face warmed as they watched her.

"Pardon me," she said softly. "Just. . . clumsy."

"Be more careful, Sybil," Lewis said.

"Yes, sir."

She collected herself, though her heart still pounded against her chest. Lewis had already redirected his attention to his wife, but Iris was still following Sybil with her eyes. Sybil went to the dresser, resolutely ignoring her mistress as she pulled out the proper petticoats.

"You knew the Percy family, didn't you, Sybil?" Iris asked.

Sybil finally met her gaze. "Yes, m'lady, we were neighbors. My parents' cottage was just outside their farmland."

Memories that she'd long kept at bay began to creep up in her mind. Big, bearded Archie, who was gone now, though she was still struggling to believe it, and his three strapping boys—Edward, Stuart, and Charles. Charles, especially since they were closest in age. The dark-haired, blue-eyed, dimpled smiled boy who'd taught her to climb a tree, even in a dress. The one who had made up stories about the stars that she never believed, but let him tell them, anyway. The one who taught her to reel while his father played the fiddle. He was also the one who left Yorkshire behind, and Sybil with it.

"Did you know Archie?" Iris asked, pulling Sybil back into the room.

"Somewhat," Sybil said, though she knew it was an understatement. Archie had acted as a second father to her. "It's been years since I've seen him. Or any of them."

Her heart gave a painful twinge. Like a bruise that would never quite heal. She could still smell the smoke from one of the last times she'd seen Archie. She could still feel his arms around her, holding her back from the blaze that consumed her childhood home.

"I suppose we will be taking that walk, after all," Iris said, getting to her feet. "We must go and see them to offer our condolences."

"M'lady, I don't think—"

"That's a waste of time. Farmers die every day," Lewis cut in.

Iris ignored him, allowing Sybil to help her step into her petticoat. As Sybil reached out to tie it around Iris's waist, she noticed her hands had a slight tremble to them. She took a deep breath to steady herself.

"The Percys have farmed that land for centuries," Iris insisted. "As a representative of the earl, I must go see them. It's what my father used to do, and what my brother would do now if he were available."

"And I thought the English were supposed to be unemotional, sensible people."

"It's sensible to show appreciation for your tenants. Running an estate like this is not the same as running a business, Lewis. After seven years, I would think you'd have figured that out by now."

He opened his mouth to retort, but another knock at the door interrupted him.

"Yes?" he called out.

"Don't speak for me in my own bedroom," Iris snapped, and then glared at the door. "Who is it?"

"It's the maids," said the muffled voice of Bridget. "We've come to turn the bed, m'lady."

"Come in," Lewis commanded, shooting his wife a sneer.

Unfortunately, the maids obeyed and entered. Sybil's heart rate picked up again, this time with panic, as they crossed the room to the bed. She tried to keep her eyes fixed on Iris's clothes, but her gaze wandered. A bead of sweat trailed from her forehead as Bridget's hand pulled back the duvet, and the darkening spot became visible.

Don't let him notice, please don't let him notice, she prayed.

"What happened there?" Lewis asked.

Iris stiffened. "It's nothing."

"It doesn't look like nothing. It looks like another miscarriage."

"Lewis, don't do this," Iris said with an exasperated wince.

"Do what?"

"What you always do. You were criticizing me moments ago for being emotional when you're the one who always makes a scene."

Bridget and Flora yanked the sheets up, rolling them in their arms as fast as they could. Sybil didn't blame them. Already, she saw the tick in Lewis's jaw as his cheeks grew red with rage. Sybil did a sweep of the room with her eyes, but there was nothing on display that he could throw that would cause any serious damage.

"How in the world are those things comparable?" he cried. "You've lost another child! This isn't some farmer you never speak to. It's our family!"

Iris rolled her eyes. "We've been trying our entire marriage. Don't you think it's time we give it up?"

"Give—" he stopped short and stepped closer, getting his face within inches of hers. Iris didn't even flinch. "Give up? I want heirs for my fortune, Iris! A fortune which saved your family from financial ruin, need I remind you!"

"You needn't," she said coolly.

"God*dammit*!"

With a shout, he turned, snatched up her jewelry box, and hurled it at the opposite wall. The box snapped at the hinge and the pieces rained down onto the carpet, decorating it in glittering jewels. Bridget and Flora scuttled out of the room and Lewis slammed the door behind them. Hands on his hips, he glowered at Sybil.

"Leave us," he ordered.

"She can stay," Iris retorted. "Need I remind you that I am called 'my lady' and you are only 'sir.' The servants answer to me."

"But I am your husband, and therefore above you! As God intended! Unless you would defy Him as well!"

"Oh, believe me, when the time comes, God will be getting an earful for sticking me with you."

Sybil had to chew her lip to hold back a snicker at that. Lewis huffed out a sigh and scrubbed a hand over his face.

"You are the most insolent, infuriating, *bitch* of a wife!" he bellowed.

"Do settle down, Lewis." Iris said as she slid her hands into her gloves. "At your age, these kinds of tantrums cannot be good for your blood pressure."

Lewis exploded, hurling insult after insult at Iris, who paid him no mind as Sybil helped her into her coat and boots. He said all the same things he usually did about her inability to bear children making her a failure, but Sybil had learned to drown it out. Iris swept out of the room with Lewis still yelling, Sybil on her heels. Once out on the landing, his voice echoed through the house, and the servants, unperturbed, went about their jobs.

CHAPTER TWO

The trail up to the Percy farmhouse appeared exactly as Sybil remembered it. Spring was not yet in full swing, so the usually green grass was still brown and dry from the chill of winter. As she walked, she could still hear Charles's laughter mixed with her own as they raced to the door the way they did as children. He usually won, but was a good sport about it. She wondered if he ever recalled those days. And if he did, was it with as much fondness as she held?

The warmth in her chest ebbed away the closer they got to the door, replaced by the frigid grip of fear. It took hold of her heart, so hard and so fast that she came to a stop.

"Sybil?" Iris said.

"I. . . I'm sorry, m'lady. I don't think I can do this. I haven't seen them in years, and I think. . . I think they might be angry with me."

"Angry with you? Whatever for?"

"Because I. . . " she trailed off and shook her head. "It doesn't matter now. We should get you back up to the house, anyway. Perhaps even call the doctor."

"Why, so he can waste his breath telling me to get rest and telling Lewis to stay out of my bed? I'd rather skip it."

"But, m'lady, I—"

The door flew open with a squeak of the aged hinges. Sybil started and whipped around. For a moment, she thought it was Archie, miraculously alive and well, upright and strong. But the longer she stared, she realized it was Edward, the eldest. He'd always most resembled their father, and he did even more now with a face full of beard and his shaggy dark hair beneath his flat cap. His eyes went first to Lady Iris, and he snatched it off his head.

"M'lady," he greeted, tucking his chin toward her.

"Mr. Percy," Iris replied. "I heard about your father. I wanted to stop by personally to let you know we will grant you the extension you requested, and to offer our sincerest condolences."

"Thank you, m'lady. It means a great deal coming from you and your family."

"Our families have worked together for years. We will honor such alliances however we can."

"Ed!" shouted a feminine voice from inside. "What are you doing hanging around the door? Don't you have some work to d—"

A woman appeared behind Edward, blonde hair piled up in a bun at the back of her head. She wore a simple brown frock with an apron to protect it. And she stopped herself mid-sentence when she took in Lady Iris.

"Oh. . . " she said softly. "Oh, m'lady. To what do we owe the pleasure?"

"She's granting us the extension, love," Edward said. He turned back to Iris. "This is my wife, Susan, m'lady. Susan, this is Lady Iris."

"It is a pleasure to formally meet you, Mrs. Percy," Iris said.

Sybil's heart ricocheted around her chest while they exchanged pleasantries. Edward hadn't gotten a good look at her. Even if he did, she wasn't sure he would recognize her in a lady's maid uniform. The last time she saw them she was fifteen, even though at twenty-six, she thought most of her features unchanged. She never told them she'd gone to work for the earl's family. Only that she had to make it on her own. All this time, she'd been close by. Would they hold it against her that she never came to visit? That she didn't see Archie before he passed? That she never asked after Charles?

"I believe you know my lady's maid, Sybil Chambers?"

Iris's voice drew Sybil out of her worry and back to the present moment. She met Edward's eyes. So deep blue, with lines beneath them that betrayed his years and the effort of running a farm and a family. Those lines crinkled up when he took in her face.

"Sybil?" he cried, a smile blooming across his bearded mouth. "My God, is that really you?"

She blinked, taken aback. "I. . . yes."

She hardly got the words out before his arms were around her and he lifted her off her feet, squeezing her so tight that she couldn't breathe. It was as if no time had passed at all. The boys had always towered over her, especially as they grew into young men.

"Oh, welcome home, love!" he went on as he released her and she gulped air back into her lungs. He pulled back to give her a once over. "And look at you! A lady's maid! You've done well for yourself, haven't you?"

She laughed nervously. "I suppose I have."

"Can I offer you both a spot of tea?" Susan offered. "I've got the kettle on."

"I really think we need to get back," Sybil said.

"Oh, please stay," Edward said. "It's been years. Stu and I'd both like to catch up. We've been wondering what became of you."

Her face flushed as she felt Iris's curious eyes on her, but she didn't dare look. "Very well."

Edward and Susan ushered them inside, though Sybil needed no directing into the kitchen. She knew where everything was in this house. And it had hardly changed since the last time she was in it. A few of the pictures were different, photographs now instead of paintings, but the furniture was unchanged. And the smell. . . that earthy scent mixed with leather and tobacco pipe. It instantly made Sybil feel right at home.

"Where is Stuart?" Sybil wondered.

"He and Linda—that's his wife—took the children to school in the village, but he should be back any minute," Edward told her. "He'll be thrilled to see you."

"Will he?"

"Of course!"

"But, Edward, I—"

"Please, take a seat," Susan said, herding them toward the table.

Somehow, Sybil ended up in the exact seat she'd been in after she'd lost everything. Archie had been the one to make the tea that night. Edward and Stuart sat on either side of her, hands rested on her shoulders with sympathy. Days later, she was gone.

"Why are you so nervous?" Iris whispered as Edward went to help his wife. "What on earth could you have done to them?"

"It's sort of a long story," Sybil hissed back.

"How d'you take your tea, m'lady?" Edward asked before Iris could press for more.

"Just a slice of lemon, if you have it," Iris answered.

"Certainly. And is it still two lumps of sugar for you, Sybil?"

Sybil blinked. "Yes, but. . . you remember how I take my tea?"

"Of course. Same as Charlie always did."

Sybil's face flushed, and she cut her gaze down to her hands resting in her lap. She recalled Charles's voice as if he was there in the room, telling her, "Two lumps, Giggles. No other way to have a cuppa tea."

Once tea was served, Stuart returned, and his face lit up like the morning sun when he saw Sybil. He knew her right away, and when she got up to shake his hand, he also engulfed her in a hug. His wife, Linda, was a schoolteacher, so she had remained behind in the village, and Stuart would go retrieve them all in the afternoon.

Within minutes, the pair were reminiscing about the childhood days they'd shared.

"We sure had some fun," Edward said wistfully, leaning back in his chair. Archie once served as the primary occupant of that chair. Edward filled it with similar grace. "We nearly lost Sybil once, you know."

Iris's eyes went wide. "Lost her? How?"

"Misplaced her," Stuart said. "Her father was ready to wring our necks for it."

"Misplaced her?"

"What they mean, m'lady, is that I was much better at hiding than they ever were at seeking," Sybil interjected. "We'd started the game after lunch, but they still hadn't found me by supper."

"Goodness!" Iris laughed.

Sybil took a moment to take in the lady's smile. It was a rare sight these days.

"Eventually, I thought they'd left me on purpose as a prank, so I went home," she explained. "Everyone was outside, absolutely frantic."

"C'mon, Sybil, we'd never played a prank on you like that," Stuart said.

"You played pranks on me all the time!" she protested.

"Such as?"

"Let's see, there was the time you put a mouse in my bonnet." They chuckled, but she continued. "There was the time you held a glass of water up to the ceiling with a broomstick, told me it was a magic trick to get me to hold it, then abandoned me there until your father got home."

The brothers burst into laughter and Susan smiled along. Even Iris snorted into her tea. She covered it up by pretending to clear her throat. Sybil shot her a knowing grin.

"It was all in good fun," Edward said. He looked at Iris. "Harmless stuff, m'lady, I assure you."

"Harmless?" Sybil challenged. "My arms were so sore the next day, I could hardly pick up a book!"

Iris sipped her tea with a chuckle.

"Then there was the worst prank of all," Sybil went on.

"Oh, do tell," Iris said.

Stuart and Edward exchanged a nervous glance.

"It was a brutally hot day," Sybil began. "Hotter than any I can remember. I was out for a walk, heading over here to see the boys, and I was already sweating. Between here and my parents' cottage, there was a lake. As I passed it, I figured it couldn't hurt to take a dip. So. . . I stripped off my clothes and got in."

"Oh, I remember this," Edward said with a smirk.

"These two," Sybil said, pointing at them in accusation. "Saw me in the water and ran off with my clothes!"

Iris clapped a hand over her mouth to stifle the laughter about to burst forth. Susan swatted her husband's arm playfully, scolding him a little, while Stuart ran a hand through his hair as he laughed. Sybil folded her arms over her chest.

"I'm still upset about that one," she said jokingly.

"After the beating we got from Charlie, I assure you, we were properly punished," Edward said.

Sybil smiled at the memory. She was twelve, standing in the lake, hugging herself from humiliation, her eyes welling up with tears. When she was about to sob, Charles appeared, her clothes bundled in his arms. His face was battered and bruised, no doubt from the scrap with his brothers. Keeping his eyes on the grass, he placed her clothes on a nearby tree stump, turned his back, and promised he wouldn't look, but he was going to stay there to make sure his brothers didn't come back to try it again. It was the first time Sybil thought about kissing that boy. Even now, she wished she had.

"He walloped us good," Stuart said. "Even with it being two on one. I'd never seen him that furious."

"If there was one thing Charlie would do, it was defend Sybil's honor," Edward agreed. "He never let us do anything that would cause you embarrassment as a lady. And believe me, we had ideas. We only got away with that because he wasn't there when we saw you."

"Sounds like a real hero," Iris said.

"He wanted to be Sybil's, that's for sure. Those two had something special. They practically came as a set."

"I see," Iris said, turning eyes on Sybil, whose face was burning as if she had a fever. "And where is Charlie now?"

A shadow of melancholy crossed the brothers' faces.

"He left about twelve years ago to take a sailing apprenticeship," Edward said. "Farm life never suited him."

"Yes, he wanted to see the world," Stuart said. "And he has, according to his letters. Though he works on steam ships now, instead of sailing. He got a job with that company—what's it called?"

"White Star Line," Edward said.

"That's wonderful." Sybil cleared her throat. "Has he. . . has he been home at all since he left?"

"Afraid not," Edward said. "We thought he might come round once Father took ill, but he was still too far away."

Her heart sank. For so long, she'd wondered if he'd ever come looking for her. That there would be something to call him home. But if his family wasn't enough, she couldn't be so self-important as to think she would be. Charles always had adventure in his heart, leaving room for little else.

"I'm sorry," Sybil said. "First, Charles ran off and then I. . . I feel terrible about how I left you. I wanted to reach out, but the longer I went without saying anything, the more unwelcome I thought it might be, and I—"

Edward held up a hand to stop her. "You were grieving, Sybil. We've never begrudged you that."

"Yeah, you're always welcome here," Stuart added. "In every way but blood, you're our sister. And whenever Charlie is ready, he'll be welcomed home just the same."

"Thank you, both." She blinked away the mist in her eyes. "I'll do better from now on, I swear."

"That's a relief," Edward said. "We should hate to lose you a second time."

She reached across the table and took one of their hands in each of hers. She got a squeeze back, and she smiled.

When they absolutely had to get to work, Iris and Sybil took their leave, thanking the Percys profusely for their hospitality. It had brightened a day which had started so grimly. As they headed back toward the main house, Iris began her questioning.

"I'm still confused as to what you might have done to upset them," she said. "It couldn't have been as bad as you thought. What happened?"

Sybil sighed. "After Charles left, I stayed in touch with them, and we saw each other often. But about a year later was. . . the fire."

"The one that took your parents?"

"Yes. The Percys took me in. After a few days, I knew I couldn't be a burden to them. I left a note and came to the big house to apply for a job as a maid. Mr. Oliver knew my parents from when they worked there, so he took me on. I moved into the servant's quarters and started my life on my own. I told myself that when it wasn't so painful, I'd go back and see them. But it never seemed like the right time."

Iris nodded. "Well, they certainly are a gracious bunch. But I understand your hesitation."

"Thank you for this, m'lady. I don't think I'd have ever gotten the courage if you hadn't forced me."

"I shall force you again as soon as I'm able," she joked. She paused for a beat. "And this Charles boy. Were you and he ever. . . romantic?"

Sybil's cheeks got pink. "Oh, no, not really. I thought maybe one day, but. . . he left. And I stopped writing after my parents died."

"How sad."

"He was my first kiss, though."

Iris came to an abrupt stop and took eager hold of Sybil's hand. "Now this is a story I *must* hear."

Sybil told her that and a few more Charles stories all the way back to the house.

When they got inside, Lewis stood in the entrance hall, another letter in his hand. He tapped his toe on the floor as he checked his pocket watch.

"Ah, there you are," he said as they came through the door.

"Another letter?" Iris questioned. "Hand it over then."

She reached for it, but he snatched it away, above his head.

"Actually," he sneered. "This one was for me. From my sister."

Iris took a step back. "And what did she have to say?"

"Evidently, she and her husband had similar. . . complications to us. She has a doctor in New York who—as she puts it—worked a miracle, which got them their son. She's made arrangements for you to see him."

"That's kind of her, but I'm not going to New York."

"Yes, you are. She already booked our passage."

"I cannot leave the estate while my brother is away."

"*Titanic* doesn't leave for two weeks. Your brother will be back by then."

Iris rolled her eyes. "I don't want to go to New York."

"I didn't ask what you want. The doctors here in Yorkshire and in London are clearly incompetent. We will go to New York and you will see this man."

She raised herself up to her full height. "You cannot order me about like some—"

"I am your *husband!*" he screamed, with such force a lock of his hair came loose and hung over his eyebrow. Sybil flinched, but Iris held her head high. "You will do as I say! You will board *Titanic* if I have to put you in chains the whole way there!"

For several agonizing moments, the pair glowered at one another. It still amazed Sybil how quickly Lewis could ruin a moment. She had hoped that after the visit to the Percy farm, that Iris could relax for the rest of the day, have some time to herself. Sybil watched him as he smoothed his hair back again and hatred rose up in her like bile. For a fleeting moment, she actually wished him dead. It riddled her with guilt, but she thought it all the same.

"Fine," Iris said, steel in her voice. "I will go with you to America. With any luck, the ship will sink and it will take you down with it."

She darted around him and fled up the stairs, Sybil behind her.

Lewis let out a humorless laugh and shouted after them. "Sorry to disappoint you, but this ship is unsinkable! Do you hear me? Unsinkable!"

CHAPTER THREE

April 10, 1912

"This might be the most difficult goodbye of all."

She let out a watery laugh, followed quickly by a sniffle. "Don't be silly."

"I'm not."

He took her chin between his thumb and forefinger and tilted her face up until her eyes met his. A curtain of tears hid the deep, warm brown he'd come to adore in those sweet doe eyes of hers. She blinked, and they spilled over down her cheeks. Her hands flew up to her face to wipe them away. His heart split down the middle, part of him eager for the adventure that awaited, the other desperate to remain home because that was where she was.

"Sybil, I—"

"Come on, Charlie, I haven't got all day!" his father called.

"One more moment, Father, please!" Charles shot back.

Sybil's gaze shifted to the cart waiting to carry him to the village, but thankfully, landed back on his face after a moment. Gazing down at her, he used his thumb to wipe away a fresh tear that was trailing down her left cheek.

"Things won't be the same around here without you," she said softly. "Who's going to tell me all those ridiculous stories about the stars?"

He chuckled. "Tell you what. I'll write down stories about the stars I see on my travels and I'll send them to you."

"I'd like that very much."

He tucked a lock of her hair behind her ear. "You'll write back, won't you?"

"Of course I will. Though I suppose my stories from here will seem terribly boring compared to what you'll be getting up to."

"You could never bore me."

"Charlie, if you aren't on this buggy in two minutes, I'll be leaving without you!" his father warned.

Charles winced and pulled Sybil into a hug. He rested his cheek atop her head, letting himself take in the smell of her hair and the feel of her in his arms. He needed to etch these details into his memory because there was no telling when he would get to experience them again. Letting her go was like leaving behind a limb.

She was the one with enough strength to finally draw back, but his arms lingered around hers, his fingers digging into the sleeves of her dress. The smile she gave him was so precious, he swore he would carry it in his heart until he died.

"Charles, I. . . " she trailed off, swallowing hard. "Such good luck."

His throat tightened, and he opened his mouth to tell her. . . something. Surely, there was something he could say.

"Charlie!" his father shouted again. "It's now or never, son!"

Sybil inhaled deeply and squeezed Charles's arms. "You'd better get going. I think he's starting to mo—"

He stopped her with a fervent kiss. It didn't matter that he lacked experience, it had all the tender passion of youth. Everything his sixteen-year-old heart could muster, he put into this kiss. Hoping to show her how much he cherished her. She stiffened at first, but eventually moved her lips with his, kissing him back, and he knew she felt the same.

He parted from her and was pleased to find her as flushed as breathless as he was. He heard the steady trot of his father's horse, and he knew he had to go. Right now. Before he missed his chance. But he took in her face one last time.

After one more peck to her lips, he took off running down the lane. He had to sprint to catch up. His heart pounded as he leaped into the cart and it rocked beneath his weight. But he had finally kissed Sybil Chambers. He could pursue his new life with no regrets.

Charles woke, his lips warm and tingling with the memory of that kiss. He somehow managed to have that dream, that memory, every time he returned to England. As if he needed a reminder of how close he was to her. And yet so far away. It still made his chest ache that she'd stopped writing.

It didn't even matter that he'd kissed quite a few other women in the twelve years since he'd last seen Sybil. Nothing could replace her. And he couldn't outrun her, no matter how far he traveled or who he met.

He threw the sheets off his body with an indignant huff. Darkness still lingered outside his window, the gray of dawn not yet touching the horizon. He stretched and yawned before getting to his feet and padding over to gaze out the window. He hoped the sun would be out today. It would make the send off for this voyage much more exciting. Plus, it might warm up the chilly April morning.

After switching the light on, he got dressed, combed through his dark curls, and as he buttoned his shirt, his mind went back to Sybil. He hoped wherever she was, she was safe and happy.

He made his way downstairs to the lobby of the hotel, slinging his sea bag over his shoulder. His trunk, containing most of his belongings, was still aboard in his quarters. While he was at home on a ship, it was nice to get his feet on solid ground for a day or two every once in a while. The excursion into Southampton allowed him to get to the post office to mail some money to his brothers back at the farm in Yorkshire. He figured it was the least he could do since he was not able to make it to their father's funeral.

If he were honest with himself, he was relieved to have missed it. There was so much he didn't want to face back home. Memories, guilt, questions. Sybil, as well. Perhaps after this voyage on *Titanic*, he'd allow himself to go back. But now, when it was so raw, he preferred to keep out of it. He could make his apologies another time.

In the lobby, a few other officers milled about, but one in particular caught his eye. Or rather, the lady in the officer's arms did. They parted from a kiss, and Charles recognized First Officer William Murdoch, a smile plastered to his face as he gazed at the lady. He reached up to give her cheek a gentle pinch.

"Well, well, well," Charles joked. "What have we here?"

"Ah, Charlie," Murdoch replied with his Scottish timbre, that delighted smile still gracing his lips. "Darling, this is Charles Percy, second officer. Charlie, this is my wife, Ada. She came down to surprise me before the journey."

Charles offered his hand, and Ada shook it.

"Lovely to meet you," she said. He recognized her accent—she was from New Zealand. He couldn't remember if that was something Murdoch had told him or not. He knew that after getting married, they had moved to Scotland near Murdoch's family.

"Likewise," Charles returned. "What a sweet gesture to come all this way."

"Couldn't help it," she said. "I already miss him, and he hasn't even gone yet."

Murdoch chuckled, gazing at his wife as if she were the only person in the world. Then he kissed her cheek as if he hardly had a choice in the matter. Charles held back a laugh. He'd never seen Murdoch so. . . smitten. Especially for a man who was eleven years Charles's senior.

"I miss you too, darling," Murdoch said. "But I'll be back soon. Before you know it, you'll be eager to be rid of me again."

She giggled and looked at him, stars in her eyes. "Never."

Murdoch finally met Charles's gaze, though his reluctance to take his eyes off his wife was clear. "Any word from the captain yet?"

"No, I think all is going to plan," Charles said.

"Good. That means I've got a few more minutes to say goodbye."

He gathered Ada up in his arms and kissed her again. She laughed into his mouth. Charles left them to it and greeted a few of the other officers with handshakes and soft "Good mornings," as they all prepared to head back onto *Titanic*. One of the newest from White Star Line, she'd been making headlines with the rumors that she was unsinkable. From the moment Charles first saw her, he thought she was grand, certainly. The largest, finest, and most luxurious he had ever sailed. And maybe she was unsinkable. But he didn't want to tempt fate by making any such declaration himself.

Murdoch joined them as they headed out to the street. It would be hours yet before passengers would board, and there was plenty to do to get her ready for her maiden voyage. Charles shot a sidelong glance at Murdoch as they walked.

"I must say, Will, I'm surprised."

"By what?"

"I never thought you were such a romantic."

Murdoch smiled and shook his head. "I call it being happily married. If you're lucky, you'll understand one day."

Charles only smirked. "Get all your goodbyes in?"

"Aye. The woman sure knows how to give a man a good send off. But nothing's better than the hello I get when I come home again."

"Oh?" Charles raised his eyebrows.

Murdoch gave him a playful shove. "Get your mind out of the gutter, lad."

Charles chuckled. "No, I want to hear more about these exceptional hellos you've been getting."

"Tell you what. Marry a girl you love, and who loves you right back, and you'll find out for yourself."

Charles's grin faded as his mind went back to Sybil and that wonderful goodbye kiss from all those years ago. *What would a hello be like between them? Or was she already married to someone else, giving that man her kisses?* Why did the thought create a *Titanic*-sized pit in his stomach?

"Charlie?"

"Sorry." Charles shook his head. "It's just. . . you know me, never one to settle down."

"I wasn't either until I met the right woman. Trust me, Charlie. When you know, you know."

"Whatever you say, Will."

After boarding, Charles went straight to his quarters. Everything was as he left it, from his carefully made bed to the photos lining his writing desk. They were family portraits from each of his brothers, with their wives and children. The nieces and nephews he had never met, but adored from afar. Sometimes, when he looked at them, a pang of jealousy went through him at the assurance their lifestyle gave them. He knew the routine of the farm to this day from how often he had participated in it growing up. And there was some comfort in knowing what chores needed to be done which day, knowing exactly what to expect, knowing who you were going to interact with throughout the week. It was safe. Sure.

When he walked back out to the boat deck, taking in the smell of the sea and feeling the breeze in his hair, he didn't regret leaving the tilled earth of Yorkshire behind. He left in pursuit of adventure, and he had found it. He was still finding it every day. He got his security with the steady pay from White Star Line, and he knew when he was supposed to be on duty and what his responsibilities were. Other than that, once a voyage was over, it was onto the next, whichever corner of the world that called to him. He'd finally achieved his dream of absolute freedom. Staring out at the horizon, with the sun peeking over and creating a gleam on the shining deck of *Titanic*, he appreciated it all over again. A new ship was an adventure in itself.

"Lovely sight, isn't it?"

Charles turned, straightening up at the sound of Captain Smith's voice. "Yes, sir."

"When I was your age, I couldn't imagine that one day I'd be looking out from a harbor for the last time," the captain replied. A wistful air claimed him as he gazed over the railing. "And here I stand."

"Don't get too down, sir. You'll sail her back from New York, right?"

"I will."

"There, you've still got one more sight to look forward to before retirement."

A smile tugged the captain's mouth up, his full, white beard and mustache following. "So I do. Thank you, Percy."

"Anytime, sir."

Captain Smith's eyes lingered on the view a moment longer before he faced Charles again. "Well, come inside. Bruce Ismay and Thomas Andrews are here for one last meeting before the passengers arrive."

"Yes, sir."

Charles followed the captain off the boat deck and into the officer's quarters. But not before he scanned the small crowd of people gathering at the dock. It was ridiculous to think he'd see Sybil there, and she probably looked different after all these years. He looked anyway.

Chapter Four

The sun shone on the streets of Southampton, warming Sybil's face through the window as she gazed out from the car. She craned her neck to try to get a glimpse of the ocean. It would be her first. Unfortunately, the street was rammed with people, and the only thing visible in the distance was the ship itself.

Titanic. The name suited, at least Sybil thought. Her mouth dropped open as she marveled at the size, the magnificence, the novelty of her. She stood in the water the way a soprano took the stage, proud and majestic. The sun was her spotlight. And there was no doubt all eyes were on her.

After Lewis's drastic declaration, Sybil and Iris researched and found some newspaper clippings that did, in fact, declare *Titanic* unsinkable. Iris told Sybil she hadn't meant what she said—she didn't want a whole ship to sink just to get rid of her husband. But perhaps if he fell overboard, it wouldn't be the worst thing. They giggled together about it and then prepared the things Iris would need for the voyage.

Sybil clamored out of the car, and the smell of salt and sea hit her like a wall. It stirred an excitement in her heart that she couldn't explain. Lewis's valet, Gordon, followed her onto the street, giving her a nudge to remind her to move, and they headed to the back to retrieve the luggage. A steward arrived to open the door of the back seat to let Lewis and Iris out.

"It's magnificent isn't it, darling?" Lewis said, gazing upon the ship with a gleam in his eye as he helped Iris down.

"I suppose." Iris maintained an indifferent expression and raised her shoulders with a shrug. "What do you think, Sybil?"

Sybil opened her mouth to say that she actually agreed with Lewis and thought the ship rather wonderful, but he cut across her.

"What are you asking a maid for?" he scoffed. "What could she possibly know about a ship like *Titanic*?"

"I ask because I value her opinion," Iris returned snappishly. "It's her first voyage. If she's not impressed, then perhaps it's just like any other ship."

They both turned expectant eyes on Sybil, who shifted on her feet at being caught in the middle.

"I suppose it's quite grand, m'lady," Sybil said. "Though I don't have another ship to compare to, so they would all seem grand to me."

Lewis blinked and then shot his wife a glare. "I still don't see why you insisted on bringing her along. My sister has plenty of servants who can tend to you during our visit."

"I already told you, I trust no one but Sybil to take care of my needs," Iris argued. "I'm not sending her back now unless you want me to go with her."

He huffed with annoyance. "Very well. Let's board, shall we?"

He put his hand on the small of Iris's back and led her toward the dock, leaving Sybil and Gordon to follow with their things. Sybil grabbed as many of Iris's bags as she could, tucking a hat box under her arm while Gordon lifted the trunks.

"Got out of that one all right," he joked.

"I expect we'll be dealing with much more of that in such close quarters."

"We'll survive it." He paused for a beat. "Is it really your first voyage?"

Sybil nodded and started walking. "It is. I've only ever accompanied Lady Iris as far as London before."

"Truly?"

"Yes." She lifted a brow. "Where have you been that's so exotic?"

"Nowhere exotic," he said with a chuckle. "But while in service to Mr. Mooring, I've been to America once. And to the continent a few times."

"Where was your favorite place?"

"Paris, I suppose."

"What did you like so much about Paris?"

"The pastries. Definitely the pastries."

Sybil giggled. "Maybe one of these days I can convince Lady Iris to take a trip there and I can try them for myself."

"You won't regret it."

They followed Lewis and Iris up the gang plank to the first class entrance. Sybil looked over the side and finally got her first sight of the ocean. It was darker than she thought it would be, more gray than blue in her opinion, but it sparkled beautifully in the sunlight. It was vast, too, stretching endlessly out toward the horizon. For the first time, she understood why Charles might have preferred this to the mundane days at home.

Stepping onto the ship, Sybil's mouth fell open at the beauty of the inside. She never imagined it would resemble an entrance hall of a manor home, but it was comparable to any that she'd seen in England when she accompanied Iris. The room stretched wide as a ballroom, and the staircase curved elegantly up toward an artfully crafted clock on the landing. Warm light flooded in from above. Waiters in white uniforms flitted through the room, offering champagne and other complimentary drinks.

Their rooms were on B Deck, in one of the parlor suites. They were every bit as beautiful as Buckland Hall. Finely upholstered furniture, hand crafted wood paneling, with a private promenade deck. Sybil could hardly wait to stand out there once the ship was moving, so she could get a proper view. For now, she had to get Iris unpacked.

"Which dress would you prefer me to leave out for dinner tonight, m'lady?" she asked.

Iris set down her hat on the vanity and removed her gloves. Before she could answer, Lewis entered the room, leaned against the door-frame, and spoke for her.

"The red one," he said. "She looks divine in that."

Sybil looked at Iris.

"All right, the red one," Iris said with a shrug.

"My word. My wife agrees with me? Has the sky fallen as well?"

"It would be easier to agree with you more often if you weren't so smug about it."

"Oh, lighten up, Iris, it was a joke."

"Jokes usually make people laugh. Is anyone laughing?"

"No one is laughing because you're being so morose. We're on the grandest ship in the world on our way to finally get some hope in regards to starting a family. You could at least be cheerful about that."

"Forgive me if I'm not dancing for joy at the prospect of being poked and prodded again by a complete stranger."

"Jesus, Iris," Lewis sighed. "Is there anything I can do that will make you happy? Or are you determined to be cross with me forever?"

"I'm only trying to be realistic," Iris shot back. "We've been to dozens of doctors and specialists, undergone countless tests, and nothing has worked. I'm not exactly optimistic. And it doesn't help that you can't give me time to recover between losses."

"We have separate rooms here, isn't that staying away?"

"But will you actually stay away? Or will you—as usual—come stumbling in here after your brandies and demand I perform my wifely duties?"

Lewis's face reddened. "We shouldn't be discussing such things in front of the servants."

"Oh, spare me that, Lewis, you know she's heard it all before."

Sybil continued with the unpacking as if she hadn't heard anything at all. But she could feel Lewis's eyes tracking her around the room. She pulled the red dress he mentioned out and laid it on the bed, but her eyes spotted a button hanging from a thread in the back. She picked it up to examine it closer.

"I'm sorry, m'lady, something must have happened in transit, this button's come loose," she said. "I think I can mend it before dinner though."

"Don't bother, I'll wear something else," Iris said with a dismissive wave of her hand.

"Are you sure? It's no trouble to reinforce a button, m'lady."

"I'm sure. Check the black one, see if that will do."

Sybil reached for the other gown hanging up and ran her hands over the buttons and beading, her eyes following to be sure all was in place.

"The black one seems to be in order, m'lady."

"Fine, black suits your temperament better anyway," Lewis scoffed. "I'm going to order champagne. At least one of us should be celebrating."

He turned and swept away to his side of the suite, the sound of his footsteps dying until they heard the sound of his bedroom door slam shut.

"I can't believe he's going to start drinking already," Iris complained. "I mean, I can believe it, I just wish he wouldn't. Now I know he'll be in here tonight."

Sybil didn't know if it was her recent rekindling of her friendship with the Percys or what, but an idea came to her. A childish one, but perhaps it could put a smile on Iris's face. Even if Lewis flew completely off the handle, it would be worth it.

"Forgive me if this is impertinent, m'lady, but. . . would you want to maybe. . . mess with him a bit?" she suggested. "Since he likes jokes so much, perhaps we play one of our own?"

Iris hoisted an eyebrow. "What did you have in mind?"

Sybil chewed her lip and cast a nervous glance across the suite. "How about we go for a walk, m'lady, and discuss it elsewhere?"

"Sounds lovely."

By the time they made it to the sprawling first class promenade deck—after taking the time to admire the stunning skylight at the top of the grand staircase—*Titanic* was pulling out of the Southampton port. The people at the harbor all blurred together at such a great distance. Especially the way they waved, their arms silhouetted among each other like a bug stuck on its back. Sybil looked back, the oddest sense of melancholy settling in her chest.

When she turned around again, she saw Iris standing by the railing, her hands curled around it and her eyes closed. They had left her hat back in the room, so the sun illuminated her fair face and made her hair shine like gold. Sybil said nothing, allowing Iris to have a moment of peace.

"I'd forgotten how much I enjoy the sea," she said after a long beat of silence. "We used to go every summer. My family."

"That must have been nice," Sybil replied.

"It was certainly a happier time. I don't remember many details, but I do recall plenty of laughter."

"I know how you feel, m'lady. It's the same when I think back to the time at the farm with the Percy boys. It's been such a pleasure to get to know them again. Maybe, once we get back, you and your brother can reconnect too."

Iris heaved a sigh and turned her back on the view. "If only it were that simple. You see, I'm still rather angry with my brother."

Sybil's face screwed up. "What for, m'lady?"

"When my family was facing. . . financial hardship, Hugh and I were both of age to get married," Iris began. "I was twenty, and he was twenty-two. But because he was in university, no one thought it was suitable for him to settle down right away. They thought he was 'too young.' Suddenly, the entire burden fell on my shoulders. When I stood to inherit no part of the estate other than a sizable dowry. It was my responsibility, anyway. My duty to my family." She toyed with the lace on the sleeves of her dress. "And Hugh didn't even offer. He was happy to let me fall on the marriage sword for him. Lewis came into the picture, fifteen years older than me with millions at his disposal, and my fate was sealed."

Sybil started to reach for Iris's hand, but drew it back. "I wish there was some way I could make it easier for you, Lady Iris. Truly."

"You already do, believe it or not," Iris said with a soft smile. "I don't think I'd survive this without you, Sybil. Much less be able to keep up this pretense about my fertility."

Sybil recalled that first night she served Lady Iris. It was directly after the wedding. Iris asked her point-blank if she knew of any way to prevent pregnancy. Unfortunately, being nineteen, unmarried, and innocent, Sybil had no idea. But she asked around. Subtly of course, checking with the other maids, embarrassed as she was to do it. But she'd never forgotten that desperate, pleading look in Iris's eyes. In that moment, she swore she'd protect this woman from whatever that man threw at her.

"Of course, m'lady. You and your family gave me purpose after I lost my parents. I'll always be there for you, however I can."

"I hope you know how much I appreciate it," Iris said, and she held out her hand. Sybil took it with a smile. "You're so much more than my lady's maid, you know."

"I know."

Iris took a deep breath. "Now, enough of all that. You must tell me about this scheme of yours."

Sybil had nearly forgotten the reason they came outside in the first place. Her smile widened at the reminder, and she allowed Iris to lead her toward the boat deck, still hand in hand. It wasn't proper, but neither cared after such a moment.

"Okay, I'm thinking, when he comes into your room tonight, let him think it's you in the bed," Sybil began. She brushed the arm of an officer walking by with two others, since the lifeboats narrowed the path to the next part of the deck. She muttered a quick, "Pardon us," to him in passing, and continued on her way. "But really, it'll be—"

"Sybil?"

She nearly stumbled at the sound, dragging Iris to a halt. She couldn't believe it. It sounded like him, but it didn't seem possible. It couldn't be. Could it? Slowly, heart pounding, she turned to face him, and there was no mistaking him. Dark wavy hair, kind blue eyes, and a dimpled smile to die for.

"Charles?"

Chapter Five

Charles watched with bated breath as the two women they'd passed turned around. It seemed to take her ages, but finally, the brunette in the black dress was facing him, and he knew. She hadn't changed a bit since he last saw her. Her beautiful brown eyes went wide as she took him in. He had to remind himself to exhale.

"Charles?"

"Sybil!" he cried, and opened his arms.

"Charles!"

She bounded over, beaming, and threw herself into him. He wrapped her up and spun her around as she squealed with delight.

"Charles, I can't believe it!" she went on, her voice muffled by his collar in her face. "Is it really you?"

He set her down so they could examine each other. She was a solid head shorter than him now, but otherwise things were fairly unchanged. His cheeks already ached with the size of the smile on his face. Her eyes sparkled.

"It's really me!" he assured her. "Is it really you?"

"It really is!"

Laughing, they embraced again. He couldn't even help himself. The years between them faded away, and they were right back in Yorkshire, two kids in happy friendship. He let himself take a deep breath to get the smell of her hair. It was exactly how he remembered it—warm with a hint of vanilla.

She pulled away so she could inspect him again, her eyes roving over his form. "Goodness, look at you! You're even taller than when you left."

"And you are just the same," he replied with a grin.

"Your brothers told me you worked for White Star Line, but I never dreamed you'd be here! And how professional you look, in your uniform and all! I can hardly believe it!"

"Believe it, Giggles. You are looking at Second Officer Charles Percy."

Her mouth fell open so adorably his knees almost buckled. "I cannot believe you called me that."

"How could I forget your favorite nickname?"

"It infuriated me and you know it. If I weren't so bloody happy to see you again, I'd thump you!"

She cast herself into his arms again, and he squeezed her with a chuckle. His eyes fell closed at her presence there. He wished his arms were walls so he could enclose her with him forever. He knew he missed her. But until that moment, he didn't realize how much. Reluctantly, he let her go once more.

"You said you've spoken to my brothers?"

She nodded. "I only went back a few weeks ago when I heard the news about your father. Lady Iris and I, we—oh, my goodness, I've forgotten myself."

Her cheeks went a rosy shade of pink, and she straightened her dress before turning toward the blonde woman watching them with an amused twinkle in her eye. Sybil cleared her throat.

"Charles, this is Lady Iris Mooring," she said. "M'lady, this is my dear friend, Charles Percy."

Charles vaguely remembered the earl having a daughter named Iris. Sybil must have followed in her parents' footsteps and taken a job in service at the house. He extended a hand toward Lady Iris, and she gave him hers, a lofty expression on her face. That proud rigidity in her shoulders would have given her away as aristocracy even if he hadn't recognized her name. But her eyes lacked that haughty look he saw in most women of her class.

"Pleasure to meet you, m'lady," he said.

"You as well," Iris returned. "It's nice to put a face to the name at last."

"You've heard of me?"

"Mostly from your brothers, but from Sybil as well."

"Sybil can be believed, but my brothers. . . seek a second opinion on anything they might have told you."

The corners of her mouth turned up into a smile. He released her hand and turned toward the two men standing behind him.

"May I introduce Captain Edward John Smith and First Officer William Murdoch," he said. "Gentlemen, this is Lady Iris, daughter of the Earl of Manfax, and her lady's maid, Sybil Chambers. Sybil and I grew up together in Yorkshire."

They greeted Iris first, and then Sybil, and Murdoch's eyes lingered on her.

"You and Charlie must be good friends indeed," he said. "That was quite the hello."

His knowing gaze slid over to Charles, who felt his ears get hot.

"I must ask," Iris said. "Why did you call her Giggles?"

"Oh, God," Sybil groaned, hiding face behind her hands.

Charles grinned. "When we were young, my brothers and I learned to play poker from our father and the neighboring farmers. So we started a game of our own. Sybil didn't think it was fair to be left out simply for being a girl—and I tended to agree—so we let her play. Only problem was, she's a terrible liar. Every time she had a good hand, she'd giggle, and we knew."

"Goodness, it really was like having brothers, wasn't it?" Iris said.

"Yes, m'lady, it was," Sybil said. "Parts of it were annoying, but mostly. . . it was wonderful."

"It was," Charles agreed, placing his hand on her shoulder. "I can't tell you how glad I am to see you. Why just this morning, I. . . " he trailed off and shook his head. "Never mind."

"Tell me."

"It's nothing. I was thinking of home, that's all."

He wondered if she remembered the kiss. He hadn't got a chance to ask her about it afterward. He thought about asking in a letter what it meant to her, but lost his nerve every time he wrote it. She never brought it up either. And of course, after a year of being away, she'd stopped writing altogether. He stole a glance at her left hand, and his heart danced a jig at seeing it bereft of a wedding band. But that didn't necessarily mean she was free.

What does it matter if she is? He reminded himself.

"Captain, will you be joining us for dinner this evening?" Iris asked.

"I will, my lady, I look forward to seeing you there," the captain replied. "Is it just you and your maid traveling?"

"No, my husband and his valet are with us as well. I'm sure he'd be delighted to meet you."

"Then I shall make a special effort to find your table."

While the captain spoke to Iris, Charles took hold of Sybil's arm and pulled her aside. Her back met the wall, and she gazed up at him. A hint of a smile still danced upon those pretty pink lips, and he longed to claim them with his own. Kiss her like the man he was now instead of the boy he was then.

"Can I see you this evening?" he asked.

"Oh, I. . . " she cut her gaze to the deck. "I don't know. I've got to get Lady Iris ready for dinner and then for bed when she gets back."

"They're at dinner for hours, we'll have time." He hooked his finger under her chin and nudged her to look at him again. "Please. I must see more of you while you're here."

Her cheeks took on that rosy tint again, and he could have melted into the woodwork.

"I'll try. But I can't promise anything."

"I can," he said. "At seven o'clock tonight, I'll be done with my rounds and right here waiting for you."

"How long will you wait?"

"Until you show up."

"Charles. . . "

She tried to glance down again, but he didn't let her.

"I've missed you, Sybil. More than you know."

"I've missed you too."

Before either of them could say more, the captain called out to him.

"Percy, are you ready?"

"Yes, sir," he said, finally tearing his eyes from Sybil's face. He stepped back from her, and felt colder than when she was close. "Good to see you again, Giggles."

With that, he returned to his fellow officers. He tipped his hat to Lady Iris in farewell, and then they continued on their way down the boat deck. He stole one last look back at Sybil's disappearing form, only to find she was peering back at him too. She smiled, and he smiled in return. He hoped it meant she would meet him.

An elbow from Murdoch made him face forward again.

"Well," he said. "I don't want any more cheek about me and my wife after that display."

Charles rolled his eyes. "Come off it, Will."

"You do seem quite taken with her, Mr. Percy," the captain added.

"We were friends a long time, sir," Charles replied.

"Well, don't get too distracted. There's lots to do here, and I cannot be an officer down."

"Of course, sir."

They walked on, but Murdoch leaned in to whisper. "It really was *quite* the hello."

CHAPTER SIX

Sybil fastened the satin buttons of Iris's gown for dinner, her heart still waltzing around inside her chest, knowing Charles was here. On the ship. And he would be waiting for her later tonight. She still wasn't sure she wanted to go meet him. Excited as she was to see him again, there was still the hurt he'd caused her by leaving in the first place. And when she stopped writing, so did he.

"Are you going to meet him?" Iris asked, as if she were inside Sybil's mind.

"I'm not sure, m'lady," Sybil replied, helping Iris get her gloves on. "There's still so much between us that feels unfinished. Questions unanswered."

"Doesn't that make it all the more imperative to have that conversation?"

"I don't know, honestly. Part of me is worried that the answers will only hurt me. And I don't want to get my hopes up."

"Get your hopes up for what, exactly?"

"Just—that he—that we could—"

"That he's unattached?" Iris finished with a teasing grin.

"Yes," Sybil admitted, face getting hot. "I should hate to think that. . . after everything. . . this is all only friendship for him."

"I can't believe you're even worried with the way he was looking at you."

Sybil's blush impossibly deepened. "I don't know what you mean, m'lady."

"Oh, yes, you do. He looked at you the way most women only dream of being looked at."

Sybil cocked her head to the side and her brows furrowed. Iris was admired wherever she went. Not only because of her wealth and the obvious ways it was displayed through her clothing and jewelry, but because she was also a strikingly beautiful woman. Sybil had been witness to men falling off bicycles, running into each other, or tripping over themselves, all because they were gawking at Iris.

"I don't understand."

Iris heaved a sigh. "Men often look at women the same way they look at jewels or ships or cars. There's a greed to it, a level of how it makes *them* look to have a certain woman at their side. Nothing to do with who she is, but *what* she is. It's how Lewis looks at me."

"But I—"

"Charles didn't look at you like a prize."

"How did he look, m'lady?"

"With reverence. The way one might look at the moon and stars."

That made Sybil recall the nights she and Charles would lie in a meadow near the farmhouse and stare up at the stars for hours. It was when he would make up his ridiculous stories about the constellations, all old gods and goddesses, tricksters and sorcerers. She always thought of him on clear nights when she would get a good view of them, a splattering of diamonds across a velvety black sky.

"You should go to him," Iris said. "In fact, I insist you do."

Sybil smiled. "Yes, m'lady."

She clasped the necklace she had picked out around Iris's neck when Lewis walked in, dressed for dinner in his white tie and tuxedo. His dark hair was combed back away from his face with pomade to hold it. He shot Iris an irritable scowl.

"Aren't you ready?" he said.

"Almost," Iris returned, glancing at herself in the mirror, touching the necklace to ensure it was secure. "This looks wonderful. Well chosen, Sybil."

Lewis frowned. "I heard you met the captain earlier."

"Yes, we ran into him while we were out walking. Sybil grew up with one of his officers."

"I don't care about that. The captain, did you tell him anything about me?"

"Only that you are my husband and you have your valet with you. We didn't have time for much else. He said he would stop by our table tonight, so any impression you'd like to make on him is entirely up to you."

"Good. Ready to go?"

He offered his arm and Iris took it. She looked back at Sybil once more before walking out of the room and winked. "I'll see you tonight, Sybil."

"Yes, m'lady," Sybil said.

When they were gone, Sybil stored Iris's day clothes away and tidied up the room before emerging into the sitting room. Gordon was on his way out.

"I'm heading to the servant's parlor for dinner," he said. "Want to come with?"

She shook her head. "Actually, I'm meeting someone."

With that, she put on her coat and left, heading for the boat deck where Charles said he'd be waiting.

True to his word, there he stood when she arrived. He was talking with Murdoch, laughing at something the first officer said. Charles appeared grown up when she saw him again, but in his smile, with those dimples, the boy she knew shone through. Had it truly been over a decade since she'd seen it? What a shame it was, for his smile created one on her own face. She slowed her walk up the steps, not wanting to interrupt.

As if sensing her presence, Charles turned his head and beamed when he saw her. "Hello there."

"Hi," she replied, her voice coming out an octave higher than usual. When had she gotten so nervous? She offered Murdoch a nod as an excuse to look away from Charles. "Good evening, Mr. Murdoch."

"Good evening, Miss Chambers," he returned. "I was just on my way."

He clapped Charles on the shoulder, nodded at Sybil, and disappeared into the wheelhouse. Charles locked eyes with Sybil.

"You made it, Giggles."

She chuckled. He was before her in two strides of his long legs, and he pulled her into another hug, every bit as warm and sincere as when they had first reunited. He smelled different than he did when they were back home. That earthy aroma of the farm no longer hung around him. Now, he smelled entirely of sea and salty air. As if it had seeped into his bloodstream. When he pulled away, she held back a shiver at the loss of his touch.

"So, would you like a tour of the ship?" he offered.

"Maybe this part of it," she said. "The whole thing might take too long, and I will need to get back to help Lady Iris."

"Certainly. We'll start here and work our way back. How's that sound?"

"Lovely."

First, he led her into what he called, "The Bridge," the control center for the ship. From there, they could look out over the well deck, forecastle deck, and all the way to the bow. Charles first showed her the wheel, which was manned by the helmsman, who greeted them politely, though it almost made her laugh to hear someone calling Charles "sir."

"This," he said, putting his hand on what appeared to be a big brass clock to Sybil. Only instead of numbers, it had words around the face such as 'stop,' 'slow,' 'stand by,' 'half,' and 'full.' "Is an engine order telegraph. It's how we communicate with the engine rooms. The bridge officer turns the handle to the speed he wants, and then the engineer will move his handle to confirm he got the order. You'd see the little hand rotate to whatever the bridge officer turned it to initially."

"Wow," she replied. "It seems so simple."

"For the most part. There's loads more that goes into it, but I don't want to bore you."

"You could never bore me," she told him, echoing some of the words he'd said to her before he left all those years ago. The smile he gave her told her he recognized them. "I'd like to see more."

He held out his hand, and she took it, warmth shooting all the way up from her fingers to her chest. "Right this way."

He led her back the way she'd come, passing the lifeboats lined up on the deck.

"We've got twenty lifeboats between these here and the collapsibles," he explained. "They're hanging on what's called a davit. In the unlikely event we need to evacuate the ship, the davit is swung out, loaded with passengers, and then lowered into the water."

"Will we need them? Or is it true that *Titanic* is unsinkable?"

"I don't know that I'd call any ship completely unsinkable. But the compartments below are water tight, which gives her a good chance at staying afloat, even if she hits something. Mr. Andrews could explain all that better than me, though."

"I see," she said. She tilted her chin up and added a teasing lilt to her voice. "Is he around? Perhaps I should be getting a tour from someone more knowledgeable."

"Oh, come on," he said with a chuckle, rolling his eyes.

Still holding her hand, he continued, leading her to the gymnasium next. It was dark inside, but warm, so they entered to escape the biting wind. Since it was after hours, Charles didn't turn on the light. The equipment was all way beyond Sybil's knowledge, but she appreciated the amount of options anyone who did want to use it had.

"Surely you could use the stationary bike," Charles said.

"I never learned to ride a bike," she admitted.

"No time like the present. I'll help you."

"What if I fall?"

"It's nailed to the floor, Sybil. I think you'll be all right."

"Charles, I—"

"Up you get."

Without warning, he wrapped an arm around her waist and lifted her onto the seat. She let out a squeal of protest, but found any struggle to be useless. He was stronger than her when he left, but she'd always stood a chance. Not anymore. His arms had doubled in size and he'd grown to stand a whole head above her. This close, she could feel the hardness of his chest as well, and it made her thankful she was facing the wall so he couldn't see her blushing.

When he had her settled, he put one hand on either side of her waist.

"There, see?" he said. "I won't let you fall."

He was standing so close, his breath tickled the back of her neck. She held back a shudder that threatened to sneak up her spine.

"One foot on each pedal," he said. "Hands on the bars."

"All right," she said shakily, and reached forward for the handles first. She looked down once she had a good grip and lifted her feet to slide her shoes on top of the pedals. One was much higher than the other, but with Charles's secure hold, she wasn't too off-balance. "Now what?"

"Push with your foot."

"Which foot?"

"Whichever is higher."

Her right was on the higher pedal, so she slowly inched it forward.

"That's it," he said. "Just move your legs in a forward circle. It's just like walking, really."

The pedals rotated underneath her feet and they all lost contact with one another, and the pedals spun out of control. Sybil let out an indignant huff.

"It's not like walking at all!"

Charles's gentle laughter eased her irritation. "Keep your feet *on* the pedals while you move them."

"That's easier said than done."

"Don't move," he said in a suddenly stern tone.

Alarm shot through her. "What is it?"

"Your dress is stuck. I'll fix it, just stay still."

"This is what I get for trusting you."

"Hey, I made no promises about the dress. Only that you won't fall, which hasn't happened, by the way."

"You are not getting away with this on a technicality, Charles Percy."

He chuckled as he squatted down and worked the hem of her dress away from the pedal. She watched him for a moment, entranced by the motion of his hands, which she could still almost feel touching her sides. Then a muffled voice caused her to look up.

There, right in front of the window, stood Lewis, a woman on his arm who was definitely not Lady Iris. This woman was of the same class, judging by her glittering dress beneath a mink coat and the jeweled combs in her dark hair. She stumbled as they walked, clutching Lewis's arm as they both burst into drunken laughter. Then he leaned in close, caging her against the window, and he kissed her. Sybil sucked in a sharp gasp.

"What is it?" Charles asked.

"Shh!"

"What?"

"Is my dress out?" she whispered.

"Yes, but why are you whispering?"

She shushed him again and gestured toward the window. He looked out, then back at her with a lifted brow.

"Do you know them?" he asked, finally lowering his voice.

"That's Lady Iris's husband," Sybil explained under her breath.

His eyes went wide. "Oh."

Chapter Seven

Sybil hopped down from the bike's seat and slunk closer to the window, Charles on her heels. She pressed her back into the wall adjacent to the window where she would be able to hear whenever they finished kissing and started talking. Charles leaned against the wall beside her.

"I can't tell you how refreshing it is to have an American woman in my arms again," Lewis said.

"What?" the woman replied in a husky voice. "The English girls aren't friendly?"

"Downright frigid. Even the servants call my wife the Ice Princess."

"You're lucky I'm here to warm you up, Mr. Mooring."

They kissed again, and Sybil ground her teeth. Charles nudged her shoulder with his elbow.

"Is that true?" he hissed. "The Ice Princess thing?"

"Yes, but. . . it's complicated."

Charles's brow furrowed, but Sybil didn't get to explain before the woman outside spoke again.

"Shall we take this somewhere more comfortable?"

Lewis groaned. "Absolutely. Though. . . I believe our servants are still in our rooms."

"You're lucky again. My rooms are servant free. And only a five minute walk from here."

"I'm lucky, indeed. Lead the way."

Giggling, they hurried away, the sound of their footsteps fading down the boat deck. Sybil's hands balled into fists and she pushed herself from the wall, already pacing back and forth.

"That wretched, rotten, *rat* of a man!" she cried. "I can't believe he's doing that out in the open! Anyone might have seen! We did see! He's a-a-a—"

"Dirty bastard?" Charles finished

"That's it."

"I've got something worse if you like, though I'd hesitate to say it in front of you."

She giggled. "Thank you, that will do."

His gaze softened. "Are you all right?"

"I think so," she said. Her eyes found his. "Could we go back outside? I want to look at the stars with you."

He cracked a wide smile. "I'd love that."

Before she knew it, they were out on the promenade deck, lying on two lounge chairs they'd pushed together, and looking up at the sky. She could see her breath form a vapor in the air each time she exhaled. She let out a contented sigh.

"There. Now we could be at home if we pretend enough."

"Not quite," he said. He lifted his hand. "We always held hands when we went stargazing back then."

He intertwined his fingers with hers. His touch eased the ire still simmering in her chest about seeing Lewis with that other woman. Charles always had that ability. Whenever she was sad or angry, he took her out to their meadow, and they reminded themselves how small their problems were in the grand scheme of things.

"Can I ask. . . how did you end up working for that man?" he asked.

"I don't really work for him, I work for Lady Iris."

"Yes, as her lady's maid. But. . . how did you get there? Doesn't it take time to become a lady's maid? I would've thought you were too young."

"I was head housemaid by the time I was eighteen," she said. "Not that I'm boasting."

"Hold on, your parents let you go to work that young?"

Her heart skipped a beat. Had his brothers not told him? A lump formed in her throat with that old, familiar hurt. "They passed away."

"Oh, Sybil, I'm so sorry."

"It's all right," she said with a sniffle. "I've managed being on my own."

"How did it happen?"

"House fire."

"And. . . when did it happen?"

"A year after you left."

He turned his face toward her. "Well, that explains another thing."

"What's that?"

"Why you stopped writing."

She blinked. "Oh. Well. I, er. . . I am sorry, Charles. I meant to, but I—"

He held up his free hand to stop her. "Quite all right, I assure you. I suppose I could have reached out, but I thought. . . "

"You thought what?"

"I thought you must have met someone. And as much as I missed you, I was happy for you. At least, that's what I kept telling myself." He paused for a beat. "So. . . how did you survive? The fire, that is."

"I wasn't at home," she said, the staggering grief of that night still a sore on her heart. But it didn't hurt as much to tell Charles. Something felt right about it. "I'd gone to our meadow to stargaze. I did that a lot whenever I was really missing you. I smelled the smoke and started back, but by the time I got there. . ." she trailed off and closed her eyes. She could still feel the heat of the blaze on her face. "Nothing could be saved. Not even Mum and Dad."

"Well," he cleared his throat and swallowed. "I suppose I'm happy to be the reason you weren't there."

"I hated you for it, you know. For quite a while."

"Fine by me." He met her gaze. "At least you were alive to hate me."

She offered a small smile. "Your father stopped me from running inside. And he took me in at the farm after. I thought about staying, but. . . I wanted to get through life on my own."

"So you went to the earl's house and demanded a job?" he teased.

"I offered my services, what they were worth," she returned firmly, but her smile lingered at the corners of her mouth. "They took me on as a housemaid, and then when Lady Iris got married, I was promoted to her lady's maid. The rest is history."

He squeezed her hand. "You're impressive, you know that?"

She cut her gaze to their clasped hands. "I'm just a servant. Nobody, really."

"You have never been nobody to me."

Her eyes flew back to his face, her heart suddenly fluttering like a hummingbird. The look in his eyes stole the breath from her lungs. His free hand came to cup her cheek, forming around her face as if it was made for her.

"I used to look at the heavens and miss you too," he said. "So much I would ache."

"I know what you mean."

The night her parents died, she had experienced that desperate yearn in her heart looking at the empty grass beside her. She felt it even more in the following days, when she had lost everything and would have sold her soul to the devil to have Charles's arms around her.

"But surely you met plenty of other people," she said in an attempt to lighten the mood. "You've been traveling so long."

"I have," he agreed. "To Africa and Australia and the Americas. Parts of Asia."

"You never met anyone special?"

"Women, you mean?"

Her cheeks got warm, but she didn't look away. "I think it's a fair question. You did kiss me, after all."

"You remember?" he asked with a raise of his brows.

"Of course I do."

He paused, and she watched a smile grace his lips.

"I did meet women in my travels," he said. "Nice ones."

Her heart sank. "I see."

"Beautiful ones too."

"I'm sure."

"Smart, funny, talented ones."

"Well, bully for you," she said, and started to sit up, but he stopped her.

"The problem was, none of them were you, Giggles."

"Oh."

Her heart went at a full gallop. This all was beginning to feel like a dream. Seeing Charles again was hardly believable, but the things he said made her head go straight up to the clouds. Above the stars and into the sun. Any moment now, she expected to wake up, back in the servant's quarters at Buckland Hall, alone, with only the memories of Charles and that kiss to comfort her.

But his hand was on her cheek again, warm and tender and real. His lips in her direct line of vision. Would he kiss her again? Would she let him? She didn't know. There was still so much to re-discover about each other. And yet, he moved closer. His eyes fell closed. Her heart was screaming at her to shut hers too and welcome him with open arms. Her head warned against it, telling her to spend more time before allowing this. But if she stopped him, would he ever try again?

"Charles, I don't know if—"

"Sybil?" Iris's voice made them jump apart, though their fingers still clung to each other. "Sybil, are you there?"

Sybil cleared her throat. "I'm here, m'lady."

Iris walked over, her heels tapping against the deck as she made her way toward them. Sybil got to her feet and Charles followed suit, without letting go of her hand. Iris's eyes went to where their fingers linked before looking at Sybil with a knowing smirk.

"I hope I'm not interrupting."

"We were just talking," Sybil blurted out. "I mean, catching up."

"If you want, you may continue, and I can get myself ready for bed."

"No, m'lady, I'll come help you."

She finally released Charles's hand, though found herself reluctant to do it. She turned to face him, drawing a blank on what to say.

"Well. . . goodnight, Charles. It's been lovely."

"It has," he agreed with a smile. "When may I see you again?"

"Oh, I'm not sure. . . "

"Tomorrow," Iris interjected. "Same time and place, if your rounds will allow it."

"Works for me. I'll see you then, Giggles."

He touched his finger to her chin, and Sybil couldn't help but smile at him. He bid them goodnight and then headed back toward the officer's quarters. Sybil watched him go and heaved a sigh.

"Don't worry," Iris said. "Tomorrow will be here before you know it."

Sybil cleared her throat. "Right. . . shall we head back to your room and get ready?"

A wicked grin claimed Iris's lips. "Absolutely."

Back in the suite, Sybil first got Iris into her bed clothes before stripping down herself. She told Iris about what she had seen with Lewis, but Iris was unfazed. She said she'd seen them leave the dining room together and knew perfectly well what would happen from there. Part of Sybil was relieved that Iris wasn't wounded. After all, it was fairly common for Lewis to stray. But it also made her sad. Iris deserved someone who truly loved her.

Before Sybil could voice this opinion, they heard the door to the cabin open. Iris started and slammed the lights off before whipping around to face Sybil.

"Show time," she whispered, barely containing a giggle.

Sybil laughed right along with her, but bit her lip to hold it back. Iris snuck into the private lavatory off her room, while Sybil pulled back the duvet and crawled into her bed. Lewis's stumbling feet could be heard slowly making their way toward the room.

He came clumsily through the door, catching himself on the doorframe before making his way over to the bed. He stubbed his toe on one of the bed posts and barked out a curse. Sybil squeezed her eyes shut and swallowed down another laugh bubbling in her chest. She felt the mattress dip behind her with his weight. The sour smell of alcohol came off him in waves, as if he was sweating out whatever he'd consumed throughout the night. He also reeked of the other woman's perfume.

"Hello, wife," he slurred, collapsing beside her with his chest pressed against her back. His hand slid up her arm and over her shoulder before stopping by her neck. He moved her hair out of the way and nuzzled his nose into her skin. "Will you deny me tonight?"

Sybil stirred like she was just waking up, rolled over, and then let out a scream. Lewis drew back with alarm. Light flooded the room as Iris came storming out of the lavatory.

"Lewis!" she cried.

"I—hold on—what the hell?"

He glanced between the pair of them, blinking rapidly as he tried to focus. Sybil held the sheet up over her chest and continued to feign offense.

"I'm willing to look the other way when you paw at the other maids and American heiresses, but Sybil? My lady's maid? How could you?"

"Iris, hold on, what is she—"

"Are there no boundaries left between us?"

Sybil had to cover her mouth to disguise her amusement. Iris was killing this performance. She was a born actress, apparently.

"There's been a misunderstanding," Lewis said. "I thought she was you!"

"Oh, because the resemblance is so uncanny!" Iris shot back. "My God, Lewis, how drunk are you?"

"I'm not drunk, I thought—"

"I think you should go. Get your grubby hands away from my lady's maid and stick to your own room for the night."

He crawled off the bed, using a post to steady himself, and glanced between them again, opening his mouth to speak, but closing it again right away. Iris's lips quivered at the corners, and Sybil knew she was about to crack. Sybil was too. She pressed her hand even harder into her face. Iris broke first. Laughter burst forth from her, and she didn't even try to contain it. Sybil joined her, and before long, they were wiping tears from their eyes.

"A practical joke, Iris, really?" Lewis said. "Of all the childish—you're the daughter of an earl, you should be above this kind of immaturity!"

"You should see your face!" Iris returned, pointing with one hand and holding her middle with the other.

He rounded on Sybil. "And you! How could you participate in something like this? Aren't you supposed to be responsible for her?"

"I'm sorry to tell you, sir, but it was my idea in the first place," Sybil admitted, still wheezing.

Lewis closed his eyes and pinched the bridge of his nose. "Foolish girls."

With that, he swept out of the room. They heard the slam of his door when he crossed the suite, but were still too entertained to flinch. Iris sighed and fell down on the bed beside Sybil. Sybil watched her, heart warming at seeing her lady so carefree and fun.

"Oh, my, that was good," Iris said. She let out another giggle. "We'll have to think of more before we get to New York."

"I'm glad you enjoyed it, m'lady," Sybil replied. "I'm sure we'll be able to get at least one more prank in before the end of the journey."

Iris rolled onto her side. "Before that, though, I want to hear how things went with Charles. I'm sure Lewis will be leaving us alone for the night."

Sybil grabbed a pillow and held it to her chest. "It was wonderful."

Chapter Eight

April 11, 1912

"You didn't!" Charles laughed as Sybil finished telling him about the prank she and Iris pulled on Lewis the night before. Seeing her giggly made his heart do flips. He didn't know Lewis, but based on the information he had so far, he wasn't a fan. The frown he put on Sybil's face was reason enough not to like him. But knowing he was unfaithful to his wife, even if it was common in their class, didn't sit right with Charles. "I can't say I feel sorry for him."

"Nor should you," Sybil replied quickly. She faltered and looked down at her hands. "I shouldn't say things like that. He's still Lady Iris's husband after all."

"Being her husband doesn't entitle him to your respect."

She smiled at him. He'd commit highway robbery for that smile.

"I suppose that's true," she said.

"Besides, it's good to know my brothers and I taught you well."

"I shall provide excellent testimony when you decide to advertise."

"We'll call it the Percy School of Mischief."

"It's perfect. It gets straight to the point. And your nieces and nephews would be star pupils, I think."

His heart gave an uncomfortable twinge. It shouldn't be possible that she'd met them while he still had not. His brothers talked about their children in their letters, but it was hardly substantial information. He forced a smile.

"Are they little devils?" he asked.

"They can be," she said. "Especially to each other. All except Nora, the youngest. She's a darling. Far more interested in books than the spats among her cousins."

"Smart girl."

"She's the one who reminds me most of you. Already, she's talking about wanting to travel the world. Says she doesn't want to just read about it, she wants to see it for herself."

"Maybe I'll write to her and give her a few tips."

"Do. She'd love it. They all would."

A beat passed, and they looked out at the darkening sky together. The sun was almost gone behind the horizon, taking the gold of dusk with it and leaving them in a world of grays and blues. He glanced sidelong at Sybil and found her even more beautiful. Her face like marble in the lighting—like art.

"Can I ask you something?" she said.

He flushed, remembering what almost took place less than a day ago. "If this is about last night, I'm sorry. I thought perhaps I was. . . I dunno, coming on a bit strong. But I thought maybe we could pick up where we left off all those years ago."

"Oh, um actually," she began, her cheeks getting a dusting of pink in them. "I was going to ask why you hadn't been home."

"Oh." He paused. There were several layers to that answer, and he could think of none of them now that he was embarrassed. "I. . . well. . . it's complicated."

"Complicated how?"

"Just that I've been busy and I don't exactly get to choose my schedule and—"

"Charles. It's been over ten years and you haven't even stepped foot in Yorkshire. Not even when your father got sick. Why?"

He heaved a sigh, forcing his mind to gather up his thoughts. "It's not as if I haven't wanted to. But, Sybil, I. . . I love my life. I love what I do."

She wrinkled her nose so adorably he wanted to kiss it. "Why should that stop you from coming home?"

He held her gaze. "I was afraid if I went home, I'd find a reason to stay."

It was hard enough to leave her the first time. If he'd gone back, it would have been impossible to do it again. Her eyes went wide, and she cut her gaze to the deck, her hands meeting in front of her as she picked needlessly at her nails. It reminded him once again that she hadn't married. So he was right not to go back.

She opened her mouth to say something, but a call from the door to the officer's quarters had them both turning their heads. Sixth Officer James Moody stood in a small puddle of light, facing them.

"Charlie!" he called again.

"Here, James," Charles replied.

"You're sure you don't want to join in tonight?"

"Join in what?" Sybil wondered from behind him.

"Poker game. It's not important—" He stopped short, an idea occurring to him. He shot Sybil a wicked grin. "How'd you like to redeem yourself, Giggles?"

She blinked. "What are you talking about?"

"Join us for the game."

"What? No, I couldn't!"

"Come on, it'll be fun." He took her hand and led her toward the door. "Deal us in, James!"

"Us?" Moody replied, tilting his head in confusion.

Sybil tried to dig her heels in, but Charles was too strong for her. He dragged her—protesting heavily—right up to the door where Moody stood, looking between them with bewilderment.

"This is my old friend, Sybil," Charles explained. "She and I will be joining the game. That is, unless she's afraid she'll lose."

Immediately, Sybil stopped struggling and glowered at him. "Excuse me?"

"I said, unless she's afraid she'll lose," he repeated slowly, teasing her with each syllable.

She narrowed her eyes at him. "You're on, Percy."

He smothered a smirk and released her hand, allowing her to go inside ahead of him. Moody shot him a questioning look, which Charles answered with only a wink.

Fourth Officer Joseph Boxhall and Fifth Officer Harold Lowe waited in the officer's smoking room. They exchanged a surprised glance when Sybil walked in, but Charles was proud to see her put her shoulders back and face them directly. She offered a nod of greeting.

"Gentlemen," she said.

"Sybil, this is Joe Boxhall and Harold Lowe," Charles told her. "Chaps, this is Sybil Chambers."

Lowe lifted an eyebrow at Charles. "Is she a passenger?"

"She is a lady's maid to a first class passenger, but more importantly," Charles said. "She is my oldest friend. We grew up together in Yorkshire. I taught her everything she knows about poker."

"Someone certainly thinks a lot of himself." Sybil rolled her eyes. "His father taught me, him, and his two brothers to play."

"But I was the one who figured out your giveaway, Giggles."

"We'll just see if you're still calling me that by the end of the night."

He chuckled at her challenge and watched with keen eyes as she took a seat beside Lowe. He started to sit on the other side of her but changed his mind and chose a chair directly across the table. He wanted to keep her in his sights all night. The days on the ship were limited, and he didn't want to waste a moment by looking elsewhere. He'd seen the ocean countless times. Sybil was the view.

Especially now, all fired up and competitive. That was the girl he remembered from Yorkshire, not the proper, withdrawn, polite lady's maid. Not that prim wasn't nice, but he enjoyed knowing that the girl he knew still existed, and he could draw her out if he wanted.

"This should be fun," Lowe joked, picking up the deck and shuffling it.

After the deal, Charles kept his gaze fixed on Sybil, sparing only a brief glance at his own hand. He studied her face, waiting for her lips to turn up into a smile or that signature giggle to come forth. But she remained stoic.

The ante was five cents, since most of the officers had exchanged their money in preparation for the trip to New York.

"Oh no, we haven't exchanged yet," Sybil said, shooting Charles an anxious glance.

"Don't worry, I'll spot you," he offered.

She frowned. "No, it must be fair. How much is the exchange?"

"About four pence," he told her.

She fished into her pocket, counted out the coins, and handed them to him. He placed a nickel into her palm.

"Thank you, sir," she said with a haughty jerk of her chin, and he chuckled.

The game began, and to his shock, she won the first hand with two pair—one of kings and one of jacks. She'd given nothing away in her face, maintaining a blank expression as she examined her cards. Her sweet laughter only came when she'd secured her winnings and scooped the pot toward herself.

"Don't worry, lads, it's only the beginning," she said with a sweet smile. "Plenty of time to win it back."

She was so adorable, he couldn't even be upset.

Unfortunately, even that smile proved to be a poker face. She won hand after hand. Not all of them, but enough for Charles to become suspicious.

"D'you think she's cheating?" Boxhall asked under his breath.

Charles considered it, but shook his head. He knew Sybil too well. Or at least, he thought he did. "No, I think this is just working out unbelievably well for her."

"What are you two whispering about over there?" Sybil challenged, picking up the cards Moody dealt her.

"Just wondering how we're going to eat once we get to New York," Charles joked.

For a fleeting moment, the color left her face, like he had accused her of robbing them at gunpoint instead of winning a poker game. She quickly schooled her expression and grinned.

"You never know what the next hand will bring," she said.

"So you keep saying," Moody sighed.

After they bet and replaced the cards they wanted, Charles's confidence grew. He had a full house, three tens and a pair of sevens. Moody heaved another sigh and folded when Charles raised. Sybil matched, followed by Lowe, and Boxhall raised again. Charles smirked and raised again. Sybil didn't back down, but Lowe did. Boxhall thought for a long moment, his gaze bouncing between Sybil and Charles, but he folded too.

"I can't afford to lose anymore," he said, defeated.

"All right, Giggles," Charles said. "Down to me and you."

The corner of her mouth ticked up for a fleeting second. Her hand had to be good. But her best hand all night had been a full house. And what were the odds of her getting another one of those or better in one game?

She raised, which he saw coming, so he raised again. She blinked, faltering for the first time all evening.

I've got her, he thought.

She resumed her aloof expression and met him. He could feel the other officer's eyes on them, but he kept his eyes fixed on Sybil's face. Something had to give eventually. He was sure of it. Her gaze collided with his and he almost drew back. Where was that burst of confidence coming from? She had to be bluffing.

"I raise," she said, and tossed a few more coins into the pot.

He barely kept his jaw from going slack and gaping at her. He cleared his throat. "Are you sure about this?"

"Dead sure."

"If you insist."

He matched her and called it. First, he laid his cards down, and he lifted an eyebrow at her. For a moment, she was still as a statue, and then—she giggled.

The blood drained from his face. "No way."

"I'm sorry to disappoint you, Charles." She laid her cards in front of her. "Royal flush."

"No way!"

He jumped to his feet and leaned over the table to see for himself. But there they were, in black and white, the ten of clubs to the ace, mocking him with their superiority. He blinked several times and ran a hand through his hair. His brow furrowed.

Sybil stiffened in her chair under his examination. "What?"

"Roll up your sleeves," he ordered.

"I beg your pardon!"

"Roll them up, I think you're hiding cards up there!"

"Are you accusing me of cheating?"

"You bet I am!"

He crossed around the table and loomed over her. She didn't draw back.

"Don't be sore, Charles, it's—hey!"

Without hesitation, he reached out for the sensitive skin of her neck and tickled her. She shriveled beneath his touch and let out a shriek of laughter. Every attempt to bat his hand away, he parried. He kept going until her cheeks were red.

"Okay, okay, I'll show you, just let me breathe, you beast!"

He relented with a stirring in the pit of his stomach at seeing her breathless beneath him. He pushed that thought away. She swallowed and unbuttoned her sleeves, cuffing and rolling them up three times on each side. He wasn't sure if it was that his mind had already gone somewhere it shouldn't because of her panting, but the exposure of her wrists had him shifting his stance.

"There, see? No cards," she said, turning her arms back and forth. She met his gaze and held it. "I'm just a much better liar than I was since the last time you saw me."

He started to smile, but it faltered. A lot had changed in the decade since they'd spoken. More than he realized. Was she the same girl he knew? Parts of her had already come through, but who was Sybil now? A damn fine poker player, for one, but what else? He supposed it was a good sign that he wanted to know.

"So you are," he said quietly, and forced a curve to his mouth to ease the curiosity in her eyes.

A knock on the door diverted all eyes to the entrance. Murdoch stood there, with Lady Iris just behind him. She looked as grand in her gold dinner dress as she had the first time Charles saw her, but he hardly noticed her when Sybil was nearby.

"Ah, here we are, my lady," Murdoch said. "Your lady's maid is safe and sound."

"I wasn't too worried since Charles was involved," Iris replied. "I've come to collect Sybil if you all can spare her."

"Certainly," Boxhall said. "Any longer, and we'd all be penniless."

Charles bit back a snicker, but Sybil looked horrified.

"I won't keep a penny of it if you disapprove, m'lady," she said.

Iris raised a brow. "How much did you win?"

"Five dollars, m'lady."

"Gracious." Iris's eyes widened. "I don't disapprove at all. Well done, Sybil."

Sybil let her shoulders drop with a breath. Charles had the strangest urge to wrap his arm around her, but contained it. She pocketed her winnings and crossed the room to join her mistress.

"Will Mr. Mooring be coming back as well?"

Iris leaned against the doorframe. "Lewis is off with his American friend tonight. He sent Gordon with a message."

Sybil deflated. "I'm sorry, m'lady."

"I'm not. If anything, I'm sorry for her. She's the one he'll be disappointing all night."

Charles coughed with surprise, and the others exchanged a shocked glance, though they'd never dream of calling a high-born lady on a vulgar comment. Even if he did find it more than a little funny.

A blush rose in Sybil's cheeks as she giggled. He was so desperate to touch that warm cheek his knees almost buckled.

"As you say, m'lady," she said.

He followed her toward the door, hardly aware he was even moving, but he found himself needing to be wherever she was. She bid the other officers goodnight over her shoulder. Charles came to a stop by the door and helped Sybil back into her coat.

"May I escort you back to your rooms?" he offered.

"We'll be all right," she said. "But thank you."

"Are you sure? I don't mind."

"I'm afraid it will be much more difficult to talk about you if you're with us, Mr. Percy," Iris interjected.

Sybil's face went beet red, but Charles only chuckled. "Understood, Lady Iris."

Sybil met his gaze. "Well. . . goodnight, Charles."

"May I see you again tomorrow?"

"Yes. I'd like to. . . pick up where we left off."

With that, she stood on her toes and pressed a kiss to his cheek. He drew in a soft gasp at the closeness, though he didn't know why it should surprise him. She used to kiss his cheek all the time. The heat it brought to his skin should have been familiar. He welcomed it back gladly. Before he could say anything more, she had slipped out the door, Lady Iris right behind her. He touched his cheek where her lips had graced it. The next day couldn't come soon enough. And yet, he wanted time to slow down. New York loomed in the distance. All they had to look forward to was this time on *Titanic*. After that. . . he couldn't say.

CHAPTER NINE

April 12, 1912

Iris was having breakfast on the private promenade deck when Lewis got back to the room. Sybil stood near the door, arms folded properly in front of her, eyes forward, but not watching. Her mind was on Charles and the fun they'd had the previous night. She could still feel the echo of his fingers from where he tickled her. But more than that, she couldn't get what he said right before they went to the game out of her mind.

I was afraid if I went home, I'd find a reason to stay.

The intensity in his eyes told her that he was talking about her. But she couldn't be sure if that was wishful thinking on her part or not. Could he really have been avoiding his home and his family for more than a decade simply because he thought he'd abandon his calling? For her? She wasn't worth that kind of sacrifice. He had to know that.

He did mention he thought she might have met someone, but he never had the courage to confirm it with his brothers. She pitied him for carrying around so much conflict. It was much the same as her own. She always hoped Charles had fulfilled his dreams and met someone who made him happy. It was part of what kept her from writing too—fear that he'd found himself a wife who wasn't rooted in a place that he was desperate to get away from.

Maybe he was talking about his family. It certainly had to be part of it; the boys were thick as thieves growing up. Of course they had their squabbles, but when push came to shove, they were brothers to the core. And Charles would be such a wonderful uncle to the children. He'd certainly make a remarkable father someday too. But did he even want that? Hadn't his admission also implied there was a large part of him still opposed to domesticity?

Then again, Sybil had hardly considered her own desires on the matter. She was happy with her life too. She couldn't imagine abandoning Lady Iris. If she had a better husband, maybe, but not with Lewis. Sybil would worry for the rest of her days if she ran off to get married and start her own family. It wasn't the most convenient life for someone in service.

But her parents had managed. It helped that they worked in the same house, but she was glad to have the memories of their family dinners each evening. After a day of playing with the Percy boys, she was ready to have a meal and then curl up on her father's lap for him to read from the Bible or whatever novels he had on hand. Sometimes, she could still hear his voice when she read, and she imagined a husband of her own reading to their child the same way.

Could that ever be Charles? Was it selfish of her to want it from him?

"Sybil, are you all right?" Iris said. "You seem deep in thought."

"I'm fine, m'lady, just remembering some things. Trying to get some feelings in order too."

"About Charles?"

Sybil nodded. "There's much to consider."

"Such as?"

"It's not important, m'lady, you can enjoy your breakfast."

"I wouldn't ask if I wasn't interested, Sybil. If you want to share, please do. I'd like to be of some help, if I can."

"Well. . ." Sybil chewed her bottom lip. "I can't help but think that, fond as I am of Charles, there isn't a future for us. Not together."

"Why ever not?"

"Our jobs, mostly. We both love what we do, and if we were to say, get married, one of us would have to make a huge sacrifice."

Iris's expression softened. "Sybil, you don't honestly think I'd insist you stay on for me if you wanted to get married and start a family, do you?"

"It wouldn't be your insistence, m'lady, it's my own want. I enjoy being in service. I especially enjoy being in service to you, and I'm not sure another lady's maid would. . ."

"Help me keep losing pregnancies?"

"Yes."

Iris stood and strode over to take Sybil's shoulders in her hands. "Darling Sybil. Do you remember what I told you the first day aboard?"

Sybil nodded. "That I'm more than a lady's maid to you."

"Exactly. Please don't ever let me stand in the way of your happiness."

Sybil swallowed through the sudden tightness in her throat. "Thank you, m'lady. I'll think about it."

Gordon opened the door, and they jumped apart. Lewis came out, still in his evening clothes but with his collar unbuttoned and his hair disheveled. He tried to run a hand through it, but it didn't help. Neat hair didn't disguise the bleary redness in his eyes or the groan stuck in his throat.

"Well, good morning to you too," Iris said coolly.

He ignored her and went straight to the table to pour himself a coffee. Another thing Iris and Lewis didn't see eye to eye on. He couldn't stand tea and she couldn't stomach coffee. Separate pots every morning.

"Iris, why is there money on the end table in the sitting room?" Lewis asked. "Are we leaving tips for the cleaning crew or something?"

"No, that's Sybil's money," Iris answered, taking her seat across from her husband. "She earned it. Rather cleverly, I must say, in a game of poker with a few of the officers."

Lewis halted his cup halfway to his mouth. "Is this another prank?"

"No. Why would I joke about that?"

"Do you even—" he stopped short and set his coffee down with such force it sloshed over the side onto the saucer. "Do you know how that makes us look? Our maid, gambling with a group of men she doesn't know? Have you considered the implications?"

"The implications? She knows one of them, and she was invited to join. I don't see what the problem is."

Sybil stiffened as Lewis rounded on her. He got to his feet and stalked toward her.

"How much was it?" he demanded.

"Five dollars, sir," she said.

"Five—Jesus Christ!" He turned on his heel and tunneled a hand through his hair again. "You have to return it to them. It isn't right for a woman to even play poker, much less beat a group of men. You will return it and apologize."

"She will do no such thing," Iris protested. "She won the money, it's only fair she gets to keep it."

"She emasculated them!"

"So what? Not everyone's ego is as fragile as yours, Lewis, they were more than all right with it."

Lewis huffed, his nostrils flaring out like a bull facing a matador instead of a man looking at his wife. He snatched his tie off from around his neck and let it hit the floor.

"Gordon!" he shouted as he stormed inside. "Get me my clothes, I have an errand to run."

Iris followed after him in a fury. "Lewis, it's not your money, it's Sybil's! You cannot take it without her consent!"

"I'm not," he snapped, and disappeared into his bedroom.

Iris shot Sybil a bewildered look. "What the devil could he mean?"

Sybil only shrugged. A minute later, Gordon emerged, apology in his eyes.

"Do you have a coin purse or something for the money? Where it would be separate from Mr. Mooring's or Lady Iris's?"

"I think I have a spare," Iris said, and she too went to her room. She returned within moments, a small beaded bag in her hand. "Here."

Sybil took it and scooped her winnings off the table and into the bag. As she pulled the strings to close it, Lewis was back, much more put together in his day clothes, and he straightened his tie.

"That's all of it?" he asked.

"Yes, sir," Sybil confirmed.

"Good. Gordon, keep my wife here. You, Sybil, are coming with me."

Before Sybil could question him, his hand wrapped around her upper arm, and with an iron grip, he yanked her toward the door. She yelped as a sharp pain shot through her arm.

"Lewis!" Iris shouted, but Gordon stepped in front of her. "Lewis, release her this instant!"

"You don't get to give me orders, Iris," Lewis said over his shoulder. "And I've had it with your adolescent behavior since we boarded. My family will operate the way *I* say, and that includes the servants!"

He slammed the door shut before Iris could retort. Sybil struggled, but there was nothing she could do to dislodge his bruising grasp. He pushed her roughly down the corridor toward the lifts, but to her horror, he led her right past them and to the grand staircase. Her neck burned with humiliation as all eyes turned on them. She looked like a misbehaving child being led to their disciplinarian.

"Mr. Mooring, please!" she cried. "You don't have to do this, I'll return everything, I—"

"It's too late for compromise now," he snapped. "When you act like an unruly teenager, you'll be treated like one."

Sybil could hear the whispers that followed them.

"She must have stolen something valuable."

"I'll bet he's taking her to the master at arms now."

"Such a shame. It's so difficult to find good help these days."

Her heart clattered around in protest, but the way Lewis was manhandling her, there was no way to stop and correct anyone. Her feet could hardly keep up with his brisk pace, and she tripped over a few of the stairs. They passed the clock, and Sybil knew they had reached the boat deck when the sky light illuminated the space above. He didn't go to the nearest door either, instead making sure a few other passengers took note before stepping outside.

Sybil struggled to catch her breath as Lewis dragged her toward the bridge. Her heart stuttered at the thought of the officers seeing this. Charles, especially. She attempted to pull free again, to no avail.

"Mr. Mooring, please!" she begged again. "I'll do as you say! You don't have to do this!"

"I believe I do."

"Please!"

"Get your hands off her!"

Lewis came to such an abrupt halt that Sybil almost collided into him. They both looked up at the newcomer, who she was surprised to see was Charles. She'd never heard him sound that angry before, nor show such command. He was raised to his full height, shoulders squared, his furious gaze fixed on Lewis.

"No to worry, Mr.. . ." Lewis trailed off.

If Sybil wasn't so embarrassed, she would have offered Charles's name, but she let Lewis flounder.

"Mr.. . . let's see. . . "

"It's Percy," Charles said shortly. "And I told you to take your hands off her."

"Mr. Percy, yes. I was told my wife's maid has given you some trouble, so I'm here to set things right. She has her winnings from last night to return to you and your fellow officers, along with my deepest apologies for such behavior. I hope you don't take it as a reflection on our family or—"

"Mr. Mooring!" Charles barked. "I will not tell you again. Get. Your. Hands. Off. Her."

Lewis blinked, as if just realizing what was being asked—no, *demanded*—of him. Lewis's grip only loosened slightly and Sybil winced. Charles took a step toward them. Murdoch emerged from behind Charles and assessed the situation carefully.

"Certainly," Lewis said. "I'll release her once the money is returned."

Sybil's eyes welled up with hot tears as she held the purse out toward Charles. She swallowed the lump in her throat. "Please accept my apology, sir. My behavior was inappropriate for someone of my station and it will not happen again."

Charles's gaze burned into her, but she couldn't bear to face him. She wished the deck would open up and swallow her down. She bit down on her lip to keep it from trembling. She couldn't cry—not now, not in front of Lewis. She couldn't give him the satisfaction.

"I do not accept the money or the apology," Charles said, and he rounded on Lewis again. "Neither are wanted."

"Shouldn't you ask your men before you decide for them?" Lewis argued.

Charles looked him up and down. "No."

Lewis rolled his eyes and then appealed to Murdoch. "Mr. Murdoch, right?"

"Aye," Murdoch said hesitantly. "We met at dinner the other night, sir."

"And I seem to remember you being a reasonable man. Perhaps you can accept the money on behalf of your men."

Murdoch shook his head. "They don't want it."

Lewis scoffed. "This is getting ridiculous."

"Finally, something we agree on," Charles shot back. "Let her go. She's done what you asked."

Lewis loosened his grip, but before Sybil could breathe with relief, he pulled her forward and shoved her. She choked on a cry. If Charles hadn't been standing there, she would have careened across the deck. Luckily, she landed in the safety of his arms.

Murdoch came flying around them. "There's no need for that, Mr. Mooring!"

Charles's eyes raked over Sybil. "Are you all right?"

"I think so," she said shakily, rubbing her sore arm.

She still couldn't look him in the eyes. It was too much, and he was being too kind.

Charles turned, keeping Sybil safely at his back, and faced Lewis.

"Mr. Mooring," he said darkly, interrupting whatever Murdoch and Lewis were saying. "If you ever walk her around this ship like a dog again, I will take your teeth out. One punch at a time."

Alarmed, Sybil peered around Charles's arm just in time to see Lewis sputter and charge toward them. She shrunk back, but kept him in her line of sight.

"Is that a threat, Percy?" Lewis said.

"It's a promise," Charles shot back.

"Charlie," Murdoch said, stepping between them. "It's all right."

"We'll see what the captain thinks of your little promise then," Lewis said. "I demand to speak with him."

"You've made enough demands for one day, Mooring," Charles practically spat. "Go back to your room."

Lewis reared back and opened his mouth to argue further, but Murdoch spoke first.

"I'll speak with the captain, sir. Please. Return to your cabin, and we will discuss it all later."

Lewis's eyes flicked between Charles and Murdoch before briefly resting on Sybil again. She ducked back behind Charles. She spotted a few other officers waiting by the bridge, Moody, Boxhall, and Lowe included, all frowning at Lewis.

"Very well," she heard Lewis say, and thought he must have seen them too. "I look forward to speaking with him."

With that, he walked away. Sybil's neck still burned with the shame of it, and she hid her face behind her hands.

Chapter Ten

Charles watched Lewis go, making sure he was out of sight before turning to Sybil. She had her face in her hands, but he could hear her unsteady breathing and the sniffles she tried to muffle. His heart clamped at the sight of her distress. He'd do anything if it meant she would smile again. They had ended the previous night on such a good note. He hoped this didn't throw a wrench into their progress.

"Sybil, it's all right, he's gone," he said, gently as he could.

"Please, don't try to comfort me, Charles, I can't bear it," she replied, finally freeing her face, but wiping at her cheeks as she did. "I'm so. . . humiliated, I can't even look at you."

"You have nothing to be ashamed of. He's the one who behaved like a monster."

She turned toward the ocean, the spring sunshine making her face glow, and tried to let out a sigh, but her bottom lip quivered and a quiet sob escaped instead. He reached for her, but she stepped back, holding out the money again.

"Please, take it," she said. "If I come back with it, it will only upset him."

"Let him die mad about it," Charles replied.

She almost laughed, but it came out shaky. "Please, Charles. Just take it."

"No, it's yours, you earned it."

"*Charles.*"

"If he has a problem, he can take it up with me."

She took a shallow breath, and he didn't wait another second before gathering her up in his arms. Thankfully, she allowed it, and buried her face in his chest.

Charles locked eyes with Murdoch and jerked his head toward the others. Murdoch nodded and ushered them away, giving Charles a moment alone with Sybil.

"I'm so sorry," she murmured. "I knew better than to even play last night, but I. . . "

She trailed off, but he didn't press her.

"It's all right," he assured her, stroking her hair. "I'm glad you joined us. We all talked about how much fun it was having you there because you're a much more graceful winner than we've ever been."

She did laugh at that and he felt her hands take hold of the back of his jacket. He rested his cheek on top of her head. He held her for several long moments without saying anything more. Her breathing evened out, and her skin cooled down. Finally, she lifted her face.

"Thank you for standing up for me that way," she said. "No one has ever defended me like you have. Like you always have."

"And I always will, Sybil," he promised.

She offered a wobbly smile. "Until we get to New York at least."

He wondered if that meant she was also questioning what would happen when they reached that harbor. He wanted to keep in touch at least. Ideally, he wanted so much more. Last night, she agreed to picking up where they left off, but what exactly did that mean for her? Unwilling to upset her any further, he tried to lighten the mood.

"I'll defend you from anywhere," he said. "Even if I'm at sea, if you're in danger, I'll sprout wings and fly to you."

She giggled. "That would be a remarkable sight."

"I'd need to make an impression if I don't know what I'm dealing with."

"The next time I'm in any sort of danger, I'll look to the skies."

He started to come back with another joke, but he could see that her smile didn't reach her eyes. And she still massaged the arm where Lewis had been holding her. Her heart wasn't in the jokes. He furrowed his brow.

"Are you certain there will be a next time?" he asked.

Her face fell, and she stepped back to hug herself. "Most likely."

He wished he'd decked Lewis when he had the chance. One good punch to send the right message. Of course, he knew it wouldn't help anything other than making himself feel better.

She gazed out at the sea again, and he tried not to get too distracted by how beautiful she looked in the morning light with the wind picking up some loose brown curls around her face. They shined like copper in the sun.

"I hate that man," she said, almost to herself. "I never thought I could feel hatred like that until he came into our lives. He does everything he can to remind us how powerless we are against him."

Charles let that percolate a moment. He hated the idea of Sybil being trapped by anyone. Lady Iris too. No one should feel their spouse had robbed them of their freedom, but he knew the way of the world, and how much harder it was for women.

"If you ever need any help, Sybil. . ."

"I know, you'll be there."

"I will."

She tried to smile, but it came out rather pinched. "I should go. I need to get Lady Iris dressed for the day. She's having tea with the

Countess of Rothes this afternoon, and I've got to mend her dinner dress before tonight."

"May I walk you back?"

She hesitated for a moment before she nodded. He offered his arm, and she took it. The whole way back to the suites, she let him do most of the talking. He wished there was a way to get off duty sooner so he wouldn't feel like he was sending her right into the lion's den when they reached the door.

***

By the time Charles got back to the bridge, Captain Smith was waiting for him, looking livid. He bit back a sigh. Murdoch must have already explained what happened. Charles held his head high. He wasn't sorry for anything he said or did.

"Captain," he said.

"Percy. My quarters, now."

Charles shot Murdoch an annoyed frown before following the captain through the door to the officer's quarters. Murdoch shrugged an apology and brought up the rear. They entered the captain's sitting room, and Murdoch closed the door.

Captain Smith whirled around. "Have you lost your mind, Percy? Threatening a passenger?"

"Did Mr. Murdoch tell you *why* I was threatening him?"

"Why?" Smith echoed. "Who cares why? There's never a reason for that!"

"He was abusing a woman!"

"You didn't like how he was treating an old friend of yours, but may I remind you that girl is his servant! It's not our business how he runs his household, not even while they are on our ship!"

"She will always be my business, sir."

"Heaven's sake, Percy! You are only old friends! She's not your family! She's not your wife!"

She's as good as, Charles thought to himself, but held his tongue. He didn't have anything else to say, so he waited. The captain sat down behind his desk. As he did, the door opened again, and Bruce Ismay, Chairman of White Star Line, stormed in. His dark eyes landed on Charles right away and his mustache twitched with obvious ire. Charles looked back at him with indifference. Ismay rounded on the captain.

"Captain, what is the meaning of this?" he demanded. "I just ran into Lewis Mooring and he told me one of your officers threatened him! Over a misunderstanding with a servant!"

"I'm handling it now," Captain Smith replied, nodding toward Charles.

Ismay glowered at him. "Do you have any idea who that man is, boy? His family put down half the railroads in America! He's married to the daughter of an earl!"

Charles did not back down. "He could be the King of England for all I care, it doesn't give him permission to push a woman around."

"Oh, for God's sake," Ismay scoffed.

"Mr. Ismay, please," the captain interjected. Then his stern gaze found Charles again. "I know you care for the girl, Percy, but do remember her place. And yours."

"Sir, I—"

"You will apologize," Ismay cut across him.

"I will not," Charles said.

"You cannot refuse."

"I'm not sorry. I meant what I told him."

Ismay drew back like he'd been slapped. "You insolent little—remove that uniform, you are no longer an employee of White Star Line!"

"Fine," Charles snapped, and shrugged off his jacket.

"Mr. Ismay, don't be rash," the captain said. "Mr. Percy is an excellent officer. He had a lapse of judgment due to his history with the girl, but that's no reason to fire him."

"And if Mr. Mooring sues?" Ismay challenged.

"He won't. I will smooth it over with him, I promise."

Ismay looked between them, unconvinced. Charles fastened the buttons on his jacket back, holding the chairman's gaze. Before they could exchange words again, a knock on the door interrupted. Murdoch opened it.

"Yes?" he asked.

Moody stood there with a piece of paper in his hand, which he gave to Murdoch. "Ice warning, sir."

"Thank you, Moody."

After the door snicked shut, Murdoch handed the paper off to the captain. "Another ice warning."

"We'll be careful," Captain Smith said, scanning it. "I don't think our speed should be a problem, however—"

"Excuse me, we have a more important issue here!" Ismay cried, and he pointed at Charles. "This man needs to face some discipline!"

"I will write a report, Mr. Ismay, but any further action will need to wait until we are in New York or back in England," the captain told him.

"Very well," Ismay sighed, defeated. He straightened his tie and shot Charles one last reproachful look. "Speaking of ice, Mr. Percy, you are on a thin layer of it. Any other issues, and you will be fired. That is a threat, too."

With that, he swept from the room, slamming the door behind him. The captain dismissed Charles and Murdoch, who headed back toward the bridge. Outside the wheelhouse, Murdoch stopped, and took Charles aside.

"Watch yourself, Charlie," he said. "I know you want to protect Sybil, but you can't lose your job over it."

"I don't care about my job if she's in danger."

"Without a job, you have nothing to offer her. Don't lose sight of the big picture."

Charles opened his mouth to argue, but had no retort. Murdoch made a good point. If Charles hoped to move forward with Sybil, he would need to provide for her. He had a good amount saved, but he couldn't live on that for long.

"All right, I'll behave," he conceded.

"Good. Now get to your rounds and put this behind you."

***

That evening, Sybil met him at the bridge as usual. She seemed to have recovered from the morning's ordeal, coming to him with a smile on her face. It warmed his heart to see it. He offered his hand, which she took, and he gave her fingers a gentle squeeze.

"Hi," she said. "I heard Mr. Mooring complained to Mr. Ismay about earlier. Are you in trouble?"

"No, the captain understood. I got a lecture, but not much else."

"That's a relief. Though I am sorry I put you in a tough spot."

"Don't worry about me, Giggles. I've been in much tougher spots than that."

She smiled again. "Shall we watch the stars again tonight?"

He shook his head. "I've got something else in mind."

She raised an eyebrow but didn't argue, following him back to the bridge and into the wheelhouse. He had already sent the helmsman away for a while. He had the idea for this moments after he left the captain's quarters, recalling how Sybil said that Lewis made her feel "powerless." Charles was determined to change that.

"What are we doing here?" she asked when they stopped in front of the wheel.

"Take the wheel," he said.

She blanched. "What?"

He took her shoulders and turned her so she stood directly in front of it. Her eyes went wide.

"What is happening right now?" she demanded.

"Go on, take the handles," he instructed, stepping up behind her. He wrapped his arms around her and placed his hands atop hers, guiding them to the right handles. She trembled against him. "Don't be nervous."

"I can't help it, you make me nervous."

"You've known me far too long for that to be true."

She huffed out a laugh. "I knew you as a boy. You're a man now."

"And you," he said, leaning until his lips were right by her ear. He could smell her sweet scent and he longed to press his lips to the sensitive skin of her neck. But this wasn't about him. "At this moment, you are the most powerful person on this ship."

She gasped as a fresh smile parted her lips. He could see the blush flood her cheeks as she looked out over the deck, but she stopped shaking. She stood securely between his arms. Her grip on the wheel tightened for a split second and then relaxed.

"I've never felt this strong," she said softly, almost laughing to herself.

"You are strong," he replied. "Strong and beautiful and kind. Everything I remember of you and so much more."

She turned her head to meet his gaze over her shoulder. "Thank you for giving me this."

"I'll give you the world, Sybil."

"Would you start with a kiss?"

It was all the permission he needed to lean in and finally claim her lips. His whole body lit up when they met, from his head down through his shoes. She tasted like everything good he'd ever known, and it made him lightheaded. To keep himself grounded and present, he took long pulls of her mouth. Something white hot coursed through his veins, so fierce and powerful, he worried he might not be able to contain it. It was beyond desire, it was an untamed need, stirring in the pit of his stomach. He could have stood there and devoured her like a starved man for the rest of their days.

They parted for air, and he already longed to kiss her again. With her lips pink and pouty and precious, his mouth tingled with want. Her heady eyes told him she felt the same. There was no running from the kiss that followed. He would never run from her again. One thing was certain, Sybil was out of his past. In fact, she was the only future he could imagine.

CHAPTER ELEVEN

Sybil came down the corridor, lips still alight with Charles's kiss. Her cheeks ached with how much smiling she'd been doing since the moment he put her hands on the wheel and reminded her that power was circumstantial. For one moment, she was even above Lewis. But it wasn't just taking the wheel that gave her that assurance. It was Charles. His kiss, his confidence. Being with him made her feel like a goddess. She could hardly believe her luck in finding him again. But with that joy came the worry about what would happen when they reached New York.

She hardly had time to consider it. As she approached Lady Iris's room, she heard muffled voices from within, shouting back and forth, each trying to outdo the other. She knew the sound well enough now to recognize Iris and Lewis in a spat. All thoughts of Charles melted away, and she slipped through the door.

"All I'm asking is for some subtlety!" Iris cried, whipping a glove off her hand and tossing it aside. Sybil scrambled to pick it up.

"You told me I'm welcome to keep whatever company I want!" Lewis shot back, unbuttoning his coat. Gordon rushed to help him shrug it off his shoulders.

"And you are, but you could at least keep it out of plain sight!" Iris continued. "Heaven's sake, Lewis, I had Molly Brown asking me about it, and—"

"Oh, and I suppose since she's new money, you find her company offensive, do you?"

Sybil hurried to Iris's side and helped her with the second glove before the latter unclipped her earrings.

"That's not what I'm saying at all! If you'd let me finish—"

"Don't bother, Iris, I know your opinion. I've known it since the day we were married!"

"I'd happily marry Mrs. Brown instead!"

"Don't be ridiculous!"

"You're the one being ridiculous! I don't want things so public that people are questioning me about our marriage! How do you think that makes us look?"

Iris stilled while Sybil made quick work of the buttons on the back of her dress.

"You weren't so concerned with how things look when your maid swindled respectable officers out of their money!"

"That's not what happened and you know it!"

Sybil found herself unable to conjure any more shame about that morning. Not after the evening she and Charles had together. The only thing missing from it was more time. She knew it wasn't proper, but she wished she could spend the entire night with him. She shook her head to return her focus to Iris, getting to work on loosening her corset. Gordon was thankfully in Lewis's bedroom, likely hanging up his dinner jacket.

"You know what might ease people's suspicions, Iris?" Lewis spat. "A child."

"Now you're blaming me for things that are in God's hands," Iris snipped. "If we're going to fight, I'd prefer to have one argument at a time."

Lewis scoffed. "Oh, please. We're always having at least two fights at any given time."

"And right now, I have the energy for none of them. I'm going to bed."

"Fine. Run away. Even though you're the one who started it!"

Sybil followed Iris into her bedroom, then darted around her to fetch her dressing down in case she decided to go back out. Iris did, tying the belt herself as she swept back into the sitting room.

"I started it because I thought I could make a simple request! I had no idea you'd turn it into this!"

"It's never a simple request with you! You wouldn't even have to make that request if you were a proper wife!"

"I would be a proper wife if you were a husband worthy of my respect!"

Lewis's cheeks reddened with rage. "Fuck you!"

He crossed the room before Sybil could blink, and in one swift motion, he reared back and slapped Iris hard across the face. Time slowed as Iris's head whipped back, her hand flying up to cup her cheek. Sybil moved at once to stand in front of her mistress, putting her arms out as a shield. Fury surged through her with each pump of her racing heart. She glowered up at Lewis, defiance drawing her mouth into a deep frown.

"Mr. Mooring, remember yourself!" she shouted.

"This is none of your concern, Sybil," Lewis said. "Stand aside."

"No, sir."

"Stand aside, Sybil."

"No, sir."

"Dammit, I said stand aside!"

He raised his hand again. Sybil squeezed her eyes shut and braced herself for the coming impact, but Gordon chose that moment to return to the sitting room. She chanced a look, cracking one eye open.

"Sir!" he cried, and Lewis froze. "Remember, you have plans tonight."

Lewis lowered his hand. He straightened his shoulders and glanced between Gordon and Sybil, as if weighing his options. Sybil rose up as well, firmly meeting his gaze. Her chest rose and fell with her panicked breaths, but she didn't care if he knew she was afraid. As long as he understood that her fear would not stop her.

"You're right, Gordon," Lewis said. "Gather my things. I won't be returning here tonight."

"Yes, sir," Gordon said quietly, and disappeared back into the room.

Lewis turned to Sybil with a sneer. "I see your officer friend has made you bolder than usual, Sybil. But understand this, come between us again, and you may find my mercy extremely limited."

Sybil said nothing, she only scowled at him. He turned on his heel and went into his room, slamming the door shut as usual. Only when she was sure he was done did Sybil finally turn to Iris.

"My lady," she said gently. "Are you all right?"

Iris trembled as she touched the angry red skin of her cheek. "I. . . I think so, I. . . he's never. . . oh, Sybil, I'm so sorry."

"Don't you worry about that. It's all right. Can I get you anything? Tea? Something stronger?"

"I. . . something stronger, thank you."

Sybil went right to the bar cart in the corner of the room and retrieved a glass and Mr. Mooring's whiskey. Iris was already halfway into her room, so Sybil followed, the bottle tucked under her arm.

She closed the door with her elbow. It shut with a soft click, and Iris collapsed on the end of the bed. Sybil dumped a healthy pour of amber liquid into the glass and carried it over to Iris. She took Iris's shaking hand in her own and wrapped it around the crystal.

"That's it, m'lady," she said, guiding the glass to Iris's lips. "One sip."

Iris let the whiskey into her mouth, and her face soured as she swallowed. Once she had, she lowered the glass and gazed at Sybil with wide eyes.

"I can't believe you did that," she said.

"Did what?" Sybil asked.

"You. . . protected me. Sybil, that was more than could be asked of any servant."

Sybil knelt to meet Iris's eyes. "I'm more than your lady's maid, Lady Iris, remember?"

"Indeed. I shall never forget again."

"Neither shall I."

Iris took another sip of the whiskey, longer than the last. "Tell me about your evening with Charles."

"M'lady, that can wait."

"I need to be distracted."

"What you need is proper rest. I don't think I can talk about Charles now, m'lady, or I'll feel like I'm boasting."

Iris raised a brow. "That good, was it?"

Sybil flushed. "It was a lovely night."

"Until you got back here. I really am sorry you saw that."

Sybil didn't answer. Iris took another long swig of her whiskey.

"I suppose you're right," she said with a sigh. "I think I want to sleep."

"Yes, m'lady."

Sybil rose and turned down the corner of the duvet before helping Lady Iris out of her dressing gown. As Sybil turned out the light and prepared to climb into her own bed, she swore she heard a sniffle from Iris.

***

April 13, 1912

Lady Iris walked into breakfast the following morning with her head held high. She did not shrink when Lewis returned, and in fact, took his arm as they filed into the dining salon. Even sporting a bruised cheek, she still managed to own the room. Sybil had to admire pride like that.

Molly Brown was the first to say something.

"My goodness, Lady Iris, who gave you the shiner?" she asked.

Iris replied with a graceful laugh. "Oh, it was all rather clumsy of me. My maid was putting away my jewelry, and I tried to unbutton my dress on my own. I tripped on the hem and ran right into my door."

"I see," Molly said, casting a sidelong glance at Lewis.

He shifted on his feet. "You'll have to be more careful, darling."

"I will be," Iris said. "I won't try that sort of thing without Sybil again."

Lewis cleared his throat and turned his gaze toward Molly. "Forgive me, Mrs. Brown, but did you need something?"

"Only to extend a friendly invitation," Molly replied with a good-natured smile. Sybil couldn't help but notice the steel in the woman's eyes. "I'm hosting a tea party this evening with a few other ladies. A little post-dinner fun."

"You're hosting a party?"

"Gals only, I'm afraid, Lewis. But hey, the second you all invite us to brandy and cigars, we'll invite you to our fun times."

Sybil didn't hear Lewis's reply as she was distracted by a tap on her shoulder. She turned, coming face to face with Charles. A grin overcame her at the sight of his kind blue eyes.

"Good morning," she said.

"Come with me," he replied, and took her hand.

He led her outside the dining room to a secluded corner by the staircase. She wondered if it would always feel warm and fuzzy when he held her hand. Once he checked there was no one around, he cradled her face between his hands and pulled her in for a kiss.

She melted against him, letting her arms make their way around his neck. Her body craved him with the same urgency it did food and water. When they parted, she let out a small whimper of protest.

"Good morning," he finally returned.

"Even better now," she said with a smirk.

He chuckled. "Listen, Sybil. Tonight, when you come to see me, I—"

"Wait, Charles. I don't know if I should tonight. Something's happened, and I'm not comfortable leaving Lady Iris alone unless I know Mr. Mooring won't be there."

His brow furrowed. "What's going on?"

Sybil bit her lip, wondering if she should say since Iris was giving out the story that she'd run into a door. But Charles could be trusted. Maybe if he knew, he might be able to help. She took handfuls of his lapels.

"He struck her last night," she said.

Charles stiffened. "That's it, I'm punching him."

He started toward the dining room, but Sybil yanked him back to her.

"No, you mustn't do anything now. It will only embarrass her!" she hissed. "Please, Charles. Say nothing."

His eyes darted between her and the door, a shadow of conflict across face. He dropped his shoulders. "Fine. For now, we'll do nothing. But this can't go on. If he's comfortable treating his own wife that way, it can't be much safer for his servants."

She opened her mouth to tell him what nearly happened, but decided against it. She didn't want him even more riled up. Especially since they had already butted heads, and Charles had received a talking to from the captain. Anything more, and he might face worse. The last thing she needed was him losing his job over Lewis's misbehavior.

"I'm all right," she assured him. "But I do worry what might happen if they're left alone."

"I thought he was seeing that woman we spotted him with."

"He is, but he stops by the room long enough for them to fight."

"Why doesn't she lock her door?"

"Believe me, when he's angry, no lock can keep him out."

His frown deepened, and he stroked her cheek with his thumb. "What sort of tyranny have you been living under, Sybil?"

"The worst sort, I'm afraid," she answered, turning her face to press her lips to his palm. "I'll find you later today when I have a moment. But for now, I've got to see Lady Iris to her table."

With that, she stood on her toes to kiss him. It was a wrench to pull away and sneak back. Even as she slid into her usual place standing behind Iris, she stole a glance out the window to spy Charles heading up the stairs, taking them two at a time.

Chapter Twelve

Whistling, Charles made his way back to the bridge. His heart was light from a kiss from Sybil, though there was still worry weighing on him. Lewis Mooring had far too much control over Sybil's situation, and there was no recourse for her or Lady Iris. It burned him up to know the man had gotten to the point of physical harm. It was imperative to get Sybil out.

He came to a stop at the bridge, where Murdoch was facing the sea. He turned when he heard Charles coming and offered a smile in greeting. Charles returned it.

"You're awfully chipper this morning," Murdoch said.

"I got a moment with Sybil before breakfast," Charles replied. "Earned a kiss for my efforts. Two, in fact."

"Aren't you lucky?"

"I am, rather."

They chuckled together and a beat of silence passed between them.

"Will, can I ask you something personal?"

Murdoch lifted an eyebrow. "Sure, I suppose."

"How did you know you were ready to get married?"

Charles did his best not to roll his eyes at the smug smile Murdoch formed at the question.

"It started with knowing I had the right woman," he answered.

"And how were you certain it was Ada?"

Murdoch heaved a wistful sigh. "I knew it was Ada, because I truly couldn't picture my life without her in it. I couldn't imagine anyone else beside me in the morning or children that didn't have her for a mother. It seemed impossible."

Charles wrinkled his nose. "Impossible?"

"Without her, there wasn't a life. Not one I was interested in living, anyway."

"And. . . how did you know she felt the same?"

"She told me," Murdoch said, chuckling to himself. "I believe her exact words were 'William Murdoch, I live and breathe for you, but if you don't propose to me soon, I'll find someone who will.'"

Charles couldn't help but laugh, especially at Murdoch's poor attempt at his wife's accent. "Sounds bold."

"I loved her all the more for it."

"That couldn't be Sybil. She's too shy."

"I *knew* this was about her," Murdoch teased, nudging Charles with his elbow. "You're thinking this seriously about her already?"

"Technically, we've known each other since we were children."

"But lots of time has passed."

"And yet it feels like hardly any. We're both different, more grown up. But deep down, we're still those kids. Now that she's near me again, I can't bear the thought of letting her go."

"I've seen the way she looks at you, Charlie. I think if you're set on proposing, you'll get the answer you want."

Charles deflated. "I'm not so sure. She's totally devoted to her job. With everything Lady Iris goes through, she is all the more determined to remain in service. As if it's her responsibility to protect Lady Iris from her husband."

"Don't overthink it. If there's something you're worried about, talk to her."

"You're right," Charles sighed. "We're just having such a lovely time together. I hate to spoil it by getting too serious."

"Marriage is serious business, lad. You're building a life together. It's not all stargazing and kissing at the wheel."

Charles's mouth fell open. "You saw that?"

"Oh, we all saw," Murdoch laughed. "I must say, it was well done."

Charles didn't bother to feel embarrassed. He would cherish that moment forever, no matter what happened with Sybil after *Titanic*. He rolled his eyes and looked back out at the sea as it glittered in the morning sun.

"I hope I'm not being selfish asking her to leave a life she clearly loves," he said. "If she's happy in service. . ."

"Lady Iris can find another maid."

"It's not about her, it's about Sybil. What she wants."

"Most men wouldn't even bother considering her wants when it comes to getting married."

"Call me a radical, but I've generally operated under the assumption that women are people, with their own ambitions and dreams, just like us men."

"Hey, I'm right there with you. Ada still teaches while I'm away," Murdoch said, putting his hands up innocently. "But, Charlie, if you never speak up and make her an offer, how will Sybil know there's another choice out there for her?"

Charles blinked and looked sidelong at his first officer. Murdoch continued.

"Talk to her. With complete honesty. Put all your cards on the table, and in all likelihood, she'll show you hers. I hear the two of you are pretty good at that."

Charles smirked, hardly believing that the poker game was less than forty-eight hours ago. Time stood still on *Titanic*, and yet, it was also flying by. They only had a few more days before they reached New York. By then, he wanted to be sure about Sybil, one way or the other.

***

Charles made his morning rounds, Murdoch's advice still in the forefront of his mind. As he walked through first class, he kept an eye out for Sybil, but didn't find her. He hoped things would work out and she would be able to see him tonight. He did see the woman who Lewis was having the affair with, and she cast a hungry look at Murdoch as they walked by, though he either didn't notice or refused to acknowledge her. Charles wondered if it was all men she was interested in or only the married ones.

Down in third class, Charles and Murdoch separated to cover more ground in less time. A group of boys were teasing a young Irish girl. They must have been older than her, as they held her doll out of reach, and any time she was about to get it back, they tossed it to the next boy. Her auburn braids flew behind her each time she whipped around, and Charles finally saw her face. Tears streamed down her freckled cheeks as she reached out.

"Give it back now!" she cried.

"Come and take it!" the boy replied through a snicker, holding it high above his head.

Moved with pity, Charles walked toward them. He'd seen Sybil in that exact predicament countless times when they were young, and he was ashamed to have played a part in it. However, his motives were different from his brothers. Even then, all he'd wanted was to get Sybil close to him. The doll was a convenient excuse. He'd hold on to it as long as he could until his brothers were screaming at him to toss it.

He approached slowly so the boy wouldn't hear his footsteps, and then plucked the doll free. The boy whirled around, indignance all over his face until he saw who had taken it. Then his eyes flew wide.

"Oh, sir, we were just—"

"I know what you were doing," Charles said sternly, and he beckoned the girl over. She stepped toward him timidly, as if afraid he was about to join in on the game. "Here you are, sweetheart."

He handed the doll back. The girl yanked it from his grasp and into her chest, holding it as tight as her spindly arms could squeeze it. She blinked owlishly up at him.

"Thank you, sir," she said.

"You're welcome." He knelt down in front of her and whispered. "And for the record, next time that happens, one swift punch to the belly, and they'll drop that doll."

He could still feel the blows from when Sybil discovered that trick. Since she wasn't around to pass on that bit of wisdom, he could do it for her. A smile erupted across the little girl's face, and she barely contained a giggle.

"I'll remember that."

"Do. I promise, it's the last thing they'll expect."

The boys were already sulking, walking away with complaints that Charles was "no craic at all," but he didn't mind. He'd heard far worse from his brothers once he decided to stick up for Sybil instead of joining them to pick on her. He patted the girl's head affectionately and sent her off, but made sure she was back with her mother before continuing on.

After his rounds, he made his way back to the bridge to have some lunch. He was heading into the officer's dining room when the voice of Captain Smith stopped him in his tracks. He backed up to the door of the captain's quarters and poked his head in.

"Percy, yes," Captain Smith said. "I wanted to let you know I've smoothed things over with Mr. Mooring today. He assured me he has no intention of taking action against White Star Line, so we're in the clear."

Charles's gut told him not to trust that. "Did he say why?"

"No, just that the girl—the maid, that is—hasn't been the easiest employee, so he wasn't surprised she was the start of the trouble."

Charles resisted rolling his eyes. There was no trouble at all until Lewis decided it was a problem that a lady's maid played a game of poker.

"Well, good to know he's not offended," Charles said. A noncommittal answer was a safe one. "Is there anything else, sir?"

Captain Smith glanced over Charles's shoulder and then waved him inside. Wary, Charles stepped over the threshold and closed the door.

"Mr. Ismay has suggested we pick up our speed," the captain said. "Light the last boilers and arrive in New York a day early."

"Why?" Charles wondered.

"For headlines, I suppose. It could be done if we want. I've already spoken with Murdoch and Wilde about it, but I wanted to get your opinion."

"What did they say?"

"Wilde was for it, Murdoch against."

"I tend to agree with Murdoch, sir. There's no need to risk it when we're making great time at our current speed. And with the ice warnings coming in, I think it's wise to err on the side of caution."

The captain ran his fingers over his beard thoughtfully. "I thought you might say so. You and Murdoch are rather alike."

"Just trying to keep the passengers in mind, sir."

"Yes, very true." He let out a sigh. "Let's see what the conditions are tomorrow. If it's clear, we may give it a go."

"As you say, sir."

Charles still wasn't convinced it was the right thing to do, but he wouldn't argue. Not with the captain, who had decades of experience. Once he was dismissed, Charles went to enjoy some lunch and a spot of tea. He didn't want to worry himself about whatever Ismay was pushing, but he couldn't help having his reservations. This was the North Atlantic in early spring. He couldn't begrudge Captain Smith for wanting to try, though. In his position, Charles might also consider pulling off something incredible and going into retirement a legend.

"Charlie, you've got a visitor," Lowe said, poking his head in.

"A visitor?"

"It's Miss Sybil, sir."

"Oh, show her in."

Charles's heart leaped at the sight of her as she entered the room, especially when she beamed brightly at him. He got to his feet to greet her. Once Lowe was gone, he pulled her in close for a kiss. She broke it off well before he was ready, though in fairness, he would have gladly kissed her until they died.

"I can't stay long," she said. "I only wanted to come by and let you know I'm able to come and see you tonight. Lady Iris is going to some party Mrs. Brown is throwing."

"She'll have a wonderful time," Charles said. "Mrs. Brown is a great lady, lots of fun."

"I'm glad to hear it. Lady Iris is due for a bit of fun."

"That she is. And perhaps Mrs. Brown can give her some encouragement too. She's a well-known advocate for women in America. Maybe she has some resources that might be helpful to Lady Iris."

Sybil's eyes went wide, excitement dancing behind them. "You mean—she could help her get a divorce?"

"Maybe. And if she can't help, she probably knows someone who can."

Her expression softened as she toyed with the lapel of his jacket. "I can hardly believe our luck in getting passage on this ship." She met his gaze. "It may have been the best thing that ever happened to us."

He reached up to tuck a flyaway hair behind her ear, wondering if perhaps it was the case for him as well. He felt like he was holding his wife in his arms. "I hope it is, Sybil."

He kissed her again, long and deep, drawing a soft moan from the back of her throat. Heat stirred in the pit of his belly, and he longed to get more out of her. What sounds would she make if he kissed her neck or nipped her ear? Would she stop him if his hands wandered, or would she let him explore her? Could he make her tremble around him?

"Charles," she sighed, and his knees nearly buckled. "I really must go."

It should have been illegal for them to have responsibilities after such a kiss, but she was right, and he conceded.

"One question," he said, finding himself breathless. "With Lady Iris at Mrs. Brown's, does this mean you're free for the whole night?"

Her cheeks took on a deep shade of rose. "I. . . yes. I'm free all night."

He grinned. "Excellent."

CHAPTER THIRTEEN

Sybil left the bridge with her skin on fire. She didn't regret being honest with Charles. She would have the whole night free to do as she pleased. And the way he smiled at her promised plenty of pleasure indeed. It wasn't proper, but, Sybil thought, perhaps for once, she could throw caution to the wind and pursue something she truly desired. Because she *wanted* Charles. Even if their time together would only last until they reached New York. There was no one she trusted more with her virtue. And there would be no one who could ever supplant him in her heart.

Before then, there was work to be done for Lady Iris. She made a mental checklist of what would need to be done by dinner, but it was difficult to keep focused with the memory of Charles's last kiss lingering. It wasn't confined to her lips, either. The desire it stirred slithered all over her body, down to her toes. A shudder went through her and she came to a stop.

Sudden weight against her back caused her knees to crumple beneath her. Her stomach lurched as she tipped forward, but she turned her body so she would land on her side instead of her face. An "oof!" escaped her when she hit the deck. Heart quickening, she looked to see what caused it. A young boy, maybe seven or eight years old, blinked sheepishly at her from where he sat, no doubt having landed there after their collision.

"I'm sorry, miss," he said in a soft American accent. "It was an accident."

Sybil pushed herself up onto her knees. "Quite all right. Are you hurt?"

He shook his head. "No, ma'am."

"I'm fine too, I think," she said and shot him a reassuring smile. "No harm done."

She got up and offered him her hand. He took it, and she almost drew back. Something yellow and slimy covered his palms. She contained a shiver at the clamminess of it against her skin. She persevered enough to get the boy to his feet, and he let go.

"What is this?" she asked, examining her hand.

"We made slime," he told her.

She peered down the walkway and saw three other boys pushing each other to get hidden behind a lifeboat.

"Out of what?" she wondered.

The boy shrugged. "Stuff."

Her lip curled with disgust at what a bunch of young boys might have discovered to put into their homemade goop, but asked no further questions. She brought it closer to her face, but it didn't have much of a scent.

"You can wipe your hands on your dress, miss," the boy told her. "It's already all over the back."

"What?" she yelped, and the boy took off down the deck to join his friends.

Sybil yanked her skirt around and saw it was true. Two little yellow handprints were along the back, and they dragged from where he'd met her knees down to the hem. She huffed out an annoyed breath.

"Lord, help me if I ever have any sons."

With that, she hurried back to the suite to get changed.

***

Unfortunately, Sybil had not packed properly. The dress she wore the first two days was already in need of a wash. She had planned on this one lasting the remainder of the journey. She had one other dress that she always carried as a spare, but she preferred not to wear it. It was her old house maid dress, complete with a white apron and cap. She sighed as she held it up in the mirror, but with no other choice, she changed into it.

Iris returned from afternoon tea and entered the bedroom as Sybil was tying the apron on. She thought about going without, but it looked too much like a plain frock, and she feared she might be mistaken for a third class passenger. Not wanting to create any trouble, she donned the apron.

"My goodness, Sybil," Iris said, blinking with surprise. Sybil whirled around. "What on earth are you wearing?"

"I. . . " Sybil trailed off. "I haven't got anything else, m'lady. This is my only clean dress since the one I was wearing got stained today."

"You can't go out wearing that, someone might mistake you for a White Star Line maid," Iris replied. "You may borrow something of mine, if you like."

Sybil's eyes went wide and her heart stuttered. "M-m'lady?"

"Is something the matter?"

"I can't wear your clothes!"

"Why ever not? We're around the same size. And with proper shoes, the longer hem shouldn't cause an issue."

"It's not the fit, m'lady, it's—well, it's not right! Your dresses are meant for a lady like yourself. And that's. . . that's not me."

Iris shook her head. "You of all people deserve to feel like a lady, even if it's only for one evening."

She went to the wardrobe and retrieved a stunning midnight blue gown. It sparkled as she draped it over the bed, the light catching the jewels sewn into the black lace and the shine of the satin beneath. She bent to pick up the black shoes that matched.

"This blue will bring out your brown eyes," Iris said.

Sybil couldn't believe her ears. "Lady Iris, I can't."

"You can if I say you can. Now, get that awful maid's dress off and I'll help you."

Sybil insisted on helping Iris get dressed first, which the latter conceded to. Then, it was Sybil's turn. The world felt tilted and backward as she allowed Iris to fasten the buttons of such an elegant dress around her body, and help her into a pair of shoes. Iris even offered some jewelry for Sybil to wear, which she initially refused, but Iris said it wouldn't be complete if she went without. She went one step further and did Sybil's hair too. Pinned up with small, wavy bits loose around her face. When Sybil looked in the mirror again, she hardly recognized herself.

"Oh. . . oh, wow."

"You look beautiful," Iris said, smiling at the reflection.

Sybil turned, glancing back at herself to get the full effect. She'd never seen so much of her back when she was dressed before, but it looked so lovely, she didn't fret over her modesty. She spent so much time gazing at herself, she didn't notice that Iris had left the room until she came back in, carrying a pair of black, satin opera gloves.

"One last thing," she said.

Sybil knew it was pointless to argue, so she simply held her arms out with a grin, and let Iris slide them on. Sybil had never had such luxurious fabric against her skin. The soft silkiness went all the way up over her elbows.

"Now all you need is a coat," Iris said.

"No," Sybil replied with a shake of her head. "I don't want to spoil it."

"Are you sure? It'll be cold tonight."

"I don't care. I want him to see me just like this."

Iris gave Sybil's shoulders a friendly squeeze. "You're going to bowl him over."

Together, they walked out to the boat deck. The sun was halfway down past the horizon, bathing the ship and her occupants in a warm orange glow. Down the deck, Sybil spotted Charles, leaning against the railing on his forearms, the ocean breeze gently rustling the black waves his hair, the light painting him with refined majesty. He turned at the sound of their footsteps. His mouth fell open and the awe in his eyes made her stop, taking her breath away. Now that he was there, she was beginning to lose her nerve.

"Go to him," Iris whispered.

Sybil tore her gaze from Charles to face her mistress. "Are you certain you don't need me to come back tonight?"

"Don't worry about me. Enjoy yourself." She pressed her hand into Sybil's before releasing it. "Have a wonderful time."

Sybil had no time to protest before Iris swept away. Sybil took a deep breath and prepared herself to meet Charles, but he was already directly in front of her. She gave a start, but quickly matched his smile.

"You look. . ." he trailed off and let out a bewildered huff.

"Like a lady?" she teased.

"Like a goddess."

She smiled and let her gaze drop to the deck. "It's Lady Iris's."

"It looks like it was made for you."

He took her hands in his. Her eyes snapped back up to his face, and she smiled.

"Sybil, I. . . " he paused to bite his bottom lip and inhale deeply. "There's much I wanted to say tonight. And now you've gone and looked so beautiful, I can't remember any of it."

A breathy giggle snuck out of her. "Perhaps a walk will jog your memory?"

"I'm not sure anything will, but we can give it a try."

He offered his arm, and her hand slid into place in the crook of his elbow. He led her away from the bridge, past the lifeboats to where the deck was clear. The silence between them was comfortable, the air vibrating with the hum of the engines and the gentle splashing of the ocean as *Titanic* cut through the water's surface. The sun continued its downward dip until the sky matched the sea. By the time they completed a lap around the boat deck, it was nearly dark.

"You look like you belong out here," Charles said as they came to a stop. "In a world of blue."

She flushed under his gaze. "It's lovely for a time. But I am looking forward to having my feet on solid ground again."

Something akin to disappointment flashed across his face, but it was gone as quick as it came. "Can I ask you something?"

"Of course."

"How come you never left Yorkshire?"

"I. . . " she trailed off. "It's my home. All I know. And there's of course the matter of affording travel and time off and—"

"Sybil," he cut across her. "Give me a real answer."

Her exhale stuttered out of her and she walked away from him. How could she make him understand when all he'd ever wanted was adventure? She took a seat on the reclining chairs they'd shared the first night aboard and hugged herself. The night air grew cold, as Iris warned it would, and Sybil shivered. A sudden warmth draped over her shoulders, and she looked up to find Charles there, wrapping his coat around her. He sat down at her side, nothing but patience in his eyes.

"Charles, I lost everything in the blink of an eye," she explained. "My parents, my home. In one moment, I had nothing but the clothes on my back. Even you were gone. I went to the big house and got myself a job because I wanted something I could count on every day. I still do."

His face fell. "I see."

"Why are you asking me this?" she pressed.

He heaved a sigh. "I wanted to see if there was any hope for. . . us, after this trip."

She noticed his cheeks flushing as he spoke, and he refused to meet her gaze. Had he taken her words as a rejection? She certainly didn't see it that way. She was concerned that the things they wanted didn't necessarily align, but if he was open to discussing it, she was too.

"Us?"

"Yes, you and me," he said. "But I'd hate to take you out of service if that's what makes you happy."

"And I'd hate to force you back to Yorkshire when being out at sea makes you happy."

"Yes. . ."

As if on instinct, they both turned their face up to the sky. A small beam of light streaked across the other stars, and Sybil gasped.

"Did you see that?"

"I did," he replied. "A shooting star."

"Did you make a wish?"

"I did."

She met his gaze. "What did you wish for?"

A sad smile claimed his lips. "I wished for us."

"Oh, Charles. . . "

He leaned in until his forehead was pressed to hers. His scent overwhelmed her, reminding her of his seafaring heart.

"I don't care if it doesn't make sense, Sybil, I want to try," he said. "I can't let you go now that I've found you again."

She drew back so she could look him in the face.

"There are things you don't know about me, Charles. Things that might make you see me differently."

"Come now, Sybil. It can't be as bad as all that."

Her throat closed up, but she swallowed through it. "You don't know what it is yet."

"I can't imagine anything so horrible that it would change my opinion of you. Did you. . . have another man in your life?"

She shook her head. "No, nothing like that, it's. . . it's difficult for me to say."

He took her hand. "Sybil, there's nothing you can't tell me. Please, I want to understand."

"Part of the reason I don't feel I can leave Lady Iris is that I'm not sure another lady's maid would. . . do the things I've done for her," Sybil said slowly. "It was difficult enough for me."

"What have you done?"

Her eyes welled up with fresh tears. "For all the years that she's been married, I've helped her lose every pregnancy she's ever gotten."

His eyes widened. "What?"

"She takes these herbs, and they make it so that she won't conceive, and if she does, it won't hold," she explained with a quivering voice. "I'm the one who found the doctor, I'm the one who goes to get them from the pharmacy, and I'm the one who puts them in her tea."

"Sybil. . . "

"And I know that I'm aiding and abetting sin, but I couldn't bear the thought of condemning a child to having *that man* for a father. Maybe I'll go to hell for it, but I can't even bring myself to be sorry for what I've done."

The tears finally spilled over and she searched his face for any sign that he understood, but all she found was shock. She sniffled and looked away. Her shoulders drooped.

"You must think I'm horrible," she said. She got to her feet and turned to go. "I'll leave you alone now, and you—"

His hand wrapped around her arm and he spun her into his arms. His eyes blazed as he looked over her face, but he said nothing. He only pulled her in for a blistering kiss that stole the stars out of the sky and sent them whirling in a waltz behind her eyes. Her breath left her lungs and for a moment, she thought she might faint. When they parted, her eyes fluttered open to meet his gaze.

"You're the bravest, most selfless person I've ever met, Sybil," he said, cupping her cheek in his hand. "I think you're extraordinary."

CHAPTER FOURTEEN

"You said you want something you can count on," he went on. The words came spilling out of him faster than he could think. "You can count on me, Sybil. You can count on my respect. You can count on my faithfulness. You can count on my love. My heart has been yours, even through the years we've been apart, and it will be yours until the last breath leaves my body. No matter what you do or where you go, you can count on that."

She blinked a few times, and her mouth shook as she opened and closed it. "I. . . I don't know what to say."

His heart sank. He'd put it all out there, and it wasn't enough for her. Taking a deep gulp of the night air, he braced himself to let her go. But she took his hand and placed it on her chest, directly over her heart. The rapid thump of it beneath his palm made his own pulse quicken.

"Do you feel it?" she asked, barely audible.

"Yes," he breathed.

"It beats for you. It always has."

He kissed her again, deeper than before, putting every ounce of affection he could muster into it. Her mouth was his new home, the place he would always return to, whether it was from New York or

New Zealand. Everything in him, from his heart to his mind was stamped with her name. She had the blueprints of his soul.

A fresh wave of desire surged in his blood, and he pulled her flush against him. Her chest pressed into his. The heat of her skin burned through that beautiful dress, and as stunning as she looked in it, he was suddenly eager to remove it. His mouth trailed down to her jaw, her neck, and her collarbone. A gasp hitched in her throat, and her hand jumped to his hair.

"Charles. . . "

"Come to bed with me."

He drew back to meet her eyes. Those tender brown eyes he was pleased to find heavily lidded as she gathered herself. He cradled her face in his hands, and her cheeks swelled with her smile.

"Yes," she said. "I want to."

Taking her hand, he led her back up toward the bridge and the officer's quarters. Before he opened the door she tugged on his arm.

"Won't people see?" she asked, glancing around.

"No one behind this door will care anything about us," he assured her with a kiss on her forehead.

With a nod, she followed him inside.

They reached his quarters without being spotted, and he watched her shoulders relax when he got the door closed behind them. She shrugged his coat off and hung it over the chair at his writing desk, where she paused, spying the photos he'd been sent of his brothers and their families.

"Oh, look at them all," she said with a smile. "How sweet of you to carry them with you."

That familiar hook wrenched in his belly, as it did whenever he looked at the pictures for too long. The guilt that ate away at him. But with Sybil there, it didn't take hold for too long.

"I wish I knew them better," he said, removing his cap and placing it beside the photos. "My nieces and nephews. Perhaps, when we go back, I'll finally get the chance."

She turned shocked eyes on him. "You mean it? You'll come back to Yorkshire?"

"For a little while, I think, to be with you. And if my brothers won't punish me for being away this long."

"They won't, Charles. They told me themselves, they'd welcome you home with open arms. Same as they did me."

"Did they?"

She nodded. "I can't promise you won't take a few jabs, but that's to be expected."

"Of course. They'd hardly be Edward and Stuart if they didn't."

She coiled her arms around his neck and leaned into him. "I can't tell you how happy I am to know you'll come back home."

"I told you that night by the wheel, I'll give you the world. Yorkshire is part of it."

"I'll take some more kisses first, if you don't mind."

"Not in the slightest."

He bent to meet her lips, feeling her smile into him. His hands met hers and he peeled off her gloves. Her ivory arms were enchanting. He slid his arms around her, hands joining at the top button of her dress. She shivered at his touch on her back. The bare skin there was enough to make him groan. He pressed a hot trail of kisses down over her shoulder so he could see what he was doing. When he heard her gulp, he pulled back to look at her.

"Are you all right?" he asked.

"A bit nervous, is all," she said, her gaze falling to the floor. "I've never done this before, so. . ."

"We'll take it slow." He tilted her chin up. "And we can stop at any time, you just say the word."

She nodded. "One more thing."

"What is it?"

"I've got to turn around or you'll never get all those buttons undone."

He chuckled, and she joined him before giving him her back. The dress fit her like a glove, and it was his turn to be nervous. A stream of tiny satin buttons flowed along her spine. He'd never been with someone in clothes that expensive, so he proceeded carefully. His heart jumped into his throat as he exposed more of her skin.

Unable to help himself, he kissed the nape of her neck and eased his way down her back until he reached her corset. Her soft sigh sent a flicker of heat straight to his lower belly. An ache shot to his groin as desire stirred. He'd never experienced want like this. Not the way he wanted Sybil.

"There," he said. "All the buttons are undone."

"That was quick," she replied. "Are you sure you haven't been a lady's maid?"

"Believe me, Giggles, that's not where I got my experience with buttons."

"I don't want to know then," she said, amusement in her voice.

Slowly, he pushed the sleeves of the gown off her shoulders. It dropped from her body like a curtain at the end of a show. But this event was only beginning.

"May I take your hair down?" he asked.

"Of course."

He spotted the first pin and plucked it out. He followed the updo with his fingers, removing each pin as he found them until her chestnut locks cascaded down her back and over her shoulders. He took a moment to inhale her scent, the scent that was uniquely Sybil and brought him home in an instant. His fingers ran through that gorgeous hair, memorizing the way the texture felt against his skin. It was soft and shiny, even finer than the satin he'd taken off her.

"I remember the last time I saw your hair like this," he said, toying with a piece.

She looked over her shoulder at him. "When was that?"

"A few days before I left. I asked you to take your plaits out while we were stargazing. And you did."

The memory came swimming into view. Sybil sitting up in the grass, two long plaits hanging over her shoulders, tied off at the end with ribbons. He told her she might look more grown up if she took them out, so she gave it a try. And he was right. For the first time, Sybil looked like a woman to him.

"You were so lovely then," he said in almost a whisper. "Though you have never been lovelier than you are now."

She twisted around to kiss him once more, and he stripped off his jacket. It hit the floor with a soft thud. Her fingers flew to his tie, fumbling to undo the knot, which she did remarkably quickly, and slipped it from around his neck. She went for his waistcoat next before freeing the tails of his shirt from his trousers. Knowing she wanted him as desperately as he wanted her made him groan into her mouth.

She paused to catch her breath, her chest heaving with each inhale. The corset put her breasts on full display, and he longed to descend on the round, white flesh, but he forced his eyes back to her face. Her gaze was fixed on his chest. Slowly, he undid his own buttons, and he saw her breathing stutter when she finally saw his bare torso. He shrugged his shirt off and it floated to join the rest of their discarded garments.

Her hand automatically reached for him, but she faltered. "Can I touch you?"

"Certainly," he said, and took her hand the rest of the way, pressing her palm into his skin. "Anywhere you want."

She explored his skin with a gentle touch, sending a shiver up his spine. It hit him even harder that this wasn't just anyone, it was Sybil. Sybil, who was braver than he ever imagined her to be, sweeter than he remembered, and more beautiful than anyone or anything he had ever seen. Her touch was magic, lighting him up from the inside out.

"So strong," she said when she reached his shoulders. "No wonder I feel safe with you."

He tried not to show how much that made him feel like a hero of Greek legend, and he pulled her close again. "You're always safe with me, Giggles."

She stifled a smile. "I wish you wouldn't call me Giggles in a moment like this, it makes me feel like a little girl."

He toyed with the stays of her corset.

"And how would you like to feel instead?" he asked, dropping his mouth to her ear so she could feel his breath. "Like a woman?"

She shivered against him. "Please, Charles."

He yanked her corset loose, and she shimmied out of it, along with her shoes, before she went up on her toes for another kiss. Finally, every soft curve of her body was in his grasp. His fingers caught sparks at the thought of her skin beneath the chemise, so he gathered the fabric and tugged it up until it bunched at her waist. Her nails dug into his shoulder and a whimper crawled from her throat when he cupped her between her thighs. The heat of her made him lightheaded.

"God, Sybil," he huffed out, his lips hovering over her shoulder.

"Please, more," she whined.

Her hips rocked against his hand. With a pained groan, he wrapped his free arm around her waist and lifted her off her feet. She let out a squeak of surprise, and then that signature giggle when he laid her on his bed. He could have melted into the mattress. Instead, he pushed her into it, settling his body on top of hers. Her eyelids went to half-mast as she gazed up at him.

"I want to see all of you," he said.

"And I want you to see."

Needing no further permission, he snaked his hand back up her body, taking her chemise with it. She raised her arms above her head, and he drew the garment up and over them. And then she was bare before him. Flush, with pink seeping from her cheeks to her chest. The bend in her waist and the shape of her legs was marvelous. Her breasts were even more perfect free of the constraints of the corset, pretty pink nipples pebbled, as if waiting for his mouth. He wasted no time before taking the right between his lips, thumbing the left so as not to keep her wanting.

Her back arched up like a bow as she gasped, her hands sinking into his hair. He didn't even mind the scrape of her nails on his scalp. The sting—along with the breathy moan of his name—went straight to his groin. He wanted more. But he would need to be sure she was ready.

"Feels so good," she said on a tight exhale.

He switched, but didn't remain there long before she took his wrist and guided it back between her legs.

"Please, touch me here again," she said.

"Whatever you want, Sybil."

He slid his middle finger through her slick heat, and she writhed beneath him. The urge to insert it was overwhelming, but first, he wanted to find that spot, that bundle of nerves that would undo her. He knew he'd landed on it when she keened, and his name tumbled from her mouth like a prayer.

"There it is," he teased.

She nodded, her teeth clamping down on her bottom lip. He warmed her up with small circles, slowly switching to his thumb for better leverage. He took her mouth in an insistent kiss, swallowing up her moan. When he plunged a finger inside, she sucked in a sharp gasp and her head tilted back into the pillow until all he could see was her delicious, alabaster neck. He nipped his way along her skin.

"Is this all right?" he murmured when he reached her ear.

"Feels good," she replied, and her legs inched further apart.

He bit back a groan at the tight squeeze of her around his finger. He started with an easy pace, letting her adjust to the intrusion, and building up to the pace of his thumb. Her breathing climbed along with the pitch of her whines. His blood raced with fresh desire. Especially as her walls fluttered against him. A refrain of his name echoed in the hot air between them. Her chest went from pink to red. And her legs began to shake.

"Charles, I—oh, God!" she sobbed, and she stiffened.

Her nails bit into his arms. She shuddered, falling apart with wave after wave of pleasure. He couldn't stop his grin of satisfaction as he gazed at her. He loved that he could unravel her, make her whimper and writhe. She was his every fantasy from the moment he knew what desire was, and having her this way was beyond even what his brain could conjure. Here, she answered to no one but him, and the way his touch captured her.

"You. Are. Beautiful," he said, accentuating each word with kisses to her forehead, both of her cheeks, and her nose.

He was desperate to taste her lips again, but he let her catch her breath. The sight of her panting was strikingly erotic. Parted lips, rosy face, brown eyes darkened to the shade of coal in her lust. He ached to be inside her. Ached like he never had before.

She swallowed. "I want you."

"We can take a break if you—"

"No, I want more," she insisted with a shake of her head. She reached up to cup his cheek. "I want that again, but with—well, you, inside me. Please."

Her hand drifted south toward his belt, but he beat her to it, quickly unclasping it and yanking it from around his waist. He pushed everything down his legs until he was naked as she was. And she smiled. A satisfied, thrilled smile as his hard member sprung free and he settled between her legs. He grinned back with delicious anticipation.

She hitched her legs up around his hips. "Now, Charles."

He entered her. Inch by agonizing inch. It made his stomach clench to go slow. His body was roaring at him to drive into her, especially with how good she felt as her sex drew him in. Soft and slick. Warm and welcoming. Her mouth fell open in a silent cry the further he pressed. He peppered her face and neck with kisses, whispering his admiration for her into her skin. He stopped when he was fully sheathed inside her.

"Are you hurt?" he asked.

"No," she said. Her eyes found his and held on. "No, I'm perfect. I'm yours."

He couldn't hold back a thrust at that, so hard and so passionate, they moved a few inches up the bed. He collected himself and went at a shallower clip, grinding into her while she held onto him with surprising need.

He'd never been close to finishing the moment he entered a woman. But, as he had often reminded himself that evening, this was not just any woman. This was Sybil, who had owned his heart without him knowing it. Only now, their bodies had caught up with their souls. And he was as much hers as she was his.

Her breaths became labored as he snapped his hips against hers.

"Sybil," he panted. "God, Sybil, you're wonderful."

"Wonderful," she repeated, high pitched and wanton.

His peak was fast approaching. He knew it when the air seized up in his lungs. But he needed to feel hers first. Needed it like he needed air. She was close, judging by the quivering of her legs and the way she babbled at him instead of forming words. He ground his teeth and drove harder into her.

With a strangled cry of his name, she climaxed. He thrust one, two, three more times, and was spent right behind her. Their lips hovered around each other, panting too much to kiss, but needing the comfort of the contact.

"I love you," he blurted, those being the first words on his mind. And he meant them. With all his being, he meant them.

Her parted lips curled up into a smile. "I love you too, Charles."

He kissed her then. It didn't matter that it only lasted a second. It was only one of a thousand kisses they would share in their lifetime. He was sure of it. She was home, the haven between her legs, his refuge.

He gently pulled out, rolling onto his side and pulling her close, until her chest pressed into his. He pushed her hair off her forehead, still speckled with sweat, and kissed her there as well. This was his life.

"*Titanic* really is the ship of dreams," Sybil said as he ran a finger across her cheek. "It brought me back to you."

Chapter Fifteen

April 14, 1912

Sybil woke, warm and satisfied, like after a good laugh with a dear friend. Being in Charles's arms helped. Her back was pressed to his chest, his arm slung lazily over her waist, their legs twisted up in the sheets. She always thought she'd feel changed after making love for the first time, but this. . . she felt like it should have been this way all along.

Eager to see his face, she rolled over. He shifted at her motion and cracked an eye open.

"Morning, Giggles," he said.

The gravel in his voice made her lower belly twist into a knot. They had gone several rounds throughout the night, it should have been impossible to want him again already. And yet she did.

"Good morning," she replied.

He stretched, and she let herself ogle his muscular form once more. When he pulled her into him for a sleepy kiss, she tangled her fingers into his hair, deepening it.

"Well," he said when they parted. "Now that you've had your way with me, I hope you're planning to propose."

A laugh burst from her and she rolled her eyes. "Shut up."

"Gladly. On one condition."

"Which is?"

"Have your way with me again."

Before she could answer, he took hold of her hips and rolled onto his back, keeping her balanced on his lap. She bent over him to take his mouth into another kiss when out of the corner of her eye, she spied the clock on the side table, and she froze.

"Sybil?"

"Heaven's sake, is that the time?"

"Yes." He raised a brow. "Is everything all right?"

"Oh, God!"

She clamored off him, kicking the sheet off her foot as she scrambled to gather her clothes. At halfway dressed, Charles was just sitting up. Out of breath, she wiggled into her corset and then turned her back to him so he could tie it. He complied without protest.

"What's the hurry?" he asked.

"I'll be late for church," she answered. "And don't you start rounds in half an hour?"

"You'd be amazed what I can accomplish in half an hour."

"Charles," she groaned, rolling her eyes again.

"Another time, then."

He finished with the corset and she flew to the mirror, winding her hair into a long braid over her shoulder. When she turned back around, Charles was already holding up the dress to help her into it. Her heart melted. She couldn't possibly love this man any more than she did, and then he made small gestures like that.

"I promise I'll be quicker about buttoning than I was with unbuttoning."

She smiled. "Thank you."

"But I can't promise I won't get distracted."

"You're impossible."

She knew it was hypocritical of her to scold him when the feeling of his hands at her back had flashes of the previous night passing through the front of her mind. The echo of his lips there sent a shiver through her. He paused, and she knew he was remembering too. Probably with a smirk on his face. When the buttons were done, he dropped a kiss to her shoulder.

"Do you need help with shoes?" he offered.

"Please."

He sat her on the bed, and that was when she noticed he'd pulled his trousers on. She held up her foot, and he slid her shoe on, buckling it for her. He did the same with the other. Then he retrieved her gloves.

"God, it's going to be terribly obvious what we've done, isn't it?" she said as she tugged them over her arms. "Walking around this early in an evening gown, with my hair undone, and my cheeks all red."

"You could wait until the service starts and sneak back while everyone's distracted."

"No, Mr. Mooring will want to attend with Lady Iris, and I can't leave them alone together."

He heaved a sigh and raked a hand through his hair. "Sybil. . . don't you ever think of yourself when it comes to those two?"

She stopped. "How do you mean?"

"I mean, you're awfully involved in this. And at some point, you have to remember that Lady Iris is just your employer."

She narrowed her eyes at him. "No, she isn't."

"Sybil—"

"No, listen. I know it's that way with most lady's maids and their mistresses, but it's not with us. I have been her only friend through everything she's endured from that man. For seven years, we have relied on each other. And after what I told you last night, I should think you'd be even more understanding."

"I do understand, believe me," he said, moving to stand close to her, but she took a step back. "It sounds to me like you keep taking risks for her, and I have yet to hear of a case where she does the same for you. Letting you borrow a pretty dress isn't on the same level."

Her mouth fell open. "I can't believe what I'm hearing."

"I don't mean to offend, I only want to make sure your generous heart isn't being taken advantage of."

"Some might argue it's you who has taken advantage of my heart," she snapped.

He drew back as if she'd slapped him, but she couldn't bring herself to feel guilty for saying it. Rage pinched her chest too tightly.

"But you know who wouldn't say that?" she went on. "Lady Iris. She's been nothing but supportive of us. And without her, I never would have reconnected with your brothers. Without her, Mr. Mooring would not have let me board this ship. Without her, there would be no us."

His eyes softened. "I didn't know. I'm sorry."

Her ire faltered, and she rubbed at her chest to ease the sting it left behind. "Right. . . "

"Sybil, I really am sorry," he said, taking her hand, which she allowed. She didn't fight it when he pulled her against him either. "I suppose I'm not used to not having you all to myself. If you say Lady Iris is your true friend, I believe you."

Her eyes searched his. "She is. And believe this as well. I love you, Charles Percy. And because I love you, so does Lady Iris. She told me she would never stand between our happiness."

"I'm happy to hear it. And I hope you forgive me."

"I forgive you," she assured him. "Now I really have to go. I've got something I must thank God for."

He grinned. "Surely He can wait until you've kissed me goodbye."

He didn't wait for her reply and claimed her lips. She yielded to him, bending the way clay conforms to an artist's hands. All her thoughts turned to sand. Everything was just Charles and his kiss. He pulled away.

"There, now you can go," he said.

Her eyes fluttered a moment, and she cleared her throat. "I'll see you tonight."

"Tonight, love."

After one last lingering look, she turned and left.

By the time she burst through the door of Lady Iris's cabin, her lungs were on fire. Lady Iris emerged from the bedroom and blinked with surprise. She was in her dressing gown, with what appeared to be a small piece of cardstock in her hand.

"Gracious, Sybil, did you run here?" she asked.

"Yes, m'lady," Sybil panted. "I was afraid I'd be late."

"I hardly expected you to come at all. I do hope Mr. Percy was considerate enough to properly ring your bell."

Sybil's cheeks burned. "My lady!"

Iris shrugged. "Why should we be coy about it?"

"He was. . . wonderful, I promise."

"Then what on earth are you doing here so early?"

"I've come to help you get ready for church, m'lady."

"I'll need to help you first," Iris said, looking her up and down. "I saw to it that your dress got cleaned yesterday, by the way."

"Thank you very much, m'lady."

Sybil followed her into the bedroom, where her regular black lady's maid uniform hung by the wardrobe. Beautiful as the gown was, she was ready to feel like herself again. While Lady Iris helped her out of it, she filled her in on the evening. Lady Iris smiled through the whole story and congratulated Sybil on her romance. As Sybil got Iris into her church clothes, she changed topics.

"And how was your evening with Mrs. Brown, m'lady?"

"Informative," Iris answered, and finally she handed the card she'd been holding to Sybil.

There, in print, it read *Hubert Herryman, Attorney*, with a London address at the bottom. Sybil gasped and gave it back.

"Does this mean what I think it means?"

"I think so," Iris said, her voice trembling. "I don't know if it's a guarantee, and I dread to think what Lewis might do if he finds out I have any intention of leaving him, but. . . it's a start."

"Everything begins that way," Sybil replied. "Where there's a start, there's hope, m'lady."

Iris heaved a sigh of relief. "I can hardly believe our luck in getting passage on *Titanic*. You have found your happily ever after, and I..." she trailed off, glancing at the card again. "I may have my ticket to mine."

The main door of the suites opened, making both women jump, but they heard Lewis call out for Gordon and relaxed.

"And to think, we may not even have to deal with him much longer," Iris said quietly.

"Let's hope so, m'lady."

"Iris!" Lewis called. "Iris, are you ready?"

Iris rolled her eyes and headed back out to the sitting room. "I'm here, Sybil's got me dressed. Are you ready?"

"I just need to change." He disappeared into his room, but left the door open, and he called out to her. "How was your night with Mrs. Brown?"

"Delightful," Iris replied. "I rather think I've made a good friend in her. She'll be sitting with us at the service today."

Lewis scoffed. "I thought the Catholic service was in steerage."

"And I thought Americans were above all that religious discrimination. Besides, it's all the same God, isn't it?"

Lewis came out, shrugging on his suit jacket. "Let's get going. I'm not about to discuss the theological differences between Catholics and Protestants with a woman."

The service was held in the dining salon. The captain stood up by the pulpit with the pastor, and Sybil found herself searching for Charles, even though she knew he was on duty. She felt like a silly schoolgirl, missing him already when she'd seen him less than an hour ago. And would be seeing him again when it was time for dinner. Even so, she wanted his company. To be at his side no matter what else was going on.

"Lady Iris!" Molly Brown greeted cheerfully as they filed into their seats. "Good to see you, honey. Thanks again for coming last night, it was a great time."

"Thank you, Molly," Iris replied. "I do hope next time, Sybil can join us."

Molly peered around at Sybil. "So this is the famous lady's maid!" She offered her hand. "Hi there, Sybil. Nice to formally meet you, I'm Molly. Molly Brown."

Sybil shook her hand. "Pleasure, Mrs. Brown."

"Molly, please. Your mistress speaks awfully highly of you. She told us about that prank you pulled—the bed switcheroo—we all laughed so hard, we were crying!"

Sybil flushed, and opened her mouth to speak, but Lewis beat her to it.

"Sybil has quite the streak of mischief in her," he said. "Just the other day, she played poker with some officers on the ship, and cheated them out of their money."

"Oh, not this again," Iris sighed, rolling her eyes.

"Begging your pardon, sir, but I didn't cheat," Sybil added. "I won a few games of cards, and none of them minded."

Molly grinned. "Even if you had cheated, well done."

She winked and Sybil stifled a giggle. Lewis only huffed and faced forward.

The service began. It passed like many others Sybil attended, only the hymns were naval in nature, and the prayers asked God to protect everyone at sea and in their travels. Sybil sent up a quick prayer in thanks, for leading her back to the love of her life.

Afterward, the passengers mingled some more, and Sybil started toward the door, already making a list of the work she would need to do that day. Iris went toward the front and approached Captain Smith. Sybil joined her.

"One of your officers, Mr. Charles Percy," Iris said. "Would it be possible to spare him for an hour or two this afternoon?"

Sybil felt the blood drain from her cheeks. What did Iris want with Charles?

The captain's brow furrowed, equally perplexed. "Why. . . certainly, my lady. Is it important?"

"Indeed, it is. I'd like to invite you both for tea."

"We'll be there, my lady."

"Excellent."

Sybil chewed her lip as she waited, holding Iris's coat up as she slid her arms through the sleeves.

"Lady Iris, what's this all about?"

"Don't worry, Sybil. I only want to know him better."

For the first time, Sybil wasn't sure that Lady Iris was telling her the whole truth.

Chapter Sixteen

"What in the world does she want with us?" Charles asked as he and the captain headed down the grand staircase toward A Deck.

Nothing could have shocked Charles more than when the captain came to him on his rounds and informed him he'd been invited to tea by Lady Iris Mooring. As much as Sybil adored the woman, Charles still had his reservations. In his experience, people of her class were concerned only with themselves, and even if they liked their servants, they kept them at arm's length. He had sympathy for her situation, but that didn't necessarily mean he trusted her as fully as Sybil did.

None of that meant he was eager to have any sort of talk with her about it. After the rebuke from Sybil that morning, he was determined to keep those reservations to himself going forward. Yet, Lady Iris was the one who organized this meeting. Perhaps she felt she had something to prove.

"Devil if I know, she didn't say much in her invitation," Captain Smith replied. "Is there anything I should know about, Percy?"

"No, sir," Charles assured him.

"And we aren't walking into an ambush about that incident with Mr. Mooring?"

"Not to my knowledge. I thought all that was handled."

"I did too. That's why I'm nervous."

They made it to B Deck, and Charles had another issue on his mind that he wanted to get out before they went into the Mooring's suite.

"I'd have thought your confidence rather intact, sir, given this morning's order."

The captain came to a stop and faced him, eyebrow raised. "You don't agree with lighting the last boilers."

It wasn't a question, but Charles answered as if it were. "Right, sir. My opinion is the same as it was when you first brought up Mr. Ismay's suggestion."

"I know." The captain sighed and let his shoulders drop an inch. "Murdoch said the same. But my gut tells me it's possible, Percy. Conditions are great."

"But the ice warnings, sir. More have come in every day."

"Anything that could damage *Titanic* will be large enough to see in time to turn."

"In the daytime, yes, sir. But at night, if the water stays this flat, we won't be able to see waves breaking against the bergs. And our lookouts are without binoculars."

"What? We had them in Southampton."

"Southampton is the last time anyone saw them, sir."

Captain Smith frowned. "Well, there's nothing to be done about it now. We'll be as careful as we can. I appreciate your concern, Percy, but do remember this is *Titanic* we're talking about. She's unlike any ship before her."

"I—" Charles stopped himself. He wanted to argue that her novelty made it all the more imperative to play it safe, but he swallowed the sentence. "As you say, sir."

"Good lad. Now, let's get through this tea."

Mr. Mooring's valet opened the door, revealing Lady Iris and Lewis Mooring waiting in the sitting room. They rose to greet their guests.

Up close, Charles could see where Iris's cheek was still bruised. She'd blended her rogue over it fairly well, but there was still some purple creeping out behind the pink. He gave Lewis's hand a hard squeeze when they shook.

"Ow!" Lewis barked, and yanked his hand away, massaging his right palm with his left.

"Sorry," Charles said with a pinched smile. "Strong grip."

Lewis returned with an equally pained grimace. "Right."

"Behave yourself," Captain Smith muttered in Charles's ear.

"Yes, sir."

"Do take a seat," Lady Iris offered.

Charles wanted to relax into the chair's cushions, but found himself rooted to the edge, sparing a sidelong, reproachful look at Lewis before facing Lady Iris again. Lewis ignored him, keeping his eyes on the captain.

"I must say, Captain, the voyage seems to be going well so far," he said. "New York will be singing your praises."

Captain Smith chuckled. "I hope so. Sailing a ship this grand almost makes me wish I wasn't retiring."

"There's no better place to go out than on top."

"Well said, Mr. Mooring."

Charles resisted the urge to roll his eyes. He was about to remark on the glaring absence of Sybil when she walked in, carrying a tray with the teapot, cups, and a few biscuits in front of her. She was back in her lady's maid uniform—black dress, hair tied up at the nape of her neck, and boots—but she was no less beautiful, in his opinion. Memories of their night together hit him hard, how she felt beneath him, the sounds she made, her mouth on his, and he had to shift in his seat. He hoped no one noticed his neck getting hot. She set the tray on the coffee table between them.

"Thank you, Sybil," Iris said, while at the same time, Lewis grumbled, "About time."

Charles frowned. He watched Sybil's smile falter before offering a small bow of her head.

"Of course, m'lady," she said. "Sorry for the wait."

"No trouble at all," Iris replied with a frigid look at her husband. "I'm sure it was Mr. Mooring's coffee that took the extra time."

"Excuse me for being a red-blooded American," Lewis grumbled.

He sipped his coffee. Sybil turned toward Charles and the captain, but her eyes were on the latter.

"I've prepared Lady Iris's and Mr. Percy's tea, sir, but I didn't know how you took yours, so I brought out cream, sugar, and lemon. I hope that will do."

"Oh, just lemon, for me, thank you," Captain Smith said.

"One moment."

She reached for his cup, but he held a hand up to stop her. "Quite all right, I can prepare it. Thank you, dear."

"Certainly." She turned to Iris. "If you need anything else from me, m'lady, I'll be in the other room."

Charles blinked and then took a second look at the tray. She had only carried out four servings. He shot her a questioning frown.

"Aren't you joining us?"

Finally, she met his gaze, but not for long. Within seconds, her eyes dropped to the floor in front of her. Lewis snorted into his coffee and laughed. A dry, humorless laugh that had Charles narrowing his eyes at him.

"Good one, Mr. Percy," Lewis carried on. "As if a servant could join us for tea."

"And why shouldn't she?" Iris spoke up. "Sybil, you are certainly welcome."

Sybil shook head. "Quite all right, m'lady. Mr. Oliver would have my hide if he got wind I'd had tea with the family. I'll be in the other room. Please. Enjoy yourselves."

Every atom of Charles's body protested against this. It didn't make sense. The ridiculous rules that separated people were based on nothing but money and bloodlines. He appreciated that Iris extended the offer, but it was only a gesture. Sybil had so much knowledge about Lady Iris, and the things she did to keep herself from a more permanent bond to Lewis, and yet she couldn't join her for tea. Charles held back a scream at the absurdity.

His anger cooled only when he felt Sybil's touch against his arm before she swept out of the room. The brush of her fingers lingered, even minutes after she left.

They returned to small talk, with Lewis asking if White Star Line was going to build more like *Titanic* and her sister ships. Captain Smith replied he wasn't sure. Charles hardly heard any of it. His mind—and his heart, too—was in the other room with Sybil. He wanted to know what she was doing. If she needed any help. If she could spare a moment for a kiss. Or ten.

"Mr. Percy?"

Lady Iris's voice drew him from his thoughts. "Yes, m'lady?"

"Might I have a private word with you on our promenade deck?" she asked.

His stomach twisted. "Er. . . " Captain Smith elbowed him in the ribs. "Certainly, Lady Iris."

"Wonderful." She looked at her husband. "We'll only be a moment."

Lewis waved a lazy hand and then went back to questioning the captain.

Iris led the way out, Charles close behind. He closed the door and Iris walked all the way to the end of the deck, as far from the door as possible. Charles followed, stopping a yard away from her.

"Do relax, Charles. This isn't an interrogation," she said with an amused smirk.

He dropped his shoulders and released some air from his lungs. "Right."

"Is Charles all right? I've noticed that many others call you Charlie."

"Sybil's the only one who calls me Charles, m'lady," he explained. "She always said Charlie sounded too boyish, so she insisted on my full name, no matter what everyone else said."

"Then I'll let that remain her privilege. Unless you'd prefer Mr. Percy, in which case, it won't matter either way."

He hesitated a moment, wondering if he wanted to draw some boundaries of his own. But as he looked at Lady Iris, he saw that, away from her husband, there was warmth in her eyes instead of ice, and an ease about her posture instead of stiff shoulders.

"Charlie's fine, m'lady."

"Excellent."

She paused and turned her gaze out the window, fidgeting with her hands. His brow furrowed. Was she nervous?

"First of all, I want to apologize for my husband," she said, facing him again. "He has all the manners of an ape."

Charles huffed out a laugh. "I wasn't going to say anything."

Her mouth ticked up into a smile that disappeared as quickly as came.

"I also wanted to discuss the matter of Sybil with you. I know you understand better than most what a treasure she is. And while

I'm immeasurably happy for her in having found you, I must say, the thought of her leaving my service... leaving *me*... it breaks my heart."

Charles took a step closer. "I know how much you rely on her, Lady Iris. As things are, she has no plans to leave service."

"I don't think you have a complete understanding, but—"

"My lady, I am *fully* aware of everything she does for you. Everything."

She held his gaze, searching his face. "I see. I hope we can rely on your discretion."

"Absolutely, m'lady."

She nodded, an appreciative expression coming over her. Then she shook her head.

"Back to Sybil," she said. "This is about her. I feel. . . a bit responsible for her, considering her parents are gone, and she has been in our household all these years. I want to make sure she's taken care of. And beyond that, more than anything, I want her to be happy. You will make her happy, won't you?"

She pinned him with a look, and he fought the urge to take a step backward. Luckily, he knew the answer.

"Yes, m'lady, I will make her happy," he said. "As long as I live and breathe, I'll do whatever I can to see to that."

She smiled then. "Good."

A beat passed.

"And you'll make an honest woman out of her?"

Charles cleared his throat and cut his gaze, heat rising up his cheeks. "I—yes, I have every intention of marrying her."

"Perfect."

Another beat of silence.

"I know you said she has no intention of leaving service right now, but I know how the world works. In your line of work, you'll want to be in a port city, not huffing it back to the heart of Yorkshire to see your wife. And once you start a family. . . well, Sybil will be the one expected to leave work. So. . . eventually, she will leave. And when that happens, I ask that you promise me one thing."

When she looked at him again, her walls were down, and he saw in her eyes—pleading. She was making herself vulnerable with this request. So much so, he couldn't even argue that he and Sybil planned to make it work as long as they could. In his heart, he knew she was right. And he could see the pain even the idea of it caused her.

"What is it, m'lady?"

"That you and Sybil will come visit me and your brothers in Yorkshire every once in a while," she said. "That I'll get a Christmas card from you each year because you will certainly get one from me. And any children you may have—" she shopped short, eyes glistening, and she swallowed. "That I will get to meet them. And they'll call me Auntie Iris. Not my lady."

"She'll always be in your life, Lady Iris," he said, heart softening. Sybil was right, too. Lady Iris cared for her far beyond being a lady's maid. Sybil was her family. "I promise you that."

"Thank you," she said. "Charlie."

Chapter Seventeen

That night, Sybil was late when she left to meet Charles. She found him pacing by the bridge, warming his hands with his breath. She might have laughed if not for the desperate relief in his eyes when he spied her making her way up the steps.

"There you are!" he cried.

"I'm sorry, there was just a bit of mending I needed to—oh!"

She yelped in surprise when he scooped her up over his shoulder. A laugh burst out of her as he opened the door of the officer's quarters.

"No stargazing tonight, eh?" she teased.

"Too cold tonight," he replied. "Luckily, I know an excellent way to get warm."

"You are a naughty boy, Charles Percy."

He kicked the door open. "I think I prefer wicked man, but either way, I'll have you in my bed."

They were in his room before she could retort. The moment he had the door closed, he placed her on her feet and pushed her against it, caging her between his arms, holding her gaze with his own. Her heart stuttered over several beats. Heat rose to her cheeks. Her breathing slowed.

His lips crashed into hers, so sudden and so passionate, a whimper escaped her throat. Charles took it for the encouragement that it was and deepened the kiss, flicking his tongue out to find her mouth. For years, Sybil overheard the other maids whisper about kissing and making love, and how clumsy it was, so it surprised her that it came easily with Charles. They didn't miss a beat when they were together. Which Sybil reasoned meant that they were a perfect match.

As they kissed, she fumbled with the buttons of his jacket, pushing it off his shoulders to get to the white shirt underneath. Through it, she could feel the strength of his arms and chest, and it made heat stir inside her.

When he trailed his kisses down to her neck, her body went molten. Charles, as if on cue, pushed his body into her hers, holding her up. Which was the least he could do since it was his fault her legs were weak. He used one hand to bunch up her skirts, making his way through the layers until he reached her bare thigh. She gasped and shivered.

"Your hands are cold," she chided.

"Whose fault is that?" he shot back with a smirk. "Don't worry, they'll get warm. You're burning up for me, Giggles."

He spoke the truth. Already, his hand was a comfortable temperature against her skin, but as he slid it higher, she shivered for a different reason—pure anticipation. Charles made her desperate in a way that she knew should make her ashamed, but there was no room for that. Not with Charles. She throbbed with need for him.

His fingers teased her entrance, and she whined, letting her head fall back against the door.

"Look at me, Sybil," he said, and she obeyed, albeit with heavily lidded eyes. "God, you're ready for me, aren't you?"

She nodded, biting her bottom lip. Her eyes flicked down to his trousers, where she could clearly see that he was ready for her as well.

She reached for his belt, but he stopped her with his free hand and shook his head. She shot him a confused look.

"I want to watch you," he said. "Just like this. In this dress, but all mine."

Her stomach did a flip.

"I could do without the dress," she sighed back with a smile.

"I can't wait. I have to touch you now."

Her center clenched, especially with his fingers prodding at her, teasing her with the lightness of his touch. She clutched at his arm, squeezing it to urge him on.

"Eyes on me, love," he reminded her, and sank two fingers inside.

Her mouth fell open with a moan, but she resisted the urge to let her head fall back again. She fixed her gaze on his face and he pumped his fingers steadily, his thumb finding her clit and applying circular pressure until her walls fluttered around him.

Her body was on fire. She could have powered the ship if she were in the engine room. The cold outside was long forgotten. Her whole world was narrowed down to Charles and his expert touch.

"You are gorgeous like this," he praised through a strained breath, his eyes ablaze. "Absolutely stunning."

She whined and rocked her hips into his hand. She wished he had taken off her dress because the room was suddenly sweltering. He sped up, and it was spinning. Or perhaps that was her head. She didn't know. Once again, she could only feel him. She could only see him. His jaw was tight as he worked her up.

Her lower belly coiled tight like a spring. Her nails dug into his arms and her legs trembled. Her toes curled in her shoes. Her gasps went up an octave with each exhale as she teetered on the edge of release. She was so, so close.

"That's it, Sybil. Let it go for me," Charles murmured. "I'm right here. I've got you."

She hit her peak and toppled over the edge with a tremor, and his name lodged in her throat. With a soothing voice, he coaxed her back down, slowing with his hand until she flinched away from his touch, and he pulled back. Then he dropped kisses all over her—from her head to her cheeks to her neck. She appreciated that he avoided her lips so she could catch her breath. Then she decided she needed his kiss more than air.

He didn't protest when she grabbed him by the neck and yanked him down, capturing his mouth. In fact, he smiled into it and held her against him.

"You're beautiful," he whispered between kisses. "My darling, Sybil."

She held his gaze for a long moment. "You make me feel beautiful, my love."

He kissed her deep and slow. Meanwhile, his fingers popped open the buttons of her dress, and he pulled it off. The air hit her damp skin, but she didn't shiver, not in the warmth of Charles's embrace. He made astonishingly quick work of her corset and undergarments as he guided her toward the bed.

The frame swept her legs out from under her, and she fell onto the mattress. Charles shed his tie, waistcoat, and undershirt. She only got to admire his strong, trim frame for a moment because he went to his knees between hers. He pressed a kiss to the inside of her thigh.

"May I make you feel beautiful again?" he asked with a smirk.

"Yes, please," she said through a giggle.

He kissed his way up her thigh, and she took her bottom lip between her teeth as she waited for him to reach the apex. When he wrapped his lips around her clit, she sucked in a sharp breath and her back arched up off the mattress. He groaned at her pleasure, the hum of it sending a rush of fresh desire up her spine. She curled her fingers into his dark hair and held him firmly in place.

He ate her slow and sweet, savoring each of her reactions to him. When he swirled his tongue, it made her dizzy, and her grip on his hair tightened. Sybil had never known bliss like this. Kissing was lovely, but mouths must have been designed for this. Nothing else sent her beyond the clouds, among the stars. It was heaven.

Her second break was upon her, and it was so intense, her legs tried to close around Charles's head, but he held her open and continued. He squeezed her thighs to ease the quake in them. Her hips rutted up of their own accord, chasing the high she knew was approaching. Charles would get her there, she had no doubt. He stayed on course, steady and sure, until it hit her and she came undone against his mouth.

Chest heaving, she came down. Charles hovered over her, placing little kisses up her tummy and on each of her nipples before making his way back to her neck.

"You're a goddess," he said.

A low chuckle sounded in her chest. She heard the clink of his belt as he unbuckled it and the shuffle of clothing as he freed himself from his trousers. He groaned with relief when he stroked himself, and she let out a whimper as she watched.

"What is it, love?" he teased. "Still needy for me?"

She nodded, then grabbed his shoulders to pull him in for another kiss. His kisses felt like the only thing tethering her to the earth. Everything else sent her skyward.

When she had him close, she flipped them so he was on his back, a feat she knew she could only accomplish when she had him distracted. But the smirk on his face told her he didn't mind being taken off guard that way. Especially once she settled on his lap, her hot center inches away from his length. A groan hitched in his throat.

"Needy for me?" she mimicked.

"Always," he said with a cheeky grin, and his hands took hold of her hips.

She braced herself on his chest and let him guide her until he breached her entrance. Inch by inch, she took him down, stretching to accommodate his size. She hissed at the delightful sting of it, relishing the fullness of him inside her. She was made for him, she was sure of it. Nothing but destiny could make this feeling so pure. So satisfying. Every path she had taken had led her to this—being his for the rest of her life.

Secure in that, she rode him into oblivion.

Chapter Eighteen

Sybil flopped onto the mattress, landing on her back next to Charles, who was as out of breath as she was. And yet somehow mustered the energy to roll on top of her and kiss her until she saw stars. When her lungs couldn't take it anymore, she gave him a gentle nudge, and he lifted up.

"You are incredible, do you know that?" he said. "Just wonderful."

"You could stand to mention it more," she teased.

He'd praised her through every moment of their love making, but she never tired of hearing it from him.

"How often would be good for you?" he joked back.

"Let's see. . . at least three times each morning. Twice that at night. And twice *that* when we're in bed together. And on special occasions, I'd like to hear what a goddess I am again. That was rather lovely."

"You don't think it'd start to lose its meaning after a while?"

"Goodness no. I fully expect to see these numbers. Else I'll worry you don't feel the same as you do now."

"Well, we can't have that."

He tucked her under his arm and she snuggled down on his chest, listening to his rapid heartbeat. With each pulse, she knew she didn't have anything to worry about. Not really. He'd crack open his ribs and carve her name on his heart if she asked him to.

"I'm dreading reaching New York," he said, breaking the silence.

She looked up at him. "Why?"

"Because it means we'll have to part. I know it won't be for long, but I'm set to sail *Titanic* back to England."

"Perhaps Lady Iris and I can get passage on the return journey. She won't stay in New York now that she plans to leave Mr. Mooring."

Charles blinked. "What?"

Sybil grinned and nodded. "She got an attorney recommended by Mrs. Brown. She wants to get back to London as soon as she can to file for divorce."

"That's great news!"

"I know. We'll be free of him at last!"

"Are you certain it will go her way?"

"It has to. She's suffered long enough."

He kissed her, long and languid. "You are awfully sweet to care for her so much."

"I hope you'll come to love her as I do."

"I'm sure I—"

A great shudder cut him off. The whole room shook with it, rattling the pictures on the desk and the light fixtures on the wall and ceiling. A metallic scraping sound echoed through the walls. Sybil held tight to Charles, her stomach plummeting as her heart skipped several beats. Charles's arm secured her to him, his free hand coming to cradle the back of her head.

Then it all went eerily still.

"What was that?" Sybil whispered.

Charles didn't answer for a painfully long moment. "I'd better go find out."

He climbed out of bed and got dressed. Sybil pulled the sheets over herself and watched him for a moment, frozen. She had never been on a ship before, so she had no idea if this was serious, but she didn't like the look on Charles's face. Worry put a crease between his brows. When he met her gaze, his expression softened, and he forced a smile.

"It's probably nothing," he said. "You can stay here and sleep if you want."

"Don't lie to me, Charles. You're concerned."

"Concern doesn't mean disaster, Giggles."

"But you *are* concerned."

"Yes, I am a little." He sighed, the mask slipping off. "We got seven ice warnings today."

"Is that a lot?"

"It's enough."

She swallowed, but found her throat suddenly dry. Throwing the sheets back, she too started to dress. "I should warn Lady Iris."

"There may be nothing to warn her of."

"I may not know about ships, but that certainly didn't feel like nothing."

"Hey," he said gently, putting his hands on her shoulders. "Don't jump to any conclusions, all right? This is *Titanic*. She's a remarkable ship. If there's any danger, I'll make sure you're all right."

"Do you promise?" she asked through the rust in her voice. "You'll come back for me?"

His warm hand embraced her cheek and her eyes fell closed to his touch. When she opened them again, she found him gazing tenderly back at her.

"I made the mistake of leaving you behind once, Sybil," he said. "I'll never do it again."

She kissed him, letting him know she understood.

Once dressed, he took her hand and led her out to the bridge. Bitterly cold air nipped Sybil's cheeks. She shivered, and Charles removed his overcoat to wrap it around her. She shot him a grateful smile.

Evidently, Captain Smith had been just ahead of them. He swept over to Murdoch, who stood by the telegraphs, his face white as a sheet, his forehead dotted with sweat. When he met the captain's gaze, he looked like he was about to be sick.

"What happened?" Captain Smith demanded.

Murdoch swallowed hard. "Iceberg, sir."

Sybil's insides froze over the longer she listened.

"We did everything we could—"

"Put her hard to starboard?"

"Yes, sir."

"Ran the engines full astern?"

"Yes, sir."

"Then what happened?"

Murdoch's mouth trembled. "We didn't see it in time. So she hit."

Captain Smith appeared to deflate, his shoulders slowly lowering and his mouth turning steadily downward.

"Jesus," Charles said under his breath. Sybil looked up at his face, but found him stoic, his eyes resolutely on the captain.

"Did you close the watertight doors?" the captain asked.

"Yes, sir, they're closed," Murdoch answered.

"Bring her to a stop. We'll need to assess the damage. Get Mr. Andrews and Mr. Ismay to my quarters right away."

Murdoch delegated to a couple stewards standing by, and they fled from the bridge. Finally, Charles turned to Sybil, an intensity in his gaze that almost made her shrink back. He pressed a kiss to her forehead.

"Get back to your room. Tell no one but Lady Iris what you've heard here," he said quietly.

"O-okay," she stammered.

"I'll come for you as soon as I can."

She nodded, gave his hand one last squeeze, and then hurried away toward the staircase. Her heart pounded. She didn't fully understand everything she'd overheard, but she recognized fear when she saw it. And it was all over Charles's face. The captain's and Murdoch's too.

A fresh bolt of worry went through her when she reached the cabin. Gordon sat on the floor in the corridor, knees drawn up to his chest, head in his hands. He looked up at the sound of her footsteps. Sybil heard muffled shouting from within the cabin and understood.

"They're fighting again?" she panted.

He answered with an affirmative grunt. "They've been at it for hours. Are you all right? You seem out of breath."

"Just the cold," she lied. "Wanted to get back inside quick. What are they fighting about?"

Gordon ran a hand through his hair and heaved a sigh. "He found the card."

Sybil stiffened. "What card?"

"You know. The attorney's card. Lady Iris admitted she wants to file for divorce. You can imagine he didn't take it too well."

Heart in her throat, Sybil burst through the door. The moment she did, something heavy and solid collided with her forehead, so hard her vision darkened around the edges. Ringing erupted in her ears, and the next thing she knew, she was on the floor. She blinked several times, willing her eyes to focus. Finally, they settled on Iris's face in front of her, a cloud of concern over her features.

"My lady?"

"Heavens, Sybil, are you all right?" Iris fretted. "I'm so sorry, he's throwing anything he can get his hands on."

Sybil opened her mouth to answer, but a throbbing pain in her head made her wince. Then, hot stickiness dripped from over her eyebrow onto her cheek. She brought her fingers to it and examined them, finding a stain of crimson.

"Oh my God, you're bleeding!" Iris gasped. She whipped around and speared her husband with a glare. "Look what you've done!"

"She shouldn't go barging into rooms—" Lewis argued, but Iris was having none of it.

"No, you shouldn't be acting like a petulant child!"

They exchanged a few more barbs and Sybil collected herself. She glanced around and found the room an absolute disaster. Iris wasn't exaggerating. Every object not nailed down was lying on the floor near a wall or was turned upside down. Beside her was a crystal ashtray, smudged where it had struck her sweaty skin. Sybil squeezed her eyes shut in an attempt to make it all stop spinning.

"Lady Iris," she said, cutting Iris off mid-insult. "I've got to tell you something."

"I'm sure it can wait, let's get you taken care of," Iris replied gently. She peered over Sybil's shoulder at Gordon. "Can you help me get her to the bedroom?"

Sybil felt a strong pair of arms beneath her, lifting her off the floor. Her head pounded in protest, and she trapped a second wince in her throat. Once she was on her feet, Iris supported her to the bedroom, where she sat Sybil down.

"Find a steward to get us some first aid and some ice," she said to Gordon. "And the Master at Arms if you can find him. I won't tolerate an attack on my lady's maid."

Gordon departed without another word.

"M'lady, it's not important," Sybil interjected. "Something serious has happened."

Iris ignored her, but looked into her eyes. "Your pupils seem normal. Are you feeling anything beyond the pain? Nausea? Dizziness?"

"Oh, do you make yourself out to be a nurse now?" Lewis sneered from the doorway.

Iris disappeared into the lavatory and came back with a damp cloth, which she pressed to Sybil's head. She also wiped away the blood that had fallen on her cheek. The cool pressure relieved some of the ache, but Sybil resisted the urge to close her eyes.

"Sybil?" Iris said. "You haven't answered."

"I'm all right, m'lady, honest. I was dizzy at first, but it's slowing down."

"Good. Hopefully Gordon can find a nurse or doctor as well."

Sybil grabbed her hand and pulled her close. She lowered her voice to barely above a whisper. "My lady, listen to me, *please*. The ship struck an iceberg."

Iris blinked, her brow furrowing. "What?"

"Didn't you feel a shudder earlier?"

"No, I was rather preoccupied evading Lewis. It can't be too serious."

Sybil held her gaze. "Charles seems worried."

"He's always worried about you."

"No, this is different, I know it."

"Did he say what we should do?"

"Not much. But I could only tell you what I heard."

Iris nodded. "Then there must be some time while they figure it out. For now, we need to get you sorted."

"What are you two whispering about?" Lewis demanded.

"If we wanted you to know, we would speak at a volume you could hear," Iris snipped.

"Don't take a tone with me, Iris. If you think making me miserable is going to get me to agree to divorce, you're sorely mistaken. You've been trying that for seven years, and I haven't left you yet."

She whirled around to face him. "Yes, well, how could I possibly outdo the master at making people miserable?"

He rolled his shoulders back, and she laughed in his face.

"Going to hit me again?" she mocked. "Go ahead. But you had better make it a good one because this time I'm fully prepared to strike back."

"Is that supposed to scare me?"

"No, it was meant to inform you."

"Is that so?"

He loomed so far over her, even Sybil shrunk back. But Iris held firm. Sybil braced herself. If Lewis tried to attack her again, Sybil knew she would need to be ready. Even if her head was still jumbled.

Before either of them could move, Gordon returned, a steward close behind him. He carried a small bucket of ice and some bandages. His eyes bounced between Iris and Lewis, neither of whom had acknowledged him. He let his gaze fall on Sybil instead.

"I assume these are for you," he said, and he set them beside her. Clearing his throat, he faced Iris and Lewis. "Begging your pardon, sir, madam." They glowered at him, but he carried on. "The captain has ordered all passengers to put on the lifebelts and make their way to the boat deck. There's no need to panic, all is in order, but do be sure to dress warmly as it is quite cold tonight."

Iris looked back at Sybil, her eyes blown wide.

CHAPTER NINETEEN

Once Sybil was out of sight, Charles followed the captain, Chief Officer Wilde, Murdoch, Thomas Andrews, and Bruce Ismay into the captain's quarters. The air in the room was thick and warm, despite the chill outside the windows. Within seconds, Mr. Andrews had the full blueprint of Titanic spread on the desk. Charles hardly recognized it. Where there were lines and numbers on the page, Charles saw people. The third class dining area where he'd seen those children pulling the age-old tactic of keep away. The parlor suites where he had discovered Lady Iris's true feelings. The boat deck and bridge where he'd gotten to know Sybil all over again. *Titanic* was a whole world.

"Five compartments," Mr. Andrews said gravely. "Five compartments breached, and water in boiler room six."

"Yes, we've determined that," Mr. Ismay replied, an irritable snap to his tone. "When can we get underway?"

Mr. Andrews rounded on him. "There will be no getting underway, Mr. Ismay."

Ismay blanched. "What the devil do you mean?"

Andrews turned slowly back toward the blueprint, his ashen face gathering a sheen of sweat across his forehead. Charles's stomach dropped. Whatever he was about to say was not good news. His mind leaped to Sybil, and how he could keep her safe.

"*Titanic* can stay afloat with four compartments breached at most," Andrews said. "With five. . . she'll go down by the head. Water will spill over the tops of the bulkheads at E Deck, and one by one, they will flood."

"What can we do?" Wilde asked, voicing the question on Charles's mind.

"We can't stop it," Andrews said.

"What about the pumps?" Captain Smith wondered.

"They'd be a waste of time at this point," Andrews answered. "They would only buy us a few minutes, and we only have an hour or two at most."

"An hour or two before what?" Ismay demanded.

Andrews held his gaze. "Before *Titanic* goes to the bottom of the Atlantic."

Charles felt like he was going to be sick. He rubbed his chest to ease the suffocating pressure on it, and his mind raced with what he needed to do. Get the lifeboats uncovered. *Make sure Sybil gets out.* Get the women and children off first. *Make sure Sybil gets out.* Prep the collapsibles in case they're needed. *Make sure Sybil gets out.* . .

"That's. . . " Ismay trailed off. "That's not possible."

"It's not only possible, Mr. Ismay, it's certain," Andrews said. "There's no saving her."

Charles looked at Murdoch, whose face had somehow paled even further. From there, his gaze slid over to Captain Smith, who was still staring at the blueprint as if it might suddenly contradict Mr. Andrews. Wilde checked his watch. The officers couldn't stand there for another second. There was no time for fear, Charles realized. They had work to do. And they needed to do it fast.

"Captain," Charles said, clearing the rust out of his voice. "Shall we get the women and children on lifeboats?"

The captain started, as if he'd forgotten there were others in the room, and looked at Charles. "I. . . yes. I need to get to the wireless room. We'll have to send a distress call."

The captain departed. A new fear unlocked inside Charles's chest. Had any other ships braved this area in these conditions with all the ice warnings out? How long would it take for rescue to arrive? Would there be enough time to ferry all the passengers onto a rescue ship before *Titanic* foundered? With less than two hours of time, it didn't seem likely.

Charles shook his head. The only thing he could do was focus on the task in front of him, and that was loading the lifeboats. He looked at Wilde for instructions.

"Percy, you take the port side, Murdoch, you take starboard," he said. "Start with first class women and children first, then see about second and third."

Charles blinked. "What the hell does it matter what their ticket says?"

"If we let everyone up to the boat deck at once, it will get out of hand," Wilde said. "Speaking of which. . . "

He headed to a cabinet in the corner, where he retrieved a few boxes. From each, he withdrew a revolver, and handed them out to Charles and Murdoch. The latter took it, but Charles only glanced between it and Wilde's face.

"I hope you're joking," he said.

"Don't be soft, Percy, crowd control might become an issue, and you'll need a way to ensure command," Wilde replied.

"People are already going to be frightened! I refuse to add to that by putting a gun in their faces!"

Wilde shoved the revolver into Charles's chest. "Do your job, Percy. Believe me, you'll need this."

"Absolutely not."

"Take it, Charlie, just in case," Murdoch spoke up, his voice thin as the edge of a knife. "You may not have to use it. And if you do, fire into the air."

Charles turned shocked eyes on him. "You aren't honestly suggesting—"

"We don't have time to argue," Murdoch said quickly. "Let's get to work."

With one last glower at Wilde, Charles stowed his newly issued sidearm away and followed Murdoch out to the bridge. They looked out at the bow, and Charles wondered if it was already dipping. He couldn't tell from there.

"It's my fault," Murdoch said quietly.

Charles raised his brows. "What?"

"I should have seen it sooner. Or maybe, if I'd let her hit head on instead of the side, we wouldn't be in this kind of danger."

"How would that be any different?"

"You heard Mr. Andrews, she could stay afloat if four or fewer compartments are breached. I should have—"

"Will," Charles said, taking his friend by the shoulders. "The what ifs will drive you mad. You did your best with the information you had at the time."

Murdoch didn't seem to hear. "I'll never work on a ship again. I'm the man who sank *Titanic*."

"Stop this!" Charles shook him. "An iceberg sank *Titanic*, not one man. Focus on your job, living through this, and getting back to Ada for one of those hellos you're always talking about."

At the mention of his wife, Murdoch softened, his eyes searching Charles's, and then his lips drew together in a resolute line.

"You're right. I'm sorry."

"I'll see you on the other side, Will."

Murdoch nodded, clapped Charles's shoulder, and left for the starboard side of the boat deck. Charles took a deep breath of the frosty air and dropped his head back to look at the heavens. The stars glittered above him. He thought once more of Sybil, and how they used to stargaze in Yorkshire. He hoped he could make good on his promise to go back with her.

The stewards had their orders to wake the passengers and get those in first class out to the boat deck. They trickled out at first, but upon feeling the cold in the air and hearing the noise of the crew darting around, shouting at each other, and swinging the davits out, they disappeared back inside. Charles kept his eyes peeled for Lady Iris and Sybil. If he could get them on a boat first, he would.

He stopped a steward heading inside.

"The boats are nearly ready, get them out here," he said. "Hurry."

The steward nodded and double timed it down the deck.

A small crowd formed as the first class passengers emerged for the second time. They chattered, and Charles even heard some laughter here and there. But they quieted as the cold hit them. Charles cupped his hands around his mouth.

"Your attention please!" he called over the remaining voices, his breath appearing like smoke in the air. They all stopped, eyes on him. "Thank you. For the time being, please have the women and children come forward. Women and children only, please."

A few stepped up, and Charles, along with Officer Lowe, helped them over the rail and into the lifeboat. But when they turned back for more, they found most of the other women hesitant. Then they fired off their questions.

"Why can't our husbands join us?"

"Are you sure it's safer in that little thing than it is on the ship?"

"Can you hold it for me so I may go back to my room for a few things?"

"Will the lifeboats be seated according to class?"

Charles held up a hand to stop them. "Your husbands will have to wait until there are boats available for the men. I'm sorry, those are the captain's orders. The lifeboats are perfectly safe, I assure you. If you go back to your room, I cannot hold a boat for you, though you may catch a later one. As of now, we are only taking first class women and children, but the longer you wait, the more likely you will be seated with passengers from second and third. Anything else, ladies?"

Silence.

"Then, please, step up, so we may help you aboard."

They surged forward. Charles took gloved hand after gloved hand and guided them up and over, into the suspended lifeboat. The children, he lifted and handed to their mothers, taking care they were secure in their seats before letting go. He turned to help the next in line, taking her hand, but she pulled against him.

"Madam, let me—"

He met her gaze and stopped, realizing the woman had tears streaming down her face.

"A moment, please," she begged, her other hand clasped tightly in her husband's. "We're newlyweds."

"One moment," he conceded, moved with sympathy.

Another woman behind her was ready, but out of the corner of his eye, he saw the newlyweds embrace, sharing a light, yet tenderly passionate kiss. He tore his gaze from them to give them a moment's privacy, but he couldn't help but overhear.

"Don't worry, darling," the husband said. "I'll get on the first boat they let me on. I promise."

"I can't bear the thought of leaving you," she replied through a sniffle. "I love you."

"I love you too. Now please, for me, get on the boat and be safe."

She nodded. "Yes, dear."

She tapped Charles on the shoulder, and he turned to assist her. She was quick about stepping into the boat, but he gave her hand an encouraging squeeze. The corners of her mouth turned up when she caught his eye, but then her gaze was trained on her husband.

Charles scanned the crowd, but there was still no sign of Sybil. He wondered if perhaps she had gone to the starboard side. But if that were the case, he was sure that Murdoch would send her to him instead so that he would know for sure. It's what Charles would have done for him. Plus, it might give him the chance to see her one last time.

He knew there were not enough lifeboats for everyone on board. If rescue didn't arrive in time, it would mean nearly half the passengers and crew would lose their lives to the freezing water. As an officer, he had a duty to see as many passengers off the ship as he could before thinking of himself. If he got Sybil onto a boat and kissed her one more time, he knew he could face that without regret.

The first boat was nearly full. He got three more women on board, some rather reluctantly, and did one last sweep for Sybil or Lady Iris. But they weren't there. He briefly considered sending a steward or Lowe to go find her, but knew that would be an abuse of his position. He had to help the people in front of him first, as much as it pained him.

He glanced at the stewards manning each side of the davit and raised his arms.

"This one's full," he said. "Lower away."

CHAPTER TWENTY

Ignoring the pounding in her head, Sybil helped Iris get dressed. For the first time, they didn't talk. Sybil anxiously waited for a knock on the suite door that would hopefully be Charles. Iris appeared trapped in her own thoughts, with her eyes glued to the floor and her head down. Sybil picked up Iris's coat and then, noticing Iris's long blonde braid still hanging loose, set it back down.

"Would you like me to fix your hair, m'lady?" she offered. "Before you go up?"

Iris blinked at her a few times. "I. . . no, I don't suppose we have time."

Sybil raised an eyebrow, the one that didn't have broken skin over it. "Are you all right, m'lady?"

"I think so. Only I'm dreadfully afraid I'm a bit responsible for this."

Sybil shook her head. "How?"

"I said I hoped the ship would sink. The day Lewis told us we were going. Perhaps this is God's way of punishing me for saying such cruel things."

"M'lady, don't do this to yourself," Sybil said, placing a gentle hand on her arm. "You said something you didn't mean in a moment of anger. If God made everything we said in such times come true, we'd be living in a much harsher world."

Iris gathered herself. "You're right, I'm being silly."

"Just so, m'lady. Now, let's get your coat on. It's freezing out."

Out in the sitting room, the steward was trying to convince Lewis to put his lifebelt on. Lewis swatted it away.

"I'm not wearing that ridiculous thing," he snapped.

"Sir, the captain said—"

"The captain can order some things, but not what I wear. The ship is unsinkable, I have no use for that, anyway."

Sybil saw the steward's mouth tighten when Lewis said "unsinkable," and her heart skipped a beat.

"Do we wear it under or over our coats?" Iris asked politely.

"Under, madam," the steward replied.

"Come, Sybil, let's set a good example."

With the steward's help, they got their lifebelts secured. It was tight across the chest, but Sybil wouldn't dare complain, not if it was something that could save her life. Gordon donned his as well, though Lewis insisted on going without.

"Second Officer Percy," Sybil said to the steward. "Where is he?"

"He's loading the boats on the port side, miss."

She tried not to be let down. Of course, his duty took precedence over coming to fetch her, but she did wish it had been him to let them know. And they could ask him how serious this really was. The steward was being so tight-lipped, he hadn't even mentioned the iceberg.

"We'll go up his way, then," Iris said.

Sybil nodded, pulling Charles's coat tighter around her.

When they first came out to the boat deck, the noise was overwhelming. The crew raced back and forth, barking orders at each other, and dodging passengers firing questions off. They hauled the canvases off the lifeboats and left them in heaps on the deck. Sybil searched the chaos for Charles.

"It's freezing," Lewis complained. "Let's go back inside."

"No, they told us to be on the boat deck," Iris replied.

"They clearly aren't loading the boats yet, so what does it matter?"

"You go back in if you want, we're staying out here."

"Like hell you are."

Sybil's pursuit of Charles was cut short when Lewis grabbed Iris by the arm, above her elbow, and yanked her away. She yelped, struggling against him to no avail. Sybil cast one last anxious look out at the boat deck before she followed them through the door.

"Let go of me, you brute," Iris demanded, tugging her arm free.

Lewis didn't put up a fight. There were too many people around for him to behave in his true manner. Iris rubbed her arm.

Molly Brown came over, her lifebelt between her mink coat and her dressing gown. She shot Lewis a glare before turning to Iris.

"You folks have any idea what's going on?" she asked. "I'm trying to get an answer from one of the stewards, but they run off like hares in rabbit season."

"We know as much as you, Molly," Iris said.

"This is ridiculous. They get us all out of bed, rush us out here in our new outfits, and then tell us there's nothing to worry about. Which is it, y'know?"

Sybil looked out the window, her eyes flying over every face, and examining each davit. She remembered Charles telling her about them the first day on board. He would likely be near one of them in order to start loading. Finally, she spotted him.

"My lady, I see Charles," she said, turning to face them.

"Geez, Sybil, what happened?" Molly said, eyes glancing at her forehead. "You run into a door too?"

Sybil shot a glare at Lewis's retreating form and looked back at Molly. "Yes, the very same door, believe it or not."

Molly frowned. "Interesting."

Sybil had no idea where Lewis was going, but she didn't care. At this point, all she wanted was to get on a lifeboat with Iris and be safe. Lewis returned, winded.

"They're already loading the lifeboats on the other side," he said. "Let's head there."

"No, we'll go to Charlie's side," Iris argued. "If we don't, he'll worry about Sybil."

"That's not my concern."

"It is mine."

"Iris, for God's sake—"

She leveled him with a scowl. "No, I know what you're doing. You don't want Charlie to see what you've done to Sybil."

"That was an accident, and I'm not worried about him. I just want to get to a lifeboat as quickly as we can."

"We will get on one of Charlie's lifeboats."

Lewis's lip curled and his eyes flashed. Sybil wondered if maybe, given the circumstances, he would throw propriety out the window and strike Iris in front of all these people. His hand balled into a fist so tight his knuckles were white.

"Iris, you're being difficult," he said through clenched teeth.

"And you're being a spineless weasel," she shot back.

"Iris!"

"Weasel!"

Under different circumstances, Sybil might have laughed. But a steward was urging everyone back outside. Iris and Lewis continued their spat, and he took hold of her wrist. Sybil's heart split in two as she watched them fight, and looked out the window to see Charles helping the first few passengers into the boats.

Molly's hand on her arm drew her attention.

"Sybil, make sure that young woman gets on a lifeboat," Molly said. "Him. . . I wouldn't worry about as much."

"I'll make sure she's safe, Mrs. Brown, thank you," Sybil said.

Molly went to the boat deck. Sybil approached the Moorings, where Gordon was trying to pry Lewis's hand from Iris's wrist. Sybil couldn't even understand what they were saying with the way they talked over each other, but the venom in each syllable was obvious.

"Stop it, both of you!" Sybil cried.

They turned shocked eyes on her.

"I'm sorry to raise my voice at you, but we don't have time for this," she continued. "Let's get to a lifeboat as fast as we can, and we'll work everything out when this is over. All right?"

They exchanged one last sour scowl, but Lewis released Iris's hand, and they walked toward the door. The port side door, to Sybil's relief.

The cold shocked her, even though it was her third venture outside that night. Each time, it got even colder. Her breath froze inside her chest, especially when she saw Charles standing on the edge of the ship, arms out to each side, moving them slowly up and down as he instructed the stewards.

"Lower away!" his voice rang out. "Steady. . . steady. . . "

People queued around the next boat, so Sybil, Gordon, and the Moorings got in line.

"Sybil!"

She whipped around. Charles was approaching from the davit.

"Charles!" she cried, and threw herself into his arms.

"God, what took you so long?" he asked after pressing a kiss on top of her head.

"I'm sorry, I—"

"What happened to your face?"

He cradled her head in his hands and examined it, his thumb running gently over the tender skin. She hissed at the contact. His brow furrowed.

"I'm all right," she assured him. "It was an accident."

"What was an accident?" he pressed.

"Don't worry about that now. Please, tell me, what's going on?"

He hesitated, casting a sidelong glance at the crowd. "It's not good."

"I knew that much. Anything new?"

He pulled her aside, but Iris and Lewis followed, hovering behind them.

"*Titanic* will sink," he said.

Sybil gasped and clapped a hand over her mouth.

"We have less than two hours. There aren't enough lifeboats, and I haven't heard any word of rescue."

"Not enough lifeboats, but. . . what does that mean?"

Charles heaved a sigh. "It means that half the people on this ship won't make it."

Her heart rate quickened into a gallop. If that was the case, did that mean Charles would have to see everyone off the ship except himself? She didn't have long to wonder before he was guiding her back to the line.

"Are we ready, Lowe?" he called.

"Yes, sir!" came the reply.

Charles pushed his way through. "Women and children to the front, please! Women and children only."

He helped the first few people in line onto the lifeboat.

"You first, m'lady," Sybil insisted, urging Iris forward.

"As long as you're right behind me," Iris said.

"Actually, I need to borrow Sybil for a moment," Lewis said. They stared at him. He stepped closer and lowered his voice. "If it's as bad as your officer friend says, there are valuables I want from the room."

Iris's eyes widened. "I hope you're joking."

"I would never joke about money. I'll need her and Gordon to help me."

"Absolutely not," Charles interjected. "Anything you lose, you can take it up with White Star Line."

"Heirlooms are irreplaceable," Lewis argued. "It won't take long."

"They're only things, Lewis," Iris said. "And it cannot be so much that you need both Gordon *and* Sybil."

"I want to recover some of your things too, Iris."

Sybil's eyes bounced between them, trying to discern what Lewis was after with this. For whatever reason, he wanted to separate her from Iris. She watched Charles a moment, catching the distress on his face as he tried to do his job and keep an eye on her. The longer they stood there and argued, the worse the situation would get. She needed to put a stop to it.

"Charles," she said, cutting Lewis off mid-sentence. "Help Lady Iris into the boat. I'll go with Mr. Mooring."

Charles and Iris both replied with a firm, "No."

"It's all right," Sybil said, putting a reassuring hand on his arm. "He said it won't take long. We'll be back here before you know it."

"Finally, someone with sense," Lewis sighed.

Sybil ignored him, holding Charles's gaze. "I'll come back to this side to get on a boat, I promise. Just make sure Lady Iris is safe for me."

"Sybil. . . " he trailed off.

"I'll be right back."

With a huff, he turned to Lady Iris and offered his hand. "My lady."

Iris wasn't looking at him. Her watery gaze was on Sybil, who she yanked into a hug. Sybil let out a small gasp of surprise, but hugged Iris back. When Iris pulled away, she had a tear rolling down her cheek.

"If you don't make it back for this boat, get on the very next one," she said.

"Of course, m'lady," Sybil replied, with a confidence she didn't feel. "As I said, I'll be right back."

Iris hesitated a long moment, gave Sybil's hand a squeeze, and then took Charles's.

"Anything for your husband?" Lewis said.

Iris looked him up and down with a gaze chillier than the surrounding air. Without a word, she stepped into the lifeboat and took a seat.

With a glower, Lewis turned on his heel, grabbed Sybil by the arm, and stormed off. His abruptness nearly took her off her feet, but she stumbled through and got her balance. She had hoped to say something to Charles, but they were halfway to the door. She glanced back and saw him getting a young girl into the lifeboat after Iris.

Before they went inside, Lewis stopped and looked at his valet.

"Gordon, head over to the starboard side and see if there are any boats letting men on over there," he said.

Gordon blinked. "Sir?"

"No time for questions, just do it."

With an apologetic look in Sybil's direction, Gordon left.

Sybil opened her mouth to ask something else, but Lewis pulled her through the door. By the time they reached the stairs, she was out of breath. She wouldn't dream of asking him to slow down though. So she struggled all the way down to B Deck, where thankfully, their rooms were right by the staircase.

Once inside the suite, a shiver went up Sybil's spine. She was alone with Lewis. No good could come of it.

He faced her with a pinched smile. "Well, well, well."

She swallowed. "Which items did you want me to save, sir?"

"Get Iris's jewelry box from the bedroom. I'll see to my own things."

"All right."

She walked into the bedroom and headed for the vanity. The moment she picked up Lady Iris's jewelry box, she heard the slam of the door and the click of the lock.

Chapter Twenty-One

"Mr. Mooring, no!" Sybil cried, and rushed to the door, the jewelry box abandoned. She tried the knob, but to her horror, he had locked it from the outside. "You can't do this!"

"I can and I will," he said, his voice muffled by the inches of wood between them.

"But the ship is sinking!"

"Convenient, isn't it?"

Her stomach dropped like a sandbag. She always knew that Lewis was cruel, with a streak of wickedness inside him that led him to bully and berate. But murder? That was a level of evil she hadn't thought him capable of.

"You've come between me and my wife for the last time, Sybil."

"I know you must be frustrated, sir, but the rift between you and Lady Iris is not my fault," she said, sounding calmer than she felt. "If you would only—"

"Don't try to placate me now. I'm no fool. For seven years, you have poisoned her against me. I don't know what you say or what you do, but it ends now. Permanently."

"If you do this, you will be taking a life."

"That's the idea."

"And you can live with that?"

Silence answered her. She thought perhaps he'd left, but she hadn't heard footsteps or the suite door open and close. She pressed her ear to the door.

"Yes," he finally said. "I can live with that."

With that, she heard him walk away. Everything in her froze over with fear until simmering rage made its way from her gut to the tips of her fingers. She didn't owe this man sympathy, understanding, or grace. Not after everything he had done. With a deep breath, she raised her fist and pounded on the door. Before she knew it, she was beating on it with both hands and a scream of, "Monster!" burst from her lungs. She threw every insult she could think of—every vile thought she'd ever had but was unable to express—at him. Non-stop, until she heard the main cabin door close.

She lowered her arms to catch her breath. Screwing her eyes shut, she pushed back the despair creeping to the forefront of her mind. There had to be a way out.

She tried throwing her body at the door. Unfortunately, she didn't have enough weight for it to give and she ended up on her backside in the middle of the room. Scrambling to her feet, she glanced around. There had to be something, anything, she could use to get free. She snatched up Lady Iris's jewelry box and slammed it against the door-knob. The brass held firm, splintering the jewelry box and scattering the pieces across the floor. Colorful gems winked up at her and she screamed in frustration.

She scanned the room again, brain awhirl with ideas, but one was clearer than the rest. She would not die here. Not now, not at the hands of Lewis Mooring. She was going to live a long, fulfilled life in Charles's arms. Give him children, keep his home, be his peace. No one was going to take that dream away from her, not without her claw marks on it.

She picked up Lady Iris's hair brush and swung it down with all her might.

***

The lifeboat filled up fast. Charles desperately kept an eye out for Sybil's return, but with the number of people crowding around, it was difficult to do. Luckily, Lady Iris was there, and he trusted she would speak up if Sybil appeared.

He took the hand of the next passenger and with a start, realized it was the American woman with whom Lewis had been carrying on his affair. Who had also batted her eyes at Murdoch during their rounds. None of it mattered now, of course. Even so, he tried to catch Iris's eye, but she was still searching the deck, craning her neck to get a better view.

"How can it be that we're safer on those things than this ship?" the woman demanded.

Iris's head whipped around, but Charles diverted his gaze. He couldn't exactly turn someone away because it would be uncomfortable.

"I don't have time to explain, madam," he said, gently as he could. "Now please, step on board."

She gulped and hesitated. Iris extended her hand.

"Here," she said. "I'll help you."

The woman looked her up and down, as if debating whether this was a prank. The woman whose husband she'd been openly flaunting her relationship with was offering a helping hand. Even Charles found it difficult to believe as he watched.

"It might be easier with the help of someone already in it," Iris went on. "And the gap is smaller than you think."

Hesitantly, she took Iris's hand, and with the assistance of the steward, got settled into a seat. She cast a sidelong glance at Iris.

"Thank you."

"You're welcome," Iris replied with a nod.

Charles barely had a moment to admire her for her grace. Everything he'd thought about Iris was wrong. Their conversation on the private promenade deck had shown him that, but this confirmed it. How she ever got the nickname Ice Princess was beyond him. The woman had a heart bigger than most. She just seldom got the chance to show it. If he lived through this, he swore he'd punch Lewis on her behalf.

He scanned the crowd again, but to his sharp dismay, Sybil wasn't there. There was no sign of Lewis either, but he wasn't sure what to make of that. His mind conjured up half a dozen horrible things a man like that might be capable of, but a bright white flare illuminated the sky, distracting him for a moment.

He started to ask for anyone else, but Iris took his hand. The remnants of the flare rained down behind her, casting her in an angelic glow.

"Charlie," she said. "We've waited as long as we can. The boat is full."

He held her gaze, her eyes reflecting his own anguish. "Are you sure?"

She nodded and her bottom lip wobbled. "Find her and keep her safe."

"I will, my lady."

He squeezed her hand, released it, and then nodded at the stewards on either side of him.

"Lower away!" he ordered. "Steady, now! Both sides together!"

He watched Iris descend until her boat hit the black water. At least one person he cared about, albeit unexpectedly, was safely off the ship. He turned to move on to the next boat, but Officer Wilde stood a yard away, his mouth tightened into a grim line. He waved Charles over.

"Lowe, keep loading them on. I'll be right back," Charles said, and Lowe nodded.

When he reached Wilde, Charles walked over to a corner where they weren't likely to be overheard.

"What's the news? Any ships nearby?" Charles asked.

"Captain says the *Carpathia* is the only one that's answered. But she's almost four hours away."

Charles' stomach twisted into a knot. "Four hours? Are you serious?"

"Afraid so."

"But we don't have—" He stopped himself. Wilde knew as well as he did how little time they had. Time that was still rapidly dwindling. "There's really no one any closer?"

"Not to my knowledge."

Charles fought the urge to kick the nearest piece of furniture or punch the wall. He couldn't be seen in distress or it would give the passengers reason to panic further. Already, the air around them buzzed with their anxiety. Another flare went off and he watched it arc over the steadily dipping bow before dying out when it hit the water.

"Fuck," he huffed out.

"I know. Just keep loading the lifeboats as fast as you can."

Charles looked at Lowe, who was persuading a young boy onto the next boat while he said a tearful goodbye to his father. With no help for four hours, he knew it might be a permanent goodbye. His mind went to his brothers, both with children of their own, and the way they spoke of them, would have gladly let them get on the first boat available. Though they wouldn't have been among this crowd. Which reminded him of something.

"Where are the third class passengers?" he wondered.

"Still downstairs," Wilde answered. "We haven't given the order to let them up yet so that the stewards have time to lock the first class doors."

Charles failed to contain a scoff. "Locking the water out?"

Wilde rolled his eyes. "Don't be cheeky, Percy. It's to keep the third class passengers from stealing anything on their way up here."

The explanation wasn't necessary, but now that he heard it aloud, he was even further disgusted. What did it matter if jewels and trinkets were lost to thieves or the ocean? Either way, they were lost. Would they be doubly lost if the thief didn't make it off the ship? He supposed if he lived, he might get to hear a solicitor make that case against White Star Line. Even as disaster loomed, they were covering themselves.

However, Sybil might still be in a room. The stewards would check for anyone inside, he was sure, but he wanted to know for himself. Now that he had Wilde there, he could ask.

"Can you take over here for a moment? I need to look for some-one."

"Your girl, I suppose?" Wilde arched an eyebrow.

"Yes."

"Sorry, Percy, but I can't. Murdoch is getting swamped over on the starboard side. I'm headed back over there."

"It would only be a moment."

"We've all got our jobs to do. If she's smart, she'll get herself on a boat. But right now, your duty is to them." He pointed to the crowd jostling around Lowe. "Get back to work."

Charles bit back a scathing retort.

"Yes, sir," he ground out.

"Third class passengers will be up soon."

"Very good, sir."

He clapped Charles on the shoulder and left, heading for the bridge to cross to the starboard side. Charles once again refrained from damaging any other parts of the ship, as much as he wanted to spite White Star Line in the moment. Taking a breath to collect himself, he walked back toward the lifeboat. A gentle tug on his arm turned him around. He came face to face with a young woman cradling a sleeping baby in her arms.

"Is there a boat?" she asked, her wide, frightened eyes darting between his face and the crowd to his right.

"Yes, right this way," he said gently, and led her to the front of the line.

Chapter Twenty-Two

The brush hadn't worked either. Hope dwindled in Sybil's chest as panic rose up to take its place. Was it possible that Lewis had won? There was only so much time before the ship was completely underwater. Was it enough for Charles to do his job and then come find her? And he *would* come find her, wouldn't he? He promised. But at what point would it be too late for him to even try?

The most frustrating part was that in the bedroom, Sybil had no idea how far the water was rising. Without that, she couldn't even begin to estimate how much time she had. All she could do was keep trying. But like the time, her options were running out. She sank to the floor and pulled her knees up to her chest.

A knock on the suite door made her snap her head up. She could hear muffled voices, but couldn't make out what they were saying. Neither sounded like Charles. No matter who it was, she had to do something.

Leaping to her feet, she pounded on the bedroom door again.

"Hello!" she shouted, loud as she could. "Hello, there's someone in here! Please, I'm trapped in the bedroom!"

She paused, giving whoever it was time to respond with her ear to the door so she wouldn't miss it. The door wasn't opening. She struck the bedroom door again.

"Hello!"

No answer. She listened carefully, controlling her breathing, and heard two clicks from the main entrance to the cabin. Her brow furrowed. What on earth did that mean? The voices faded even further. Her heart skipped a beat.

"No! No wait! Please, there's someone here!"

The sides of her hands ached with all the battering she was doing, but she didn't stop. Not until the voices were completely gone. It was certainly not Charles. If it were him, he would have come into the suite to be sure. He would have checked everywhere for her. If only he could get away, for even a moment.

She pressed her back to the door and scoured the room again. She had already tried the jewelry box, the hairbrush, and even one of Lady Iris's more durable shoes. All to no avail. She ran to the nightstand, snatched up the brass clock there, and brought it over. Maybe metal on metal would do the trick.

She hit the doorknob with all her might. Nothing. Her eyes stung with fresh tears.

"Dammit!" she sobbed, hurling the clock across the room.

It struck the vanity mirror, cracking it right down the middle. Then she saw them. Hair pins, strewn across the top of the vanity, left behind when Lady Iris refused to have her hair done to go up to the boat deck. Perhaps brute force wasn't what she needed after all. As with everything else she had done to thwart Lewis, it would take some cleverness and using whatever tools she had on hand. Thinking like a lady's maid.

She took a hair pin, went to her knees, and brought it to the keyhole. It had been years since she had picked a lock—probably since she and Charles were children—but maybe with some patience, she could do it.

The first few tries were abysmal. The dim lighting didn't help, as she couldn't see what she was doing once the pin was inserted. It was all trial and error. But she kept trying. And trying and trying. When she was about to curse again, she heard it.

Click.

Heart in her throat, she tried the knob. And it turned.

"Thank God!" she cried, and kissed the pin. "I shall never be without one of these again."

She raced toward the door that was the entrance to the suite and did the same, jimmying the lock until it snapped and she heard the click. With triumph in her heart, she grasped the knob and turned it, preparing to step out and race back up to the boat deck. It turned, but when she pulled, the door didn't budge. Her heart stopped.

"No. . ."

She yanked as hard as she could. But once again, found herself trapped behind the door.

The people she heard earlier must have been crew members securing the first class rooms. It was a silly precaution to take, considering everything within them was doomed, anyway. And now it had doomed her as well.

She chewed her lip to keep back the tears pricking at the corners of her eyes. At least now she was where she might be heard by someone in the corridor. Surely, there would be another round to check for stragglers. There was still hope.

She put her ear to the door, but didn't hear anything beyond it. She turned and crossed the room, heading out to the promenade deck to check if she could see the water line. To her horror, it cut diagonally across the window.

Don't panic, Sybil, she told herself. *It's still outside the window, at least. You've got some time.*

Turning her back to the sight, she returned inside, pushing the image of the water bursting through and flooding the room to the farthest reaches of her mind. She approached the door again, prepared to knock and knock and knock until someone heard. As she raised her fist, a couple more voices floated from down the hall. This time, she could just make out what they were saying.

"Are you sure this is the right way, love?" a feminine voice asked.

"Of course," a masculine one replied. "I helped build this ship up from her bones. I know my way around."

"It still feels like we're not supposed to be here."

"We aren't, technically, but I'm not gonna let you and Maisie miss out on a boat just because we don't have first class tickets."

They were Irish, by the sound of their accents, and fast approaching. Sybil beat on the door.

"Hello!" she called. "Hello, there's someone in here!"

The woman shrieked in surprise and she heard a heavy stumble that must have been the man, and he muttered, "Sweet, suffering Jesus!"

"I'm sorry to startle you," Sybil continued. "But please, I've been locked inside!"

They took such a long moment to reply, Sybil thought they must have run off.

"What's your name, darlin'?" the man finally asked.

"Sybil," she said with a sigh of relief. "Sybil Chambers."

"How'd you get locked in a room, Sybil?" the woman wondered.

"It's quite a long story, and I'm afraid we haven't much time. Please, tell me who you are."

"I'm Killian," the man said. "This is my wife, Siobhan."

"Don't forget me, Da," came a third, higher voice.

"And our daughter, Maisie, of course."

Sybil smiled in spite of herself. "You're angels for stopping. I know you must be anxious to get to a boat."

"Not so anxious that we'd leave someone behind," Killian replied. "Have you tried the door already?"

"I have, but I think the stewards have turned a latch or something to secure it. You said you helped build the ship, Killian, yes?"

"Aye, so I did, but I never heard about extra locks or anything of that sort."

She heard the brush of a hand over the door, near the jamb. He must have been feeling for it. A second hand went over the hinges, so Siobhan must have been helping. Sybil held her breath, hoping beyond hope that one of them would locate whatever it was that would set her free.

The scrape of the furniture against the wood floor made her jump and whip around. The coffee table scooted an inch closer to the fireplace. The ship was leaning even more than she thought.

"We don't see anything, Sybil," Killian called from the hall. "Stand back, darlin'. I'm gonna give breaking it down a go."

Sybil took a few cautious steps, unsteady on her feet with the floor slanted beneath her.

"Watch yourself, love," she heard Siobhan warn him. "Don't go breaking you now."

Sybil braced herself as if she were the one about to go barging into the door. She heard Killian's body collide into it with a heavy thud, but the door held firm. He grunted and tried again. The door groaned beneath his weight, but still didn't budge. The third try met the same result.

"Here, let me help. Some extra weight might do it," Siobhan said.

"All right, but be careful, love," Killian replied.

They slammed into the door together. Sybil's heart leaped when she heard a crack from deep inside the wood. Killian and Siobhan laughed with triumph. Sybil almost joined them, but motion to her left caught her eye. At first, she thought it was the furniture sliding again, but it was going the opposite direction. When she looked, she saw it was water, slowly sweeping in from the front bedroom. She gasped.

"Da!" Maisie cried, and Sybil heard a small splash.

It must have been coming up the corridor, too.

"Don't worry, Sybil," Killian said. "One more good shove and the door should split."

He threw his body at it again. It creaked, but still did not splinter.

"Come on, damn you, give!" Killian grunted, pushing with all his might.

"Killian, don't worry about me, save your energy," Sybil said, her heart breaking at what she was about to say. "You must get yourselves to a boat."

"We can't leave you here, it's not right."

"You've done all you can." She swallowed and blinked, letting a tear slide down her cheek. "Please. Don't trap yourselves on my account."

"But we can do it, Sybil, if we just—"

"There's no time! Please, save yourselves!"

She heard the water shift as his feet moved, so she knew he was stepping back. Though whether that was to head up to the boat deck or to try to ram the door again, she had no idea. She hoped he would listen. She didn't want them to miss their chance on her account.

The water seeped further into the sitting room, pooling beneath her feet. She could feel the cold even through the soles of her boots. It was biting and harsh, making her shiver all the way up to her head. And it moved much faster than she was comfortable with.

"It's freezing," Siobhan said quietly.

"We'll get you and Maisie to a boat, love," Killian assured her. "Listen, Sybil, we'll send for some help once we get up top."

Help. . .

"Oh, yes, please do!" she cried. "Go to the port side of the boat deck. You'll find Second Officer Charles Percy loading the lifeboats. Tell him I'm in Lady Iris's rooms, and he'll know where I am. And he'll get you on a boat."

"An officer? He won't ask to see our tickets, will he? Most of third class hasn't been allowed up yet."

"Why on earth—" she shook her head. She could question not letting passengers up later. "No, he won't check your tickets, I promise."

"We'll tell him," Siobhan assured her. "Come on, Killian. Let's hurry."

"We'll send him, Sybil," Killian said as she heard the splash of their steps down the hall. "He'll be here!"

Hope flickered inside her chest, dim, but burning. But as the ice cold water rose up to her ankles in the mere seconds that passed since Killian and his family's departure, she wondered if she could keep it alive. Or even keep herself alive. By the time they made it up and found Charles, would she still be standing?

The life with Charles she imagined was slipping from her grasp. How foolish she was to count her blessings, to call herself lucky for getting passage on *Titanic*, when it was clearly to be the end of her.

CHAPTER TWENTY-THREE

Charles's control over loading the lifeboats was hanging on by a thread. Third class passengers were making their way up to the boat deck, and as the number of lifeboats dwindled, panic rose in the air, especially among the men. Many were leaping into the icy abyss to take their chances with the ocean rather than go down with the ship. The ones who still had their loved ones aboard were clamoring for the remaining boats. Charles had nearly been knocked overboard by a bout of pushing and shoving as fathers and husbands tried to get their families to safety. A feeling Charles understood. He was still desperately searching for Sybil, but hadn't so much as caught a glimpse of her.

No doubt it was Lewis's doing. Sybil promised she would return to his side of the ship to get on a lifeboat, and nothing short of foul play could have made her do otherwise. Had Lewis taken her off the ship? Or worse, was she somewhere inside, trapped with him? It made Charles's stomach turn.

As if summoned by the thought of him, Lewis appeared on the deck, joining the crowd of men surrounding the lifeboat Lewis was loading. Initially, the sight awakened hope in Charles's chest, but upon closer inspection, he saw that Sybil was not with him. Charles and Lowe continued helping women and children onto the lifeboat until the crowd around them was mostly men. Lewis pushed his way to the front.

Charles rounded on him. "You've got some nerve showing up here without her."

"Who, Sybil? She'll be along," Lewis replied, craning his neck to peer into the lifeboat. "Any room for men yet?"

"Women and children only," Charles said firmly. "Where is Sybil?"

"She's coming, I'm sure, just grabbing a few last minute things."

"You're lying. What have you done to her?"

Lewis's lip curled up into a sneer. "Now, Mr. Percy. Why would you assume that?"

"You have given me every reason to suspect you, Mooring. There's no time for games. Tell me where she is."

"For all I know, she's gone over to the other side. Though she won't have much luck there, all their lifeboats are gone."

That explained Lewis coming back to this side. He was running out of options. He dug into the inside pocket of his jacket and pulled out a thick wad of paper bills. They fluttered in the chilly breeze. Charles glanced between the cash and Lewis's face, bile rising in his throat.

"Can I interest you in a business deal, Percy?"

"No," Charles said flatly.

"Are you sure?" Lewis pressed. "With this much, things could be very comfortable for you when all this is over. You could take care of Sybil. And your brothers too, for that matter."

"No amount of money is worth my honor."

"Be reasonable, Percy. This is life and death."

"Let me make one thing perfectly clear, Mooring. I don't trust you. I don't trust your money. You've done nothing but harm people I care about, and if you don't back away from this lifeboat right now, I will throw you overboard myself."

Lewis scowled and tucked the money away. "For God's sake, this is ridiculous." He turned around and addressed the men behind him. "Listen, men! There's more of us than there are officers! Don't we deserve to live as much as our wives and children? What's to become of them without us? I say we band together and get on this lifeboat!"

Charles's stomach dropped as the men gave a shout of approval and surged forward, jostling him and Lowe toward the railing. Charles pushed them back with all his might, while Lowe tried to guide frightened women and children forward, shielding them with his arms.

"GET BACK!" Charles bellowed. "GET BACK, I SAY!"

Their collective roar of protest in reply could have drowned out his own thoughts. He was able to pick out a few clear statements among them.

"Give us a chance, you limey bastard!"

"These are the last of the boats!"

"We just want to live!"

His knees buckled under the pressure and he stumbled back a step. His mind went to the revolver Wilde issued, and for the first time, he thought about using it. It wasn't loaded, but maybe showing it would be enough to restore some sense of order. He locked eyes with a man directly in front of him, the stranger's eyes wide and clouded with fear, and he forgot the gun.

Charles planted his feet firmly on the deck, rose to his full height, and grabbed his whistle from around his neck. Bringing it to his lips, he blew, the sound ringing out sharp and piercing. He absurdly noticed the metal was warm from being tucked inside his sweater, in harsh contrast to his cold lips.

The men drew back, covering their ears. After three quick bursts, Charles relented, assured they were paying attention.

"Listen to me!" he cried. "None of us will survive if we don't have order. Women and children must come first, or we cannot call ourselves men. So please, stay calm, and allow the women and children to come forward."

There were a few grumbles, but otherwise, they settled. Charles helped the next woman aboard and as he did, saw Lewis Mooring in one of the seats, eyes straight ahead, refusing to acknowledge anyone still on the boat deck.

Rage coursed through Charles like an avalanche. Seeing red, he reached into the lifeboat, grabbed Lewis by the collar, and with his free hand, retrieved the revolver. Lewis jumped as the metal of the muzzle collided with his temple.

"Get out of my goddamn lifeboat," Charles warned.

Lewis trembled. "I—now, just a minute, Percy—"

"I SAID GET OUT!"

Lewis leaped to his feet. Charles hauled him back onto *Titanic* and threw him to the deck. With a shared gasp, the crowd parted as Lewis careened across the wood. He scrambled onto his knees, but Charles was already looming over him, sidearm raised.

"If I catch you in a boat before I've allowed men on, I'll put you overboard with a bullet in your skull."

Lewis held up his hands as if in surrender, and for the first time, the mask of arrogance dropped. The surrounding air had impossibly thinned as all eyes watched the scene unfold.

"Now, Percy, don't do anything rash," Lewis said, a tremor to his voice.

"I won't if you don't give me a reason. Do not let me catch you on another boat."

"Of course."

Charles turned his back to the man and reached into his pocket for a handful of bullets. He loaded the still empty chambers with shaking hands. He wasn't afraid to fire a weapon. He'd grown up around guns and had even put down a horse at the command of his father when he was fourteen. He was so damn angry. Angry that Lewis had attempted to turn the crowd against him. Angry that Sybil was still nowhere to be found. And angry that no matter what he did now, there was no chance of him saving even half the number of people standing there. There were two lifeboats left, and one was nearly full.

Stowing his weapon, he ordered the stewards to lower it.

He watched it descend. Suddenly, a figure flew out from the A Deck promenade and grabbed onto the lifeboat, making it sway and swing out. Several passengers inside screamed, while others rushed to grab onto the stowaway before they slipped off.

"Stop!" Charles ordered, and the stewards held the ropes fast.

A woman hung from the side of the lifeboat, clinging on for dear life. She'd seen a chance and taken it. For a moment, Charles let himself believe it was Sybil, having escaped whatever happened to her with Lewis. But as the other passengers pulled the woman aboard and she took a seat, he knew it wasn't her. This woman was older, with blonde hair piled on her head in a bun. She turned toward *Titanic* in her seat and blew a kiss toward someone still on deck.

"Lower away!" Charles commanded once she was secure.

The lifeboat hit the water, and it felt like Charles's heart had too. He'd come to the last lifeboat, not counting the collapsibles above the officer's quarters, which, looking down the deck, were fast approaching the rising sea. He schooled his face before turning back to the crowd.

"Women and children first," he reminded them.

Many stepped forward, and he and Lowe helped them aboard. But the men had become impatient, jostling each other as they all tried to get to the front to be first. Charles swallowed. The moment he said he would allow men, he was sure all hell would break loose as each man made a mad dash for the boat. He craned his neck.

"Are there any more women and children?" he called.

"No, dammit, now let us board!" one of them shot back.

Suddenly, Lewis was in front of him again, grabbing his arm and pulling him close.

"I know we've had our differences, Percy, but if you let me on board now, I'll tell you what's become of Sybil," he said.

Charles narrowed his eyes and shoved him away. "So you have done something."

"I'll only tell you if you let me on the lifeboat this instant."

Charles wanted to scream. He briefly imagined taking Lewis by the neck and hurling him into the frigid waters just to hear him scream all the way down. And if one of his limbs hit the hull and broke, well, that wouldn't be so bad either. He shook his head. Violent thoughts weren't going to help him. He either had to give this worm a shot at living or find out what happened to Sybil on his own, which could take time he didn't have.

"Oi, there's a woman and child here!" someone cried.

Charles turned his head. A young family ran up the deck, and the daughter, he recognized, not only by her freckled face, but by the doll she held in her arms. Panting, they slowed to a stop. The girl caught his eye.

"Mammy, that's the nice man," she said, pointing at him. "He got me my doll back."

"Don't point, love, it's not polite," her mother scolded through deep breaths.

The father glanced between his girls and Charles. "You wouldn't happen to be Second Officer Charles Percy, would you?"

Charles's eyebrows shot up. "I. . . yes, I am."

"There's a woman trapped on B Deck, Sybil Chambers, she said her name was," the man said. "She got locked in her room somehow."

Charles turned dangerous eyes on Lewis, who was looking sheepishly at the deck. But Charles wasn't going to let him get away with that. He seized a handful of his collar, reared back with his free hand, and punched that low life twice—once on the cheek, and once on the chin. One for Lady Iris and one for Sybil. The mother gasped and shielded her daughter from the sight. Charles released Lewis and let him crumple into a heap. Then he faced the family.

"Thank you for telling me," he said, and led them toward the lifeboat. "Right this way."

The wife and daughter stepped on first, but more women and children arrived, so the father refused to get on, which Charles respected. Somehow, he managed to fill it with the straggling women and children as third class passengers had made their way to the boat deck en masse. Charles loaded them as quickly as he could, all while his heart pounded for Sybil, whose room was probably already flooding with freezing water.

"Lowe," he said once the boat was full. "Get on this one."

Lowe searched his face. "Are you sure?"

"I've got to get Sybil. Climb aboard and take charge. I'll try for the collapsibles once I've got her."

"Yes, sir."

Lowe stepped over the rail and into the lifeboat. Charles ordered it lowered. When it reached the water, he released a breath he didn't even know he was holding. Now free, he turned and hurtled down the deck, stumbling with the slant of it, and went through the door closest to the forward staircase. It was nearest to the Mooring's parlor suite.

A Deck was remarkably still dry, and as Charles descended the grand staircase, more passengers scrambled past him toward the boat deck. He heard the roar of the water coming up B Deck before he saw it. Pale green ocean with white foam at the helm surged toward him. The chill coming from it pricked at his skin, and he shivered. There was no time for hesitation. He continued down and plunged into the icy water.

It hit him like a wall of needles, cutting him from the waist down. He sucked in a shocked breath at the prickling of his skin, but he didn't dare stop. He trudged through it, biting back curses as he fought the current, heading for Sybil. He hoped she was all right.

Chapter Twenty-Four

Oddly, as Sybil shivered in freezing, waist high water that she was now certain would be the last thing she ever saw, she thought about her mother. She thought of her father too, but the night of the fire, her mother had been awake. Which Sybil only knew because as she snuck out to her and Charles's favorite spot in the meadow, she glanced back at the house. A candle was still lit in her mother's sewing room and then the curtain dropped closed. Sybil had smiled to herself. Her father had never approved of a young girl going out late. While her mother understood that Sybil missed her dear friend, and she never betrayed her to her father.

She wondered now if her mother had been waiting up for her that night. Did Effie Chambers look on in horror as the unstoppable force of nature consumed everything around her before it claimed her as well? As Sybil did now? Did she thank God that Sybil had gotten away? As Sybil did that Lady Iris had? Did she wake her husband so that they would be together in facing their demise? Which Sybil now did alone?

She absurdly thought about what she might say to her parents when she found them in heaven. The Chambers family, eradicated by fire and water. Every bit as devastating as it sounded. And yet, it would be nice to see them again. They'd smile at her and take her in their arms.

There would be no more Lewis, no more fear, no more cold. And she could watch over Lady Iris and Charles, she reasoned. Maybe letting go wasn't such a bad idea.

Pressing herself against the wall, she closed her eyes. She had one more thing to thank God for—getting to see Charles again before she died. And that she got to love him.

Maybe it was the thought of him that made her hear his voice. She swore she heard him calling her name over the rush of the water and the pounding of her own heart. She didn't mind. If anything was to be the last thing she heard, she was happy for it to be her name on Charles's lips. Imagined or not.

"Sybil!"

She blinked. His voice was growing louder.

"Sybil!"

Louder still. Could it be possible that Killian and his family succeeded? And the real Charles was making his way to her door? Hope stirred within her again.

"Sybil, are you there?"

Fighting the pressure of the rising water, she made her way to the door. The wood was loose where Killian struck it, but it wasn't enough for her to break through. And she had tried.

"I'm here, Charles!" she cried, her voice breaking over his name.

"Sybil!" he replied, and she could hear the relief in his voice as his hand hit the other side of the door. "God, Sybil, are you all right?"

"I-I think so! Charles, it's so cold!"

"I know, my love, I know. Listen, I need you to stand back or to the side, I'm gonna get you out!"

She swallowed through her tight throat. "I don't know if it's possible."

"Don't you doubt me, Giggles."

She clapped a hand over her mouth to stifle a whimper at hearing the endearment. He sounded so sure. So confident. And to her own surprise, she believed him.

She nodded but, remembering he couldn't hear that, she shuffled over to the side of the door and rooted to the spot.

"I'm out of the way!" she called.

She barely got the words out before Charles rammed into the door. The crack that Killian created was nothing compared to the blast from Charles's contact. He walloped it one, two, three times until finally it burst like a ripped seam. His familiar form stepped through the splintered wood and his eyes found hers.

Time stopped. The rumble of the water went silent, and they were the only two people in the world. They waded toward each other, and Sybil collapsed into his arms with a sob.

Everything moved again, but she was safe in his arms. He kissed her everywhere his lips could reach—her head, cheeks, mouth, and neck. All while murmuring soft words of comfort. He was there, he had her, he loved her. She clutched his jacket like a lifeline. Tears spilled over the edges of her eyes and rolled freely down her face.

"You came back for me," she croaked out.

"Of course I did," he replied, stroking her hair. "I promised you."

They held each other only a moment longer before Charles drew back.

"We've got to get back to the boat deck," he said. "The lifeboats are gone, but there are some collapsibles over the officer's quarters I want to try to launch."

"Do we have time?"

"We've got to try."

She nodded and followed him into the hall. The rushing water swept her feet out from under her. Her stomach dropped and she let out a scream. Charles didn't even let her head go under before he pulled her back to her feet.

"Hold tight to my hand!" he called.

"I will!"

She grabbed onto his whole arm. With Charles as her anchor, they slogged against the current toward the staircase, the beautiful wood getting rapidly swallowed up as the ocean rose up. It was already halfway underwater.

Muscles screaming, Sybil followed Charles up the steps, racing the water which nipped at their heels. They made it up to A Deck among a clamoring crowd, and still she struggled to catch her breath. Her clothes hung wet and heavy on her body. Her arms hurt from beating on the doors in the suite. And her burning lungs couldn't hold enough air. Charles practically dragged her up the next flight of stairs, and she had to yank him to a halt when they reached the clock.

"Please, please, I need a moment," she panted.

Charles's eyes darted toward the exit before landing back on her face. "I know you're tired, Sybil, but I need you to push through. We have to get back to the deck before the officer's quarters are underwater."

"I'm sorry."

"It's all right. I'll help you, just keep holding onto me."

She took a deep breath and nodded. "Okay."

Somehow, she forced her aching legs onward and out the door to the boat deck. She wondered how it could possibly be the same door she'd come through countless times on her way to see Charles, and on her way back to Lady Iris. She'd gone through it for the last time.

The boat deck was absolute chaos. A man running toward the stern barreled past Sybil, knocking into her shoulder. He would have sent her flying if not for her grip on Charles. He shot her a questioning look to make sure she was all right, and she nodded to let him know she was. Another man launched himself off the side of the ship. From somewhere farther off, a woman screamed. Or maybe several. Sybil couldn't distinguish them. And to her left, the band was playing.

She blinked at them, transfixed by the calm movement of their arms with their bows, and how gently "Nearer, My God, To Thee" floated from the strings. A serene, mournful melody amid a tumultuous scramble for life. It brought Sybil's mind back to her parents. Then to Lady Iris, floating somewhere out in the cold. The photos of Charles's siblings, likely sliding to the floor and shattering before they would be lost. And then, every moment she had shared with him since finding him that first day flashed before her eyes as a reel of film. *Titanic* would take those memories with her to the bottom of the Atlantic, carried on only in Sybil and Charles's hearts.

Fresh tears stung her eyes, and she shivered, suddenly colder than she remembered.

"Captain!"

Charles's voice drew her out of her reverie. She turned her head, and Captain Smith was before them, a somber shadow over his face. His lips ticked up into a fleeting smile when he looked at Charles.

"That day at port. . . I was right," he said.

"Sir?" Charles questioned.

"It was my last look at that horizon."

Charles's eyes went wide. "Sir, there is no obligation to go down with the ship."

Smith shook his head. "I will see as many people off as I can."

"But you needn't—"

"Will you tell my girls how sorry I am?"

Charles stared at him for a long moment, and Sybil swore she could see his heart breaking. Hers was in pieces.

"I will, sir," Charles said stiffly.

They shook hands, and the captain's watery eyes flicked between them. "Good luck to you both."

Sybil wanted to say something, but was lost for words.

Charles urged her onward, toward the submerged bow. A crowd of men converged on what looked like a lifeboat outside the bridge, only it was upside down. Chief Officer Wilde stood atop it, barking instructions, but no one was listening. He raised his gun in the air and fired off three shots. Sybil screamed, clamped her hands over her ears, and buried her face in Charles's chest.

"Listen up!" Wilde shouted. "We can get the collapsible turned back over, but we need to work together. Starting with cutting it loose. Does anyone have a knife?"

"I do!" Charles spoke up and reached into his pocket to retrieve a switchblade.

Sybil looked up at him. A few other men jumped in with knives of their own, clamoring over the collapsible to reach the ropes, where they started sawing. The water approached fast.

"Percy!" Wilde cried, jumping down, but grasping a rope to keep himself upright on the slanted deck. "Can you handle things here? I've got to get back to the starboard side."

"Murdoch hasn't launched the collapsible over there yet?" Charles asked.

Wilde's lips turned down, and he shook his head. "No, he. . . " He trailed off.

Charles swallowed hard. "Don't say it."

"I'm sorry, Percy."

"Are you certain?"

Wilde nodded. "I'm certain."

Charles swore under his breath. "All right. I'll handle things here."

"I'll see you," Wilde replied, clapping Charles's shoulder before he departed.

Charles took hold of Sybil's hand again, and his grip was tighter than before. She wondered how much of this she could take. Murdoch was Charles's friend and had been kind to her as well. And he was gone. Just as the captain would be. Just as they would be if they didn't hurry.

Together, they approached the capsized collapsible, and Sybil let go of his hand to hold a rope taut so he could cut through it more easily. The water climbed steadily toward them, and she chanced a glance. Her heart nearly stopped.

"Charles!" she warned.

He didn't look. "I know!"

It was close enough that the spray dusted her numbing cheeks. Charles glanced up.

"Everyone!" he called over the din. "We don't have time to turn it over, just push!"

Sybil placed her hands on the boat, and with the crowd, shoved it toward the water. She was surprised she had any strength left, and yet, she knew she would need more in the moments to come. This was far from over.

The ocean swept under the boat and carried it out to sea. She went to follow it with some of the others, but Charles grabbed her around the waist and yanked her away.

"Charles, what—"

"We can't go that way or the suction will take us," he explained.

She watched as the sea swallowed up the people directly behind the lifeboat, the suction sound making her stomach turn. They were underwater before they could even scream.

Charles pulled her further toward him. "Back up, back up!"

Together, they fought gravity up the slanted deck, the water threatening as it climbed higher. When there was at least a yard between them and the water, Charles stopped, and Sybil took a breath.

"Do you trust me, Sybil?" Charles asked.

She held his gaze. "Of course."

"Then jump."

Her eyes went wide. "What?"

"Take my hand, and jump as far out as you can!"

She didn't hesitate. Locking her fingers with his, they climbed over the railing, stood on the edge of *Titanic's* dropping deck, and together, they leaped into the black abyss of the sea.

CHAPTER TWENTY-FIVE

Charles might have found some relief in the moment of quiet beneath the surface of the water if it hadn't been for the penetrating cold. It seeped through every layer of clothing, every stitch on him, pricking his skin and sinking deep. It went all the way to his bones. He forced some air out through his nose and kicked up for the surface. Luckily, they had jumped far enough that the suction of the ship was only a gentle tug, as opposed to a hard drag.

He sucked in a gulping breath when he broke through the surface, and—thank God—Sybil did the same to his right. Treading water, he looked at her. All the color had retreated from her cheeks and lips, leaving her face a ghostly white. She swam closer to him and he could hear her teeth chattering.

"Are you all right?" he asked, giving her a once over.

"C-cold," she stammered.

"I know," he replied, gently as he could. There would be no relief from it. Not for hours yet, if it was still true that *Carpathia* was the closest ship available for rescue. "Swim this way, Sybil. Come on, with me."

To speed things up, he took hold of the shoulder strap on her lifebelt, and pulled her along behind him. She did not protest, and to her credit, neither did she complain. She even kicked her feet and paddled with her hands to help. They swam toward the lifeboat they had helped launch, now a faint white spot in the dark. Charles was grateful there was some distance, it meant the lifeboat wouldn't be sucked down with *Titanic*. However, it would be a difficult swim to reach it with their tired and freezing limbs.

A few other jumpers were making their way away from the hull of *Titanic*. Some, who had jumped straight down instead of out, were snatched back through the broken windows by the rushing water. One of the survivors was the Irishman who told Charles where Sybil was.

"Mr. Percy," he said with a nod then turned to Sybil. "You must be Sybil."

"Killian?" she questioned.

"Aye. Glad to see he got to you in time."

She offered a shaky smile in reply.

"There's a boat this way," Charles said. "Come with us."

Killian shook his head. "I'm gonna swim on, see if I can find the boat my girls are in."

"That could take longer than your body can stand," Charles said. "That boat went from close to the stern, and they'll have rowed hundreds of yards away by now."

"I've got to try. Good luck to you."

"You as well," Charles returned, trying not to sound too defeated.

Killian swam the opposite direction. Then, a metallic groan sounded from the ship. The ropes holding one of the smokestacks came loose with a heavy ping, and the funnel leaned toward the port side. Charles's stomach dropped. It was going to fall.

"Swim, Sybil!" he shouted. "Hard as you can, this way!"

"But Killian!"

"Don't look!"

They raced along with a few others, out of the shadow of the smokestack as it came down over the water and the dozens of people in it. Screams were cut short. Those still aboard *Titanic* wailed and pointed. The wake from the fall launched Charles and Sybil forward several yards. Somehow, he managed to keep hold of her lifebelt, despite the waves rolling over his head and making him sputter for breath.

Surfacing again, he called out for Sybil, and heard her spitting and coughing in response. At least that meant she was still breathing. The smokestack had given them a boost as far as reaching the lifeboat.

"Keep swimming, Sybil," Charles said.

She nodded and kicked her legs. The water sloshed around them as they moved through it, and Charles kept his eyes fixed on the lifeboat up ahead. It seemed like it would never get any closer, as if they were back on that stationary bike in the gymnasium, but he recognized his fatigue and pushed it down. He couldn't rest now. Not until Sybil was safe.

The lights on *Titanic* flickered, and he came to a stop. He and Sybil both turned and watched as the mighty ship's lights went out, plunging them all into absolute darkness.

The screams on board intensified. Sybil let out a cry of alarm too, and her hand shot out of the water, clutching at him.

"I'm here," he assured her, pulling her closer.

His own heart rate accelerated without being able to see her. For several agonizing moments, all he knew was Sybil's hands, and the devastated shrieks of the unfortunates still aboard. When his eyes adjusted to the darkness, he focused on Sybil's face. It had crumpled into tears.

"Sybil?"

"I'm sorry," she sniffled. "It's all too much. Killian and Captain Smith and Mr. Murdoch. . . they're all gone. The lifeboat's so far away and I'm so tired and cold. I can't keep going, Charles."

"Listen to me," he said sternly, and he could see his breath in the air. "You can, and you must. Lady Iris is waiting for us. Our life together is waiting for us, Sybil."

She choked on a sob. "Charles. . . "

"I won't let you give up now. But we can lighten the load."

She still wore his overcoat, so he reached out and tugged it off her. It wouldn't keep her warm anyway, as waterlogged as it was. It sank the moment it left her body.

"Better?" he asked.

Her colorless lips trembled as she nodded.

She was significantly lighter, which helped him to swim on, his numb fingers still wrapped around her lifebelt. He understood her despair. His own was gnawing at his insides, but he caged it away. He had to be strong now. For himself, and for her.

When they reached the lifeboat, it was still overturned. There were already half a dozen people on it, clinging to the beam across the bottom to get as far out of the water as they could. Summoning every ounce of strength left, Charles heaved Sybil up. Her trembling fingers struggled to find purchase, and she slid back down into the water on the first try. She found her grip with his help. He dragged himself up next. Finally, his muscles relaxed.

All he could make out of *Titanic* from there was the silhouette of her stern against the horizon. The screaming was still audible, but faint. A minor relief in such a moment. The others who had taken refuge on this lifeboat shivered as they huddled together. No one spoke, all eyes on the ship they had escaped. Charles wondered how many of them knew someone still aboard. Or had all their loved ones gotten to a lifeboat?

Glancing around, he saw that all the people on the collapsible were men, except Sybil. There was one man wearing a tuxedo beneath his lifebelt. He must have been a first class passenger. Next to him, Charles saw one of the men who worked the boiler rooms. Water had smeared the coal and soot around his face. It was almost funny. If not for the disaster, those two would never have crossed paths. They would have sailed right into New York, the first class man would have disembarked, never knowing that the man beside him now had fueled his journey there. Now they had an equal shot at living or dying.

The whole group was a mixture of everyone aboard. There were two men opposite Charles and Sybil, with dark curly hair and brown eyes, so alike Charles thought they must have been brothers. They reminded him sharply of his own. The pair wore white uniforms of the first class restaurant staff.

There was also a steward, and what appeared to be a third class passenger holding on to the end of the boat.

A thunderous, deafening *crack* had Charles and everyone around him turn their eyes back to *Titanic*. He blinked a few times to be sure he was seeing it right, but it appeared that the hull was. . . breaking?

With crashes, snaps, and pops, it fractured, sending debris flying in every direction. A wooden piece of what must have been the deck sailed toward them, landing with a plop in the water a few feet away. Charles put an arm around Sybil's shoulders and a hand on her head to protect her. Her face was buried in his chest, her eyes squeezed shut.

He had to watch. To see it for himself. The greatest ship he'd ever worked on—hell, the greatest he'd ever seen in all his years at sea—splintered. His heart pounded so loud, he could hardly register the cries of the people on board. He watched as the stern took a swan dive back toward the water, surely flattening anyone or anything beneath it. Sybil winced beside him.

The break must not have been clean, because the stern rose up again, this time going almost completely vertical. *Titanic* descended into the water like the lifts that had carried passengers between decks, and Charles saw small shadows springing away from her still. Whether they were people or parts, he had no idea. He wondered if any of them were Captain Smith or Officer Wilde, making one, last-ditch effort to survive.

The ship seemed small now, with so little of her left. A sight that was considered impossible less than a week prior, back in Southampton. Back when Sybil was only a memory. The journey had brought him one thing to be grateful for, and that was bringing her out of his mind and into his arms. He gave her shoulders a squeeze, and he watched in somber awe as *Titanic* took her last bow, her stern finally disappearing beneath the Atlantic.

Chapter Twenty-Six

Sybil could feel her strength draining steadily from her, as if it seeped out of her fingers and toes, disappearing into the dark, frigid waters. She shivered where Charles held her against him, for there was no warmth to share with them soaked to the bone from their swim. Her shallow breaths appeared in the air, and she watched each puff for something to keep her eyes on. She couldn't bear to watch the ship go down. And her heart ached to hear the screams of everyone in the water, cold and frightened, just as she was.

She envied her parents now. While the pain of burning must have been comparable to the sting of the chill in the North Atlantic, at least the fire took them quickly. She was going to have to cling to life as best she could, for God only knew how long. All while listening to the people around her do the same.

"The lifeboats will come back," Charles said through stuttering breaths. "It won't be long now."

She only had enough energy to nod. Even as she thought about everyone who was lost, she could no longer muster up tears. The only thing her body was capable of was quaking with cold. Perhaps, if she lived through this, she would be able to cry, to mourn, but now, her mind could only comprehend the cold and the dark. And Charles beside her. That she could always rely on.

She realized she would not have survived this without him. Even if it was Killian who broke her out of the parlor suite, she would never have made it to the collapsible, and the ship would have sucked her under. It was Charles's strength that got her up the stairs, off the ship, and to the safety of this overturned lifeboat. And it was his presence that made her feel she could not let herself succumb to the cold or the fatigue that consumed her every muscle.

Our life together is waiting for us, he'd said. Could she hold on for it?

A couple of swimmers who managed to escape the suction found their way to their lifeboat and joined them, pulling as much of their bodies out of the water as they could manage. One man's weight caused Sybil's grip on the boat to slip, but Charles held on, keeping his arm around her so she wouldn't go under. With stiff, numb fingers, she held on to him instead.

The screaming faded after a while, though Sybil had no idea how much time had passed. Eerie silence fell over their corner of the North Atlantic.

"S-Sybil," Charles stammered quietly.

She turned her face up toward him. "Hm?"

"Will you marry me?"

She stared at him. A proposal while they froze in the middle of the ocean? It was hardly any woman's dream scenario, and she might have thumped him if they were anywhere else and she had the strength. "Have you gone m-mad?"

He shook his head, and the ice clinging to the ends of his hair rattled. "I need to know that you will. And if we don't live through this, that you would have."

It was the first time he'd spoken of the possibility of them not surviving. Though she supposed, even with his resilience, he had to know there was a chance it wouldn't be enough. *And,* she thought, *it was nice to know for sure that was what he wanted.* She could certainly make peace with that.

"Y-yes," she agreed through chattering teeth. "I will marry you."

His blue lips turned up into a smile and he pressed them to her forehead, but she couldn't feel the kiss.

***

Hours passed that felt like years. Charles kept a watchful eye on Sybil, as her body kept going limp against his. Even her teeth were no longer knocking together with the frequency they had before. Her eyelids drooped slowly closed, but each time they did, he gave her a gentle shake. She had a bump on her head on top of the cold to fight. If he let her fall asleep, he feared there would be no waking her up again.

Her eyes fell closed, and she held them there, so he nudged her. "Sybil, stay awake, love."

"I can't," she murmured.

"You must."

"Please, I'm so tired."

"I'm sorry, I can't let you."

It broke his heart to deny her. He could hear the exhaustion in her voice. He knew she must be thinking it would be a relief to slip into sleep. He was tempted himself. To close his eyes, shut out the cold and misery around him. To no longer concern himself with what was to come. But if he did, he sacrificed the dream he was still holding onto. Even harder than he held onto the lifeboat.

He looked up at the stars. Stiffly, given his neck was sore and frozen, but it brought him back to Yorkshire. And for a moment, it was a muggy summer night. Sybil was at his side, their fingers barely touching in the grass as they gazed up. And he told her stories to make her laugh.

"Do you remember the stars in Yorkshire, Sybil?" he asked, his voice hoarse.

She answered with a noncommittal hum.

"Do you remember the stories I told you?"

"Mhm."

"Would it help if I told one now?"

She nodded.

He couldn't remember the exact ones he'd told, so he turned his eyes skyward and tried to let his imagination create something new. Making them up on the fly was part of the charm, after all.

"There once was a boy who loved a goddess," he began. "He spent every day trying to get a glimpse of her, and when he did, all he wanted was to please her, for her laughter was magic. It made the sun shine and the flowers bloom. It was even powerful enough to dry tears. Even though he was mortal, he hoped to marry her. But being a third born son to a farmer, he felt he had nothing to offer her."

He glanced down to find her eyes, half-lidded, but open and on his face.

"So, with a heavy heart, he left his home behind and took to the seas on a quest to become worthy. After all, that was what the heroes he read about did. He wasn't sure what would do the trick—wealth, experience, and knowledge all stood to be gained on such a journey. But was any of that enough to make him worthy of his goddess? He wasn't sure."

He checked on Sybil again. Her eyes were closed, so he nudged her awake once more.

"Sorry," she said, her voice barely above a whisper. "What happens next?"

"He traveled and traveled, to nearly every corner of the world," Charles continued. "And still, he didn't feel like he could return to her. And the longer he was gone, the more he convinced himself she was out of his reach. So. . . he stayed away."

"S-silly fool."

"I agree. The goddess, unable to be contained, set out on her own adventure. Little did the boy—now a man—know, he would face her for the first time in years. And he was not prepared for the way his old love surged back into his heart. The moment he laid eyes on her, he was no longer his own person. He was hers—mind, body, and soul. The goddess, touched by his devotion, gave herself to him, forsaking her immortal life to spend her days at his side. It utterly humbled him."

Sybil gave another shiver. "She was quite a forgiving goddess."

"Quite," he agreed. "And he never forgot it. They built a home together, a cozy little place with a big fireplace, so they never went cold. And he made sure to have everything she ever wanted inside—a kitchen to die for, a sewing room, a small library. And most importantly, a nursery."

The corners of her mouth twitched up.

"They had several children," he went on. "A girl first, as fair and gentle as her mother. Two boys after that, and they were rambunctious little monsters. And then another girl. Incidentally, also a rambunctious little monster."

She blew out a shaky laugh. "H-happily ever after?"

"Yes. They lived happily ever after. Long, full lives, in each other's arms."

"Sounds lovely. . . "

Charles kept talking. Coming up with story after story, each more far-fetched than the last. He would ask her questions in the middle to make sure she was following along. Often having to wake her up. She kept resting her head on his shoulder, and he gave her a moment before urging her upright so she wouldn't fall asleep. At one point, she gave him a miserable little moan that made him feel like the biggest bully, but he knew it was for the best.

"Sybil?" he asked when she failed to answer him on a previous question. "Sybil, are you with me?"

She didn't respond. Panic seized his chest.

"Sybil."

He shook her gently but her head lolled back onto his shoulder. Her eyes were closed, flecks of ice clinging to her lashes.

"Sybil, love, wake up," he said, failing to keep the desperation out of his voice. "Sybil. Sybil!"

Still nothing. He lowered his face toward hers, and he could barely hear her breathing. He couldn't feel her breath, though he couldn't be sure if that was due to the weakness of her breath or the numbness of his own face. He hoped it was the latter.

Another faint sound made him turn his head. It sounded like a voice, though he couldn't be sure. He peered into the darkness, and in the distance, spied a small light. It wasn't a star, it was too low and too bright for that. It had to be a torch. As it turned back and forth across the water, the reflection following it. The voice called out again, and Charles barely distinguished what was said.

"Is anyone alive out there?"

He cleared his throat.

"Boat!" he yelled. It came out wheezy, so he cleared his throat again. "Boat, ahoy!"

The light stopped, pointed in his direction. It was getting closer. He roused the others on his lifeboat. Those who didn't stir, he prayed, were still alive.

"Come on," he said. "Call out, so they can hear us."

Out of the dozen or so that had taken refuge, only three had the strength to join him. Within a few minutes, a lifeboat arrived, Officer Lowe at the helm with a flashlight, and a few passengers rowing the oars.

"Charlie?" Lowe said, eyes going wide.

"Hello, H-Harold," Charles replied.

"What?" gasped the woman rowing behind him, who poked her blonde head around, revealing herself to be Lady Iris. Her cheeks and nose were pink with cold. "Charlie, oh my God!"

She threw herself toward the edge, stretching her hand out.

"Get Sybil first," Charles said, dragging her through the water by her lifebelt.

"Oh, Sybil!" Iris cried, grasping the strap and pulling up.

Lowe helped, and together, they hauled Sybil up and over the side. The sloshing of the water was so loud in the dense silence, Charles flinched at the sound. They got him in the lifeboat next, and Charles realized it was empty.

"How did you do this?" he asked as he rubbed his stiff shoulders.

"We linked up with a few other boats and combined them as much as we could. We're taking the empty ones back to the wreck site," Lowe explained, and his face fell. "You're the first survivors we've seen. We may have waited too long."

Charles wanted to say something comforting, but Iris threw a blanket over him, cutting off his train of thought. Then she knelt down beside Sybil, hands cupping her cheeks.

"God, she's like ice," she said quietly.

"Is she. . . " Lowe trailed off, glancing between Sybil and Charles.

"She's alive," Charles said.

Iris pressed two fingers to the side of Sybil's neck. "She has a pulse. A weak one, but it's there."

While Lowe and a steward helped the others out of the water, Charles reached for Sybil, but Iris slapped his hand away.

"We have to warm her up," she said, throwing more blankets over her. "I'm sorry, Charlie, but until you're back to a regular temperature, you won't be any help." She paused to gaze at Sybil. "She looks like a ghost. Where did you find her?"

"In your suite," Charles said. "Lewis had locked her inside."

She whipped around. "He wh—oh, I'm so sorry."

"I'm the one who should be sorry," he replied, and he nodded toward Sybil. "I told you I'd keep her safe."

If Sybil didn't make it, the only consolation Charles had was the knowledge that they wouldn't be parted for long because surely, Iris would kill him. As it was, she only took his hand, her flesh so warm against his skin, it itched, but he didn't let go.

"In that regard, you've done your duty," Iris said. "It's not over yet."

Chapter Twenty-Seven

Small waves lapped at the sides of the lifeboat as it slowly plodded through the water. With Iris watching Sybil, Charles was free to look out or at Lowe, who continued scanning the ghostly faces of the people floating by the wreck site. Still, except for the bobbing of the water as the lifeboat approached. Charles shivered and kept searching, hoping to spy Captain Smith or Murdoch.

He didn't have any luck with those two, but he did spot Wilde. His frozen arms still held onto a lounge chair from the promenade deck, his whistle in his mouth, wide eyes unblinking. Charles sighed. Wilde's wife had died a couple of years prior. *Titanic* had made orphans of their children. And Charles was sure they weren't the only ones. The ship no doubt made orphans and widows en masse. So many families changed forever in a matter of a few hours.

"I suppose this makes you in charge now, Charlie," Lowe said quietly. "You're the highest ranking officer to survive."

Charles blinked as that percolated through him. Lowe might as well have strapped boulders to Charles's shoulders and threw him overboard. He was responsible now. He would have to answer for and represent the officers and crew of *Titanic* when the news of the sinking broke. It was going to be a nightmare. But he couldn't think about that now. Not while he had Sybil to worry about.

"I. . . " he trailed off and shook his head. "Let's keep looking."

His heart told him it was no use.

They carefully made their way through the crowd, checking each body for signs of life. Only a handful did, and no one Charles recognized. He gave the order that anyone with a pulse had to be pulled from the water. If there was a chance, they had to take it.

Iris was surprisingly resilient. She rowed, bent over the side to check people, and helped pull anyone up that she could. All while checking on Sybil every few minutes, minding her pulse, ensuring she was breathing, and keeping blankets on her.

"I wish I could tell if she was warming up," she said with a sigh, pressing her palm to Sybil's cheeks and forehead. "The air's too cold."

"You're doing well, my lady," Charles said. "I'm impressed."

She met his gaze. "Impressed?"

"I never thought an earl's daughter could be hardy enough to row a lifeboat and drag people into it."

"I should tell you, she insisted on coming along," Lowe added. "We originally said only stewards should row, but she wouldn't hear of it."

Charles raised his brows at Iris, who flushed, despite her cheeks already having a rosy tint from the cold and the effort she was putting in.

"I wanted to find you both if I could," she said, uncharacteristically sheepish. "I couldn't bear the thought of waiting around any longer."

"That's admirable," Charles said. "Thank you for coming for us."

She only nodded, picked up a blanket, and wrapped it around another shivering man.

"We've got another survivor!" the steward rowing opposite Iris called.

"Pull him up!" Lowe ordered.

Iris crossed the lifeboat to help. Charles had offered to help with the first few, but found himself too weak after being in the water for so long and keeping Sybil pressed to him. So he watched as Iris and the steward lifted a dark-haired gentleman halfway out of the water. The man lifted his head, and the moment he did, Charles's stomach turned.

"Lewis!" Iris gasped and dropped him.

Lewis sputtered and water splashed as the steward struggled to hold on to him. He didn't manage, and Lewis slipped back into the sea with a curse.

"Leave him," Charles said.

The steward and Lowe turned shocked eyes on Charles.

"Sir?" the steward questioned.

"Leave him behind," Charles repeated.

"But you said—"

"I'm ordering you to leave him!"

Iris was already bending back down, much to Charles's shock. She only got Lewis as far as hooking his arms over the side of the lifeboat on her own, and then the steward moved to help her. She held out a hand to stop him.

"Wait!"

The steward froze. Iris turned chilling eyes on her husband.

"I'm going to save your life now," she said. "Nod if you understand."

Lewis managed to glower at her through his frosted features, and he nodded.

"It comes with a condition," Iris went on. "Promise me now. You will grant me the divorce when we get home. You won't contest it. You won't dispute my claims. You will simply sign the papers and leave me alone for the rest of your miserable life. If you don't, I'll drop you back in this water and leave you to freeze."

His mouth fell open. He didn't answer for a long moment.

"I don't like this, Charlie," Lowe said. "I know their marriage wasn't exactly happy, but this is his life we're talking about. We should stop this."

"Do what she says," Charles said, his tone clipped as he waited for Lewis's answer.

Iris shook him. "Promise to leave me!"

"I promise," Lewis finally choked out.

Iris nodded at the steward. "Help me pull him up."

Charles made no attempt to hide his displeasure. It didn't even satisfy him to see the bruises blooming on Lewis's face where Charles had gotten his punches in. That seemed like a lifetime ago now, though the rage at what that man had done to Sybil was as fresh as an open wound. He briefly considered defying them all and putting Lewis back in the water, anyway. It was what Lewis would have done. But Charles bowed to his respect for Iris, which far outweighed his hatred of Lewis.

Lewis huddled away toward the stern. The steward got him a blanket and then left him alone. Thankfully, Lewis made no attempt to speak to Iris or Charles. He cast a wary look at Sybil, but then fixed his gaze outward. That suited Charles fine. He wasn't sure he could take hearing an apology or some weak attempt at making amends.

It wasn't fair that Lewis should be able to sit on his own while Sybil was barely breathing. If it weren't for him, Sybil would have been put safely on a lifeboat, not hanging somewhere between life and death. And he did it to keep control over his marriage to Iris, which was ending regardless. Charles ground his teeth to keep the insults he wanted to hurl at bay.

He focused on Sybil instead, willing the color to come back to her cheeks or her eyes to open. Something to give him even a glimmer of hope. But she remained still as ever. For the first time in his life, he understood Shakespeare's Romeo, and his desire to end it all upon seeing his love in the crypt. Shaking his head, he reminded himself that all was not lost. Iris was right. It wasn't over yet.

When they were certain they had rescued any remaining survivors, they rowed away again, back toward the other lifeboats Lowe had secured together. There were a few glad reunions, but far more disappointed frowns as the women craned their necks, only to find their loved one was not among those returning. Charles and Iris remained in their boat so they wouldn't have to move Sybil. Iris held Sybil's hand, sitting on the floor.

"Was there any word of rescue?" she asked.

"The *Carpathia* said she was four hours away when we sent out the first few distress calls," Charles answered. "But I wasn't given any updates after that."

He lifted his arm to check his watch, but found it missing from his wrist. It must have come off when he and Sybil jumped. Or perhaps with the force of the wake from the smokestack falling. Whatever the case, it was gone. Which riddled him with guilt, as that was a parting gift from his brothers when he'd left Yorkshire. The photographs they'd sent were gone, too. His two links to home, taken to the bottom of the sea. Though, he supposed, he had an even greater link than either of those things in Sybil.

Even so, a trip home was in his future now. A brush with death made him realize how much he missed his family. He resolved to never be away from them for so long again. And when he was, he would be better about writing. He would be a better brother and uncle.

He had no idea how long they waited before the sky turned gray with dawn's arrival. When he saw a glow on Sybil's cheeks, he initially believed she was waking up, but it was the low morning sun shining on her face. The light revealed the field of ice around them. Bright, white giants looming over the surface of the water, immovable and dangerous. And then, between them, dark puffs of smoke, and the outline of a steamship. *Carpathia* made her way steadily toward them. Help had finally arrived. As Charles looked at Sybil's pale face, he hoped it was in enough time.

CHAPTER TWENTY-EIGHT

April 15, 1912

The women and children boarded first, same as when they unceremoniously disembarked from *Titanic*. Sybil was not the only one who was unconscious, so she, and the others in similar condition, were carried carefully up the ladders on stretchers by the *Carpathia's* crew. Charles's first instinct was to go with her, but he knew she would be safe with Lady Iris. With a pit in his stomach, he waited his turn.

By some miracle, he had enough strength to get himself up the ladder. Warmth slowly returned to his body, though his clothes were still cold and damp. The passengers of *Titanic* swarmed the boat deck, demanding to know if their family members had survived. Charles pitied the crew of *Carpathia*, for they had no more answers than he could have given them himself. Some openly wept, others dabbed at their faces in as dignified a manner as they could muster, but most sat with blank, numb stares, hardly even glancing up to accept a warm cup of coffee.

He glanced around for Sybil, with no luck. When he stopped a steward to ask where any sick and wounded would be taken, he felt a hand on his shoulder. He turned, coming face to face with *Carpathia's* captain. He was tall and slender, his clean-shaven face shadowed with compassion.

"Second Officer Percy?" he asked.

"That's me," Charles said.

"Captain Arthur Rostron. One of the junior officers gave me your name. They also said you're the highest ranking surviving officer."

Charles swallowed. "Yes. We lost the captain, chief, and first officer."

Their faces swam before his eyes, and he blinked away the mist that gathered at their memory.

"You best come with me, son. We have a lot to discuss. Then we'll let you get some rest, I promise."

Charles nodded and followed Captain Rostron to his quarters. They weren't as grand as Captain Smith's on *Titanic*, but Charles hardly expected them to be. *Titanic* was meant to be the height of luxury, after all.

He sank into a chair indicated by Rostron, and for the first time, Charles realized his own exhaustion. His muscles were heavy as lead. He wanted to fade into the cushion of that chair and surrender to the pull of sleep. Perhaps forever.

A warm mug of tea was placed in his hands, and he forced his gaze up to thank the junior officer who'd brought it. Only it wasn't any of *Carpathia's* officers. It was Bruce Ismay.

The shock at the sight of him sapped all the weariness from Charles's body and he stiffened. Ismay had none of the signs of being in the water. His clothes were dry, and his skin had warmth and color to it. His hair, while not neatly combed, was dry as well. He looked tired, certainly, but otherwise completely unharmed. Which told Charles the man had gotten away on a lifeboat.

Ismay at least had the decency to look ashamed. After an apologetic look, he sharply cut his eyes from Charles and backed away, taking a seat in the other chair, but not relaxing. He sat on the edge, pulling his dressing gown tighter around him.

"I suppose the question on everyone's mind is. . . what happened?" Rostron said.

Charles tore his disdainful gaze from Ismay and locked eyes with the captain. "We struck an iceberg, sir."

"How?"

"I don't know the details. I was. . . not on duty at the time."

"Where were you?"

He cleared his throat and shifted in his seat. How was he supposed to answer? He was in bed with Sybil. Good Lord, how was that less than twelve hours ago? And now he may never make love to her again. He needed to see her. As soon as he could.

"I was in my quarters," he said simply. "I felt the impact, but that's all. I didn't know what happened until Captain Smith called us all together for a briefing."

"Can you tell me about the briefing?"

Charles relayed everything he could remember. How Murdoch reported the collision, what Mr. Andrews said to confirm the ship would sink, and the timeframe they had to get the lifeboats loaded. He talked until his mouth went dry, and he finally took a sip of tea. It warmed him like a brandy, sliding down his throat and into his belly.

"Did you not receive any of the ice warnings about the area?" Rostron asked.

"We got seven of them, but. . . " he cast a sidelong glance at Ismay. "It was suggested that we light the last boilers to pick up speed and arrive in New York a day early."

Rostron shook his head. "It's odd that Smith would take that kind of risk."

"With the information we had, it was difficult to imagine anything truly dangerous happening," Charles said. "Everything he knew at the time indicated little risk."

Rostron nodded and turned to Ismay. "Anything to add, Mr. Ismay? You are the representative for White Star Line."

Ismay started at being addressed and stared back at Rostron with such wide eyes, Charles thought he looked owlish.

"I. . . " he trailed off. "No, nothing to add. Mr. Percy has spoken true. Of course, I will need to consult with the board before making any official statements."

"Of course," Rostron said.

A soft knock at the door made Charles and Rostron turn their heads, but Ismay did not, keeping his eyes resolutely on the floor in front of him. A junior officer stood in the doorway, a bundle of folded clothes tucked in the crook of his arm.

"The fresh clothes you requested, sir," he said.

"Thank you," Rostron replied. "I took the liberty of getting something for you to wear, Mr. Percy. You'll need to change out of your wet things."

Charles could have wept for the kindness. Even the tea hadn't fully banished the cold, and he knew nothing would until he got dry. He got to his feet and took the outfit.

"Thank you."

The officer nodded and departed the room.

"You're free to change in here, and you may use my quarters to have a lie down," Rostron offered. "You'll need your strength for what comes next."

Charles raked a hand through his hair. "An inquiry, you mean."

"Yes. I've never dealt with one myself, but White Star Line is about to be under some serious scrutiny. And in your position, you'll be the one to answer for much of it."

"I can't think about that now," Charles sighed.

"Of course. We'll leave you to get some rest."

He turned to leave, gesturing for Ismay to leave as well, but Charles called out to stop him.

"Before you go, can you tell me where they're taking the people sick or hurt?" Charles asked. "My fiancé. . . she wasn't conscious when we boarded."

Rostron blinked. "Your fiancé was with you?"

"She's a lady's maid, and was traveling with her mistress on *Titanic*."

"I see. I know a few first class passengers have given up their rooms, so I'll ask around. What's her name?"

"Sybil. Sybil Chambers. She'll be with Lady Iris Mooring."

"Understood."

He left, Ismay not far behind. The latter hesitated at the door and opened his mouth as if to say something more. Then he shook his head, muttered something to himself, and was gone. Charles was sure he hadn't seen the last of Bruce Ismay. He had a feeling the next time they met, they would be facing that scrutiny that Rostron warned about.

Shaking his head to clear it, Charles got changed. The clothes were civilian, and a close fit for him, but not exact. It hardly mattered. He would have put on a corset and an evening gown as long as they were dry.

Well, perhaps not the corset.

He draped his uniform over the backs of a couple of chairs to dry. Then, his body and heart were at war. His aching muscles screamed at him to crawl into the bed and sleep. But his heart called Sybil's name. His mind told him even if he did lie down, without seeing her, sleep would never come. He couldn't wait around for Rostron to return. So he headed out.

He shielded his eyes against the bright sunshine, and checked out around the deck, but it was largely clear of the haggard survivors of *Titanic*. Some lingered by the railing, eyes scanning the sea. Probably looking for any sign of their loved ones that were missing. There, in the area designated for steerage passengers, he saw two faces he recognized. Killian's wife and daughter.

His gut twisted up, but he knew he should tell them. So they could stop leaning over the railing and face the grief that was coming. Sybil would have to wait a moment longer. He had to tell them now before he lost them in the crowd because there would be no way to find them again. He hadn't even gotten their names back on *Titanic*.

He descended the steps, got stopped by a steward, but explained who he was, and was allowed to pass. A goose egg in his throat, he approached them.

"Excuse me," he said.

They turned their heads.

"Oh, Mr. Percy," the wife said. "You made it. Did you find your Sybil all right?"

"I did, yes." He cleared his throat. "Listen, um. . . "

"Siobhan," she said gracefully. "And this is Maisie. She told me how you won her doll back for her. It was a gift from her father, so. . . "

Oh, this was going to be much harder than he thought. "About Killian. We saw him in the water when we got off the ship. He was heading for you when. . . "

He stopped when he met Maisie's eyes. How could he say this in front of her? Siobhan clocked his hesitation.

"Maisie, love, why don't you take your doll and play over by the other children?" she suggested, jerking her chin toward a group of girls huddled in a corner, seemingly unfazed by what they had survived. Maisie glanced between them and departed without argument. Siobhan met Charles's gaze again, her eyes welling up. "How did it happen?"

"We can leave it at this if it's too much."

"No, please. Tell me."

He sighed. "One of the smokestacks. It fell sideways from the ship, and. . . Killian was underneath it. I'm so sorry."

She blinked, and a tear raced down her cheek. She swiped at it with the back of her hand, but a second came right behind it on the other side. Charles wished he could take this away from her. This splitting heartbreak he knew she must be feeling. And she was not the only widow he would be offering his condolences too. Already, he could picture Ada's smiling face, and that starry-eyed look he'd seen her give Murdoch back in Southampton, crumpling.

"Thank you for telling me," Siobhan said. "It would've been agony to wait."

"If there's anything I can do for you and Maisie, please let me know," Charles said.

She nodded and swallowed hard. He searched for something more to say, but there was nothing. Nothing that could truly console her now. Yet he hesitated to leave. He wondered if it was appropriate to reach for her, to place a hand on her shoulder or something, but he had no idea. The woman was pretty much a stranger. And yet they had this horrific thing in common.

"Charlie!"

He turned his head at the voice he now knew to be Lady Iris. She stood at the top of the stairs and waved him over. He glanced at

Siobhan, who nodded, and he had to believe she would be all right. Then he raced up the stairs, opened the gate, and closed it behind him to join Lady Iris in the first class section of the ship.

"Where is she?" he asked, holding her gaze.

"I'll take you to our room. This way."

She started to lead the way, but Charles took her arm and turned her to face him again.

"And. . . how is she?"

"You should see her," Iris said. "She's much the same, but I know you'll feel better once you've clapped eyes on her."

He almost smiled. "You'd be right."

"Come on, then."

She led him inside.

Chapter Twenty-Nine

Iris was right, Sybil was about the same as she had the last time Charles saw her. The ice pellets had melted out of her chocolate brown curls, and she was in fresh clothes, but her sweet, round face was still colorless and cold. The rise and fall of her chest gave him some comfort. He took a seat on the edge of the bed and reached for her hand. It was freezing.

"Has anyone come to see her?" he asked.

"There is a doctor on board who's been making some rounds," Iris answered. "He says the cold exposure is dangerous, especially with the injury to her head, but he can't say just now which way she'll go."

"What can we do?"

"Keep her warm and comfortable."

"Sounds a lot like 'nothing' to me."

Iris heaved a sigh, and he felt her hand on his shoulder. Warm, and in stark comparison to Sybil's. She squeezed gently. He was comforted in spite of himself.

"Some things are simply out of our hands," she said.

He wanted to argue with her. There was always something to be done. The whole bloody ship had gone down and by sheer force of will, he'd come through it with Sybil in tow. It hadn't been luck or a miracle. It was his own resourcefulness, his own determination that he was going to live. He was going to marry Sybil and be her husband before he was anything else ever again.

"The bump on her head," he said. "How did it happen?"

"It was Lewis," Iris answered, and he appreciated her matter-of-fact honesty. "He and I were in the middle of a fight, he threw a crystal ashtray, and it struck Sybil as she was coming in the door. So, yes, it was an accident, but if he wasn't just the worst person to ever exist, it wouldn't have happened."

He almost laughed. And he might have if it weren't Sybil lying there unconscious. "We should have left him in the water."

"I considered it. But I thought I'd much rather get rid of him myself than let nature do it for me. It will wound him all the more."

Sybil's still hand led Charles to agree. Better for Lewis to live and face the consequences of his actions.

"You should go sleep," Iris said, interrupting his thoughts. "You look dreadful, you know."

He might have been offended if he didn't detect the humor in her voice. And he knew there was some truth to it. He hadn't bothered to look at himself while he was in the captain's quarters, even though there was a mirror on the wall. He feared what he might find staring back at him.

"I'm not leaving her," he replied.

"You must at some point. I'm not so particular, but if I allow a man to stay overnight in my rooms, there will be more than one story hitting the London papers this week."

He sat back with a groan, finally taking his eyes off Sybil to look at Iris. "You don't think they've told the press yet, do you? About the sinking?"

"Devil if I know," she said with a shrug. "If they haven't yet, it won't be long."

"Bloody hell," he sighed, running a hand through his hair.

"All the more reason for you to get some sleep."

"Don't send me away, Iris," he pleaded. "I can't leave her."

She regarded him with a smirk. "That's the first time you've ever called me Iris."

He blinked. "What?"

"Just now, you dropped the honorific."

He opened his mouth to apologize, but her pleased expression made him stop. There weren't many in her class who would take kindly to what was usually perceived as disrespect. He hadn't meant it that way, it was something he forgot in his weariness. But she was still smiling.

"You may stay here, Charlie," she said. "I'll see about getting some food and tea."

He raised his brows. "You're certain you don't mind?"

"Quite certain. We're friends now, after all."

With that, she left, closing the door softly behind her.

***

Charles woke hours later to a sore neck and a numb arm from where his head had been resting on it. Flexing his fingers, pricking tingles shot up and down his arm, waking up the same as he had. He blinked back the grogginess in his eyes to find Sybil, exactly as he'd left her—still, pale, and unconscious. He heaved a sigh. It would never get easier to see her this way.

His stomach rumbled, and he realized he was famished. Glancing at the clock, he saw it was almost four in the afternoon, and he hadn't eaten since dinner the previous night on *Titanic*. He looked at the door, preparing to call for Iris, but saw a tray situated on the dresser. It was stacked with some bread and cheese, and a biscuit off to the side next to the teapot. He got to his feet and stretched his aching body.

When he padded over to the dresser, he spied a note in neat script. Picking it up, his eyes scanned it.

When you wake up, the captain wants to speak to you. I'll keep an eye on Sybil while you're busy. –Iris

He nodded to himself and stuffed a piece of bread into his mouth with ravenous vigor. After the first few bites, he forced himself to slow down. These were his last moments of peace before the work began. He would need to enjoy them.

***

The days aboard *Carpathia* passed in a blur. Charles had frequent meetings with Captain Rostron, putting together the pieces of the night of April 14th. A daunting task since he was not the officer on duty. With Murdoch and Wilde gone, they had only the stewards and junior officers, who were hardly better informed than Charles. The meetings became increasingly redundant, going over what was said immediately after striking the iceberg again and again. Rostron had informed the press ahead of the New York arrival, so he wanted answers.

In search of them, Charles also spent time talking to *Titanic's* surviving passengers and crew, jotting down anything they saw or heard the night of the sinking. He spent most of his energy with those that worked on the lowest decks and in the boiler rooms. Their testimony mostly consisted of running for their lives when the water came through. Anyone on the boat deck or promenade decks saw some ice falling and felt the same shudder Charles and Sybil had. Third class passengers made some disturbing reports about being locked below E Deck as the ship went down, with stewards not even allowing women and children up.

Charles sought out Siobhan when he heard this, and she confirmed the story.

"The only reason we found Sybil was because we snuck up a crew staircase Killian knew about from building the ship," she said. Her voice broke over her late husband's name, so she cleared her throat and tucked her hair behind her ear. "How is Sybil by the way?"

"The same," he told her, biting back a sigh.

He was at Sybil's bedside whenever he had a free moment. Each time he came into the room, he hoped to find her sitting up, eyes bright, and maybe even talking. But he was disappointed. The only person who changed was Lady Iris, and whatever book she was reading to pass the time while she kept faithful watch.

"I hope she gets better soon," Siobhan said. She pressed a hand to her chest and rubbed it. "Lord knows I wouldn't wish what I'm feeling on anyone."

Charles retrieved some stationery from his pocket where he'd written his home address in Yorkshire. He held it out to her, but she didn't take it right away, her eyes flicking between the paper and his face.

"What's this?"

"Where to reach me," he told her. "I meant it when I said if there's anything you need to let me know. As soon as I'm back in England, this is where I'll be."

She took it with a shaking hand, then met his gaze again. "Anything?"

"Anything. Even if it's just a friend."

She blinked slowly. "Thank you."

He left her to continue his interviews, and after he handed his notes off to Captain Rostron, he went straight back to Sybil. Iris was asleep in the chair next to the bed, her feet up on the edge of the mattress and her head slumped against the wingback. The book she was reading lay splayed over her lap with her hands resting daintily on the pages. Charles approached, placing a light hand on her knee so as not to startle her.

Her eyes slowly opened, and she smiled at him. She said something that resembled "Hello" through a yawn and deep stretch, and he nodded in reply.

"That book must not be any good," he joked.

"I've read it before," she returned.

"What is it?"

"*Sense and Sensibility.*"

"Ah, Jane Austen. Classic."

"I was reading it aloud to Sybil. The doctor says she can hear us, and I don't want her to think she's alone. So I started trying to sort out which of us is Elinor and which of us is Marianne."

"And what did you determine?" he asked.

"We're both Elinor's, actually. You're Marianne."

He blinked. "What?"

"I don't mean to imply that you're frivolous or gullible," she added quickly as he chuckled. "Just that you're a romantic. Full of hope and all that. And it did take you an awfully long while to realize that what you needed was something you had all along."

"I can't argue with you there," he conceded, taking Sybil's hand.

His brow furrowed. Her palm was warm against his fingers.

Warm.

His eyes snapped to her face, where he saw that her lips were nearly back to their rosy shade of pink. They were still chapped and dry, but the color was there. His heart quickened. He brought his free hand to her cheek and again, felt warmth.

"Iris, she's—she's warm," he said.

Iris leaped to her feet, the book falling to the floor with a thud. She reached for Sybil's other cheek and put the back of her hand to it. She checked her forehead too, careful to avoid the bruise.

"She *is* warm!" Iris gasped. "Sybil. Sybil, can you hear me?"

They called her name, the two of them creating a chorus of it. But Sybil gave no indication she heard them. No squeeze of the hand or motion behind her eyelids. They stopped calling for her and exchanged defeated looks.

"I suppose it's a good sign that her temperature is getting back to normal," Iris said. "Perhaps it means she's truly on the mend."

Charles took a seat in the chair, his eyes still fixed on Sybil's face, willing her to respond. Iris put a hand on his shoulder.

"I'll get us something to eat. Be patient, Charlie. She'll get there."

He patted her hand and then she slipped out of the room. He wondered if what she said was true and Sybil could hear them. If so, why hadn't she responded to her name? They would arrive in New York within a day. Would Sybil disembark on her own two feet or would she be carried off on a stretcher the way she boarded? It made his stomach turn to imagine. He couldn't bear the thought of sitting at a hospital for days—maybe even weeks—on end, waiting for some sign from her. Or worse, if she declined again. It would drive him mad.

"I can't do this," he murmured, stroking the back of her hand with his thumb. "I need you, Giggles."

She stirred. His heart leaped into his throat. And then, slowly, her eyelids fluttered, and she gazed at him through those beautiful brown doe eyes once more. Half-lidded and weary, but open.

"Charles?" she croaked.

His eyes burned with emotion. "Sybil. . . "

"I knew you'd be here."

CHAPTER THIRTY

Charles cupped Sybil's face between his hands, still in disbelief that she was awake at last. Speaking and smiling. He felt like getting on his knees and praising God or leaping to his feet and dancing a quickstep. He wasn't sure which more accurately conveyed his elation at seeing her thus. She blinked slowly at him and her smile widened.

"Of course I'm here," he said. He was loath to take his eyes off her sweet face, but he needed Iris, so he called for her over his shoulder. "Iris!"

She trotted into the room. "What is it?"

"Sybil's awake," he said. "Get the doctor, right away."

"She's—" Iris stopped short and crossed the room to see for herself. "Sybil, my goodness!"

"My lady," Sybil replied with a weary grin. "I'm glad you're here."

"Not as glad as I am to see your eyes," Iris returned. She patted Charles's shoulder. "I'll run and get the doctor."

She hurtled out of the room. Sybil brought her hands up to wrap her fingers around Charles's palms, and he marveled at her strength to do even that. Holding his hands, she let her eyes wander around the room, taking in the fine suite.

"Where are we?" she asked.

"Aboard *Carpathia*," he told her. "They arrived just before dawn after the sinking."

"How long have I been asleep?"

"About three days."

She nodded. His chest was ten times lighter than it had been since they boarded. She had come back to him at last. Now, they only needed the doctor to confirm all was well, and they could move on to their lives together. He had to blink away the mist in his eyes.

"Charles," she said seriously.

"Yes, love?"

"Did you really propose to me while we were in the water or did I dream that?"

He chuckled. "I really proposed. Did you mean it when you said yes or were you that delirious?"

"Of course I meant it," she said gently. "I love you, Charles."

"I love you too, darling."

She squeezed his hand, and he thanked God that he could feel that again. He was grateful for every breath she took, every motion of her body, and for every day he would have by her side. He would never take those things for granted. Never again.

The door creaked open and a white-haired gentleman with horn-rimmed glasses and a tweed suit walked in, a smile plastered to his face beneath his handlebar mustache.

"I hear someone is awake at last," he said cheerfully. "I'm Dr. Barkle. It's a pleasure to formally meet you, Miss Chambers."

"Hello, Dr. Barkle," Sybil replied.

Dr. Barkle looked at Charles. "A moment, please, Mr. Percy."

Charles reluctantly rose from his place at Sybil's side and stood away from the bed. His hands felt cold where they were no longer touching Sybil, and he flexed his fingers to rid them of their yearning to be near her again. He hovered by her bed throughout the examination, where Dr. Barkle asked Sybil questions about what she was able to remember last, and basics about where she was and her full name and birthday and hometown. All of which she answered perfectly. He carefully inspected her eyes, shining a small light in them to see the size of her pupils. He also had her follow the light to test her focus. He gently prodded at the bump on her head. She winced, setting Charles's teeth on edge, but he took a deep breath to remind himself it was the doctor's job. He hated to see her even the least bit uncomfortable after everything she had endured.

The doctor tucked away his flashlight and straightened his jacket.

"All looks well with you, Miss Chambers," he said. "I recommend getting a more thorough going over when we get to New York to be sure, but your recovery is promising. Keep resting, and let me know if anything changes."

He shook hands with everyone and left, and Charles was back beside Sybil in a flash.

Iris beamed at them. "I'll give you two a moment. I've been working on a letter to your brothers, and I'll have to add this happy bit of news."

She left again, and Sybil watched her go with sleepy eyes.

"Charles," she said, blinking up at him. "You're going to take me home now, aren't you?"

"Yes, Sybil. As soon as we can, we'll go straight back to England."

"And we'll live happily ever after."

He pressed his lips to the back of her hand. "Happily ever after, indeed."

***

June, 1912

For the first time in over a decade, Charles walked the old, familiar pathway up to the farmhouse where he'd grown up. Little had changed about it, reinforcing that what had truly changed was Charles himself. This land, his home, wasn't wild like the sea or ever-changing as the technology they had to navigate it. The only difference was he could no longer see the outline of the Chambers's roof in the distance.

Sybil took his hand, and the metallic cold of her wedding band burned against his palm. After weeks of delay due to the inquiry conducted by the US officials regarding *Titanic's* sinking, they finally managed to get back on English soil. Once they did, they wasted no time. In London, while the British inquiry went on, they got married, with Lady Iris as a witness. One thing the disaster taught them was there was no time like the present.

The drawback was that both Mrs. Murdoch and Mrs. Smith had been waiting in London, and Charles delivered the news of their husbands' deaths personally. He'd been dreading it, knowing he would face their tears and their questions, which he answered to the best of his ability. And as he did with Siobhan, he offered his help in any way they could use it. They answered with watery, grateful smiles, and he promised to write.

Somehow, *that* was not as nerve wracking as the prospect of seeing his brothers again after all this time away.

"I don't know whether to brace myself for a hug or a punch," he said.

Sybil giggled beside him. "I already told you, they'll be happy to see you."

"That doesn't mean I'm not getting punched."

"I won't let them punch you."

"I can't hide behind my wife, they'll never let me live it down."

"You're being dramatic."

"I am not. They'd take the mickey out of me for the rest of my life. I'd have to go back to never visiting."

"Charles," Sybil said sternly, and he met her warm gaze. "They're your brothers, and they love you. Almost as much as I do."

She stood on her toes and pressed a light kiss to his lips. He cradled the back of her head in his hands to keep her close. He kissed her again, longer and deeper than hers, until he heard a soft moan from the back of her throat.

"Don't distract me," she said, pulling back enough so she could look him in the eyes. "You're going up to that door."

"Shame," he said with a shrug. "We could make much better use of our old stargazing spot now that we're man and wife."

She swatted his arm, and he chuckled. With a wry grin, she said, "Another time."

When she took his hand again, she tugged him forward, and he followed her, all the way up to the door. It felt silly to raise his hand and knock. He'd barged through it a million times as a child. But it wasn't his home anymore, a fact which made his stomach sink like a rock. He rapped his knuckles against the door three times.

A frazzled blonde woman answered, her face still hidden behind the door as she scolded a child off in another room. Wiping her hands on her apron, she faced Charles, who gulped. He recognized her from the family portrait he'd lost—his eldest sister-in-law, Susan. Edward's wife. Mother to his nephews, Bertie and Joe, and niece, Nora. His family. And he was a stranger to all of them.

Susan was even prettier in person, with her soft round face and blue eyes. She blinked at him for several moments before her lips turned up into a kind smile.

"Charlie," she said, with welcome in her voice.

"I—"

"Ed! Stu!" she called over her shoulder before Charles could say anything back. "You'd better come see who's here!"

The unmistakable, hulking frames of his big brothers appeared in the hallway, shooing two laughing little boys back into the kitchen. They came to a halt when their eyes landed on Charles. He shifted under their gaze, a bead of sweat rolling down the back of his neck.

He cleared his throat. "Hello."

Edward and Stuart thundered down the hall, Susan stepping out of the way just in time. Before Charles knew it, he was engulfed in his brothers' arms. They ruffled his hair and pinched his cheeks and clapped his back, and suddenly he was a scrawny twelve-year-old again, struggling to defend himself against a pair of burly teenagers. They said a lot, much of which included insults and indignation at his being gone all these years. But he picked up, "Welcome home," several times out of all of it.

Finally, Edward detached and went to hug Sybil, with whom he was a great deal gentler, but he gave her a squeeze.

"Come in, the pair of you," he said, keeping his arm around Sybil's shoulders. "We've got a lot to catch up on."

They were ushered into the kitchen, where Charles met his other sister-in-law, Linda, who already had the kettle on. The children were not shy about greeting their Uncle Charlie, aided by the gifts he and Sybil brought from London. They did, however, have an extremely important game of hide and seek to get to, so they thanked their aunt and uncle for the gifts, and then raced outside. Nora gave Charles an extra hug before she did.

Charles blinked to get rid of the stinging in his eyes, and then Linda placed a cup of tea in front of him.

"Thank you," he said.

"You're welcome," she replied, and then moved to perch on Stuart's knee.

The sight of the table was so different, it could have knocked Charles over. What was once occupied by three boys and their father, was now surrounded with three men and their wives, two of the three now fathers themselves. A thought which brought Charles to the first thing he wanted to say.

"I'm sorry," he began. "For missing Father's funeral."

"S'all right," Edward said with a wave of his hand. "We understood."

"Still, I should have made the effort. I hope you can forgive me."

"We forgave you a long time ago," Stuart said. "And now that we know you were on the ship that would bring you to Sybil, how could we be upset?"

Charles glanced sidelong at Sybil and grinned.

"We were grateful to get the letter from Lady Iris letting us know you were all right," Linda added. "Once we heard about the sinking, that is. We hardly slept with worry."

"It was touch and go with Sybil for a few days," Charles said with a sigh. "But thankfully, she pulled through."

She curled her fingers around his hand. "We're also sorry about eloping. We couldn't wait another second to get married, or we would have had a proper ceremony with everyone there."

"We more than understand that, we had courthouse weddings ourselves," Edward said, looking fondly at Susan. "Once you know, what's the use in waiting, anyway?"

"Right you are, love," she agreed, and kissed his cheek. Then she turned back to Charles and Sybil. "What will you two do now?"

"Stay at the farm, of course," Stuart answered.

Charles and Sybil exchanged a look.

"For a little while," Charles said, facing his family. "We want to have a good long visit with you all before we settle."

"Settle where?" Edward asked.

"Liverpool," they answered in unison before falling into laughter together.

"It puts Charles in a port city so he can keep working, but close enough to home that I won't get lonely while he's away," Sybil said.

"You want to keep sailing?" Stuart questioned. "After what you went through on *Titanic*?"

"Sybil asked the same thing," Charles said with a half smile. "I know it seems mad, but the sea is in my blood. I can't let what happened keep me from doing what I love. For now, I'll remain with White Star Line."

"And Sybil? What about your job?" Linda asked.

"I've talked it over with Lady Iris, and I'll be leaving her service at the month's end," Sybil answered, and Charles could hear the ache in her voice. "Her divorce proceedings have started, so I'll help her pack up his things and train a new lady's maid, but then I'll be ready to set up housekeeping."

"You've found a place then?" Stuart wondered.

"Yes," Charles said. "A cozy little row house, with a big fireplace."

"And a kitchen to die for," Sybil added. "A sewing room, too."

"With space for a small library, if we want."

"And—when we're ready—a nursery."

Charles would never forget seeing the listing in the paper. He and Sybil had taken a detour to go see it on their way to Yorkshire, and were as smitten with it as they were with each other. He could picture it all—the holidays, the dinners, the children. But most of all, Sybil, who would make a simple house into a dream home. And for the first time, Charles was not looking forward to the next time he set foot on a ship. From now on, he'd be leaving a piece of himself behind. The goodbye would never be easy. And then he reminded himself the hellos would be all the sweeter with something real to return to. His Sybil. His wife. His best friend. For the rest of his life.

Epilogue

December, 1918

"Here," Sybil said, wadding up the sheet she'd stripped from the bed, and tossing it to a sergeant. "You can get rid of this one, there's blood on it."

"Yes, Nurse Percy," he replied, and stuffed it into the bag beside him.

He hoisted it over his shoulder and marched out of the room, which was slowly becoming the library again. Lady Iris's brother, Hugh, the current Earl of Manfax, had allowed the British military to use his estate as a convalescent home for recovering wounded coming back from the continent. Sybil volunteered to be a nurse the moment it opened up, and she'd been serving there for most of the Great War. Now, the last of the remaining soldiers had been sent home, and Sybil was helping the staff put the home back to its original state.

It satisfied her to be working again after a couple years managing her own home. And to see Lady Iris more regularly. Though she had made herself busy as well, becoming a leader of the suffragette movement in Britain, attending protests and rallies, even getting herself arrested a few times. Sybil would never forget the shock at seeing the headline *EARL'S SISTER CLAPPED IN IRONS AT RALLY FOR*

WOMEN'S VOTES, and then Iris's mugshot, with her winking at the camera. Iris later informed her that she'd also been giving the middle finger, but the paper cropped that out.

Sybil admired the courage of those women, and part of her wished she could participate. But between nursing and taking care of her children, she hardly had time. Her daughter, named Effie after her mother, was born in 1914, just before the war broke out and Charles went to active duty with the Royal Navy. Nine months after Charles was home on leave, their son, John, arrived in 1916. His full name was William John, in honor of Murdoch and Captain Smith, but John was the name that stuck with everyone that met him. And it was easier for him to say as he learned to talk.

Her children grew up in the estate's nursery, alongside the earl's son, Robert, while Sybil served the wounded. Something Sybil initially said was not necessary, but Iris insisted. The nanny was more than happy to take on the extra children, since Robert was so easy, and he enjoyed having playmates.

"Nurse Percy."

The voice of Dr. Barkle drew Sybil's attention. He'd come back to England after the war broke out to offer his services and was delighted to be assigned the convalescent home. Especially when he saw Sybil, alive and thriving. He'd been the doctor to deliver John into the world, so Sybil felt even further indebted to him. He was out of uniform now, back in a suit and white coat, another reminder that the war was over. With Charles still gone, it didn't quite feel like it to Sybil.

"Yes?" she asked.

"I wanted to say thank you for all your hard work these years," Dr. Barkle said. "Who could have guessed that the shivering girl I met after *Titanic* would be one of the strongest nurses I ever had on my staff."

"Thank you, doctor," she replied, warmth coming to her cheeks. "Like anyone else, I only wanted to do my part for king and country."

"You've done more than enough."

She inspected her hands. "The only problem is I hardly know what to do with myself now that it's all over."

He hooked his finger under her chin to tilt her head up, and her gaze fell upon the yard outside. Lady Iris was out there with the children, teaching her niece and nephews a game of some sort, the picnic they'd taken abandoned on the blanket in the grass. Effie let out a shriek of laughter as she chased Iris around, the dimples she'd inherited from Charles on full display. John waved his hands as he toddled after them. Robert was counting on his fingers. Sybil had no idea what game this was, but clearly, they were having fun.

"Now you get to just live," Dr. Barkle said. "Live and enjoy these blessings."

As if on cue, the sun peered out from behind the clouds, warming Sybil's face. Sunshine. Her children's laughter. Her life, without despair.

"You should join them," Dr. Barkle went on. "Fresh air would do you some good."

He gave her cheek a paternal pinch, and departed. Heaving a sigh, she removed her cap and apron, laying them to rest on the window sill. With one last look out, she turned her back to the window and followed the doctor's advice.

It turned out, the sun was deceptively warm. As she walked outside, the brisk December air cooled her skin. For a moment, it brought her back to the frigid nights on the boat deck of *Titanic*, but it wasn't quite that cold. Winter hadn't fully set in yet.

Even so, the children were bundled up, though hats and scarves were dumped on the picnic blanket. Red spotted their cheeks and the tips of their noses. Their laughter appeared in the air in little gray puffs before dissolving. Effie was the first to spot her.

"Mummy!" she cried, beaming.

She sprinted over, John on her heels, and Sybil crouched down to wrap them in her arms as they came careening into her. They almost knocked her over, but she managed to stay upright and give them affectionate squeezes.

"My darlings!" she replied, kissing each of their heads. "Are you being good for your Auntie Iris?"

"Yes, of course," Effie said. "She's teaching us a game, d'you want to play?"

"I'd love to."

The game was absolute nonsense, with Iris allowing the children to make up rules as they went along. Eventually it was clear the goal was to make the other players appear as silly as possible. Sybil ended up hopping on one foot while patting her head, when a figure in the distance made her freeze.

"Sybil?" Iris questioned on the end of a breathless laugh.

Sybil squinted and shielded her eyes from the sun with her hand. Silhouetted on the gravel drive, a person was walking toward the house. A man if she had to guess, judging by the shape of his hat and the length of his stride.

"Sybil, are you all right?" Iris pressed.

Sybil opened her mouth to ask if Iris could see the man too, but he finally stepped into the sunshine from the shadow of the trees, and Sybil saw his face. A face she would know from any distance. Her heart took a flying leap, and so did she, tearing across the lawn as fast as her legs could carry her.

She was only a couple yards away when he finally saw her, and she locked eyes with her husband for the first time in nearly two years. His familiar, blue eyes and his sweet dimpled smile and his strong arms opening up to receive her.

"Hello, Giggles," he managed to say before she flung herself into his embrace and kissed him like her life depended on it.

Her legs hooked around his waist, and he stumbled back from the force of her, but he didn't fall or break the kiss. He held her close. Her heart had slotted back into place. Her world was upright again, after years of being off-kilter, slanted beneath her feet. Her fingers buried themselves in his hair, knocking his hat to the ground so she could be even closer. She kissed him and kissed him and kissed him.

"Welcome home, my love," she said when they parted for air.

Her forehead came to rest against his, and she inhaled his scent. He smelled of fresh soap and clean clothes, but the sea clung to him through all of it. A touch of salty air that would never fully go away.

"Hard as it is to be away, I so look forward to your hellos," he said with a grin.

"Will you be going away again?" she asked, holding back a pout.

"No, love. Not for a long time yet. I'm ready to be home."

She stroked his cheek with her thumb. "And home is ready to have you."

With that, he placed her gently on her feet, took her hand, and went to the family they created together. They would return to Liverpool after the holidays, but for a while, they enjoyed the land of their youth, where their story began. Sybil watched Charles lift his son into his arms and they smiled at each other, and she knew—there was no end in sight.

Acknowledgements

First, I must start with my usual gratitude for my continuously supportive family. You have believed in me since the beginning, and the fact that you all are willing to take time out of your work, parenting, and fabulous hobby schedules to read my little books is humbling. Thank you so much.

Second, my best friend, Christy. I will thank you in every book because you are vital to every book. Your encouragement, feedback, and love enriches not only my writing, but also my life. You are my biggest fan, and I am grateful every day for you. Especially when I text you at ungodly hours because I'm wondering if something in the plot works. You're a saint.

Third, my author friends. I have no idea how I would get by without y'all. This journey has been confusing and hurtful at times, but I know I can pop into our group chat and complain to my heart's desire, and y'all are always there for me. Thank you so much.

Fourth, thank you to my editor, Emma. Your feedback made this book everything I believed it could be. I couldn't be prouder, and I'm so looking forward to what's next.

Fifth, my cover designer, Lorissa. I had an incredibly vague idea for what I wanted for this cover, and you created something more beautiful than I could have imagined. I love it. As I write this, it is still the background of my phone. Thank you so, so much for your creativity.

Finally, I must thank you, the reader. Every time you take a chance on an indie book, we have something to look forward to. Thank you for taking a chance on me and this book. Because of you, I get to call myself an author. Thank you for being part of that dream.

ABOUT THE AUTHOR

Thanks again for reading!

I grew up in Charlotte, NC, where I sill live today, and have been writing since the tender age of six. While my stories have matured, my passion for them has never faded. I'm a lifelong reader as well as writer. I'm also an avid soccer/football fan and amateur ballroom dancer.

Keep up with my upcoming books on my website, www.kelseyp ainterbooks.com and be sure to follow me on Instagram for the latest updates (@authorkelseypainter).

Also by Kelsey Painter

Stanmore FC Soulmates Series

We'll Meet Again

The Keeper and I

Made in the USA
Middletown, DE
03 August 2024

58172511R00154